FOREVER CHRISTMAS ON

SUGARPLUM LANE

ISLAND COUNTY SERIES #16

Karice Bolton

Cover Design by Didi Wahyudi, Interior: Adobe

Stock © grigvovan

Interior Formatting: BB Formatting Adobe Stock © Aleksandr

Edited by Valorie Clifton

DEDICATION

Thank you, readers! When I started writing Island County, I had no idea we'd be at sixteen books in the series. You've made it possible. And to my incredible family for giving me all the happiness and joy in the world. I love you more than words will every say...

Chapter One

Skye

A snowflake danced through the night sky and landed on the tip of my nose as I clapped my hands and held them up to the sky. A surge of happiness flowed through my veins at the thought of my latest adventure.

"Now, this is what I'm talking about."

Silence.

"What the heck?" I spun around to see nothing.

No one.

"Where did he go?" I craned my neck down the street, only to see the taillights of the driver's electric car dashing away.

Oh, well.

The story of my life, men who hightail it out of my life the first chance they get.

But I refused to believe I had anything to do with it.

I walked up to the tiny cottage and entered the key code to let me inside.

The moment I opened the door, the scent of vanilla sugar cookies drifted toward me, and I suddenly wanted to bake cookies all night and forget about my new temp job tomorrow.

"Probably not a wise idea. Money is always handy," I muttered as I wandered back outside and pulled my bags into the entryway.

The office I was starting at tomorrow was only a quick walk down the block. The rideshare guy pointed out the building to me before dumping me off and, apparently, dashing off Fireweed Island.

I let out a blissful sigh and glanced around the house I'd be calling home for the holidays. The décor in the entry was bright white with fresh sprigs of fir laid on the foyer's table. A light pine floor led me into the open kitchen and dinette that probably overlooked the water. Since it was dark outside, it was only a guess based on the home's proximity to Puget Sound. Regardless, part of the deal with this temp job was free housing, and this was a pleasant surprise. I'd dreaded what would greet me, but this was fantastic.

My phone buzzed, and I spotted a text from my mom.

Did you get there yet? Why haven't you texted?
Have you been kidnapped?

I chuckled to myself as I walked deeper into the kitchen and smelled the vanilla from out front, only stronger. When I spotted a platter full of cookies, I knew I had the perfect place to stay. I'd never had a host leave out cookies before, and I'd taken plenty of trips in recent years to know.

Me, myself, and I excelled at vacationing and finding jobs anywhere other than Maine, where I'd grown up and had most of my family and an ex I'd rather forget.

I glanced at my phone and reached for a cookie.

It wasn't that I didn't love my home state, but I was surrounded by loved ones who all stared at me with two questions in mind—*When are you going to settle down with a guy? Where are our grandchildren and nieces and nephews?*

But I wasn't like them. I'd never had the overly gushy feeling swell over me or the urge to find a soul mate and settle down. The moment my high school boyfriend talked to me about moving in together for college, I knew I wasn't built like my sister. When he'd brought it up, she was ecstatic for me, while the thought of living with him panicked me. He was a great guy and perfect for attending all the dances we had senior year, but it never occurred to me that there would be more. I couldn't even remember his name now. Was it Blake or Ben? I had no idea, but it had been fifteen years ago.

I smiled and took a bite of the cookie when a bitterness twisted my tongue into a contortion of revulsion as a chemical taste spread through my entire mouth. I dashed to the sink and spat out the uncookie into the sink and stared at the thing in my hand while swishing water from the kitchen tap inside my mouth. All I could do was swish and spit, swish and spit as tears streamed down my cheeks.

"Blech. Pfft." I grimaced as I wiped my tongue with a towel and tossed the poison onto the counter, finally realizing it was a wax candle. I just hadn't seen the wick without my glasses.

The doorbell rang, and I groaned as I wiped my mouth on my arm and prayed for the taste to go away.

On the way to the door, my phone buzzed again, and I laughed, seeing the next text, but this time, the message was from my sister.

Do you love your cottage? Please answer me, or Mom will hound me as much as you. Give me something to tell her.

I laughed and shook my head. Even though I didn't want to live next door to my family, we were extremely close. In fact, they were all headed out here for Christmas since none of them had ever been to the West Coast. Hopefully, Fireweed Island would be a great place to spend the holidays. Licking more of the chemical taste onto my sleeve, I clenched my eyes shut and gave a last blech before typing back to my sister.

I just ate a candle thinking it was a cookie, so I'd say I'm not off to a great start. But the cottage is beautiful, and I'm headed out to grab something to eat and get the terrible flavor out of my mouth. I'll text Mom, but someone's at the door.

I then texted my mom back a slightly different version.

The driver dropped me off, and the house is gorgeous. You'll love it for the holidays. I can't see the water, but I'm sure it's there. Love you and Dad. Hugs.

I set my phone down and opened the door to see an

extremely sexy man staring at me with two paper bags full of groceries. He was dressed in a pair of worn jeans, a red flannel rolled up at the sleeves, and shades were propped on his head even though it was pitch-black and snowing.

My lips felt numb from the earlier debacle, but I smiled. "I didn't order any groceries. Sorry. Wrong house."

The man's dark brows scowled as he cocked his head. "Marcy asked me to drop these by. She was supposed to do it."

Ah! Marcy was the one who'd hired me for the temp job. The puzzle pieces were starting to click.

"Oh, I see." I smiled, hoping drool from the uncookie experience wasn't puddling down my chin. "Well, that was sweet of her."

My phone buzzed, and I saw a text come over from the woman of the hour, Marcy.

Hey, just a heads up. Max should be bringing over some groceries to get you settled in. He's harmless even though his mouth doesn't seem like it. I'm stuck in Vermont, or I would have stocked your fridge earlier.

I brought my gaze back to harmless Max.

"It was, except she got stuck in Vermont because her

flight was canceled, so I got stuck having to deliver this to you." He stared at me.

My jaw dropped open at his rudeness just as I pulled the grocery bags from his arms.

"Stuck? Are you her son or BFF or something?"

He looked taken aback. "Gawd, no."

His hazel eyes stayed connected with mine, and I felt my body sputter into uncertainty. He was extremely good-looking. But I had no idea who he was. Should I just shut the door on him and his rudeness, or invite him in for a drink?

I wasn't sure, but he wasn't leaving.

And there were no sparks, witty banter, or flirting to be had—hot or not.

And I desperately needed to wash the uncookie from my mouth.

He shoved his hands into his pockets and looked annoyingly charming for someone so rude. "Marcy is stuck back there because she visited her family with her boyfriend for Thanksgiving."

"Oh, God forbid," I muttered.

He smiled, looking somewhat confused. "Pardon?"

I shifted the groceries, wondering if he'd get the hint. "Just some people like the holidays, like their family around for the holidays."

7

"Regardless, the weather had to throw a wrench in things, and here I am."

"At least she's with family for the holiday instead of being stuck here with me delivering my groceries. I'm sure she didn't mind the delay too much," I said, smiling and attempting to balance the grocery bags on my hips.

He shrugged. "I suppose."

"You don't sound convinced." My eyes started watering from the bad taste in my mouth, but he kept going.

"These holidays are just made-up reasons for people to spend money," he nearly growled.

I scowled and chuckled. Not sure if the bad taste in my mouth was from the uncookie or the man standing in front of me.

"Do you need help getting the bags to the kitchen?" he asked.

The desperate need for a drink of water to get the bitter taste out of my mouth was overwhelming. Without thinking, I nodded, and he reached for the grocery bags, snagged them, and scooted past me while I shut the door.

"It looks like you know where you're going," I called after him, secretly wiping my tongue on my sleeve before I followed him.

I wiped my eyes with my fingers and wandered into

the kitchen, where he'd set the grocery bags on the counter.

"This was really nice of Marcy to go grocery shopping for me."

"Uh-uh." He waggled his finger. "I went shopping for you. I also came by earlier and lit some of the candles to make the place smell good."

"Of course you did." I reached for a glass on one of the open shelves and filled it up. "But the grocery stop was her idea."

"But I did the actual labor of getting the groceries."

Did it really matter who got the credit?

I clenched my eyes shut when I realized the water only spread the bad taste around.

"You okay?" he asked, coming over quickly.

"Yeah. Fine."

"You don't look fine."

I opened one eye. "It's a long story."

His gaze fell to the rogue uncookie on the counter. "Did you try to eat the candle? Who would do that?"

I swished more water around my mouth as I started putting the groceries away.

"I didn't know it was a candle."

"How could you not know it was a candle?"

"There was a pile of them on a plate, just like real

cookies." I frowned. "And I didn't have my glasses on."

Max attempted to hide a smile, but he failed miserably. "That is my cue to exit. I hope you figure out a way to wash the taste out."

He turned and started toward the front door.

"Thanks. I plan on finding a place with some good food and tangy liquor."

He laughed. "Shouldn't be too hard."

"Good to hear." I followed him down the hall to the front door.

Max turned around, smiling. "So, I take it you're not going to use the groceries tonight?"

"I'm sure I'll eat something out of the groceries you were so kind to pick up on my behalf."

"Have a good night," he said before turning and heading out the door, leaving me very puzzled.

I made my way back to the kitchen and hoped he wasn't a sign of what was to come on Fireweed Island.

I glanced at the kitchen, which was so crisp and beautiful. I could now clearly see that what I'd eaten was meant for the décor, but I was starving, and the yummy smell had confused me. My stomach growled as I reached for the binder left by the host and opened it up to where it listed their favorite places.

I sighed happily. "Mudflat Tavern it is." Marcy had written a note about their homemade French fries with chili cheese sauce, so obviously, I wasn't going to turn that down. Plus, it was only a short walk down the road.

Quickly rifling through my bag, I found my hairbrush—and dashed to the bathroom since it had been so long—and combed my hair. I looked in the mirror.

It would have to do. There was no doubt I looked like a woman who'd had her connecting flight delayed by three hours, but at least my luggage made it. The same couldn't be said for my poor aisle mate.

I zipped my coat and dashed out the door to see a sparkling white carpet of fresh snow. It probably wasn't more than a half-inch or so, but it had stuck, and it was beautiful. As I carefully made my way down the sidewalk, I couldn't help but notice how beautiful and serene the little island was. Christmas lights had been strung around the lamp posts, and large red bows had been stuck to the doors of the city hall.

When Mudflats came into view, my step quickened. Even though it was Sunday night, the place looked to be hopping, and it didn't look anything like a tavern. As I watched a family of four wander inside, I realized it wasn't really a tavern. When I got closer, I could smell the heavenly scents of garlic and onion wafting my way.

When I went inside, a hostess greeted me immediately and asked if I wanted to sit in the restaurant or the bar. I scanned the restaurant, which was covered in nautical décor, and noticed the darker lighting in the bar. In my current state, the bar was probably best.

"The bar would be great." I grinned. "Is it a full menu? Because I've heard the fries are a must."

The hostess smiled and handed me a menu. "Sure is. Go on in and find a place to sit."

"Thanks." I nearly skipped to a booth near the windows that called to me. It was tucked in the corner, but I could still feel like I was in the action.

As soon as I sat down, the bartender appeared and slid a coaster in front of me. "What would you like to drink?"

"Well, I just ate a candle I thought was a cookie, so something strong to wash out my mouth and kill anything left behind. Maybe something spicy and with a lot of kick."

He nervously laughed as if he'd never heard of someone chowing down a candle before and nodded as I opened the menu and scoped out the fries. The blue cheese cheeseburger sounded amazing, too, with crispy fried onions.

Sold.

I glanced out the window and saw the gentle glow from several yachts bobbing softly in the water. It looked so peaceful and was exactly what I needed after my last temp job.

When the bartender returned, he slid a clear drink in front of me. "This is one of our specials. It's the Tipsy Tidal Wave. It's got gin, lime, and crushed hot peppers."

"Nice. It looks quite festive. If that doesn't change the flavor in my mouth, nothing will." The clear liquid had sliced cayenne peppers settling on the bottom and a lime wedge on the glass. It was quite beautiful.

"Ready to order?"

I nodded and recited my choices as I felt a different pair of eyes on me. The bartender headed back behind the counter when I spotted one of the sexiest men I'd ever laid eyes on.

Again.

It was Max!

But he looked way different.

Yet, the same.

Wishful thinking, since his personality left something to be desired.

Oddly, I had felt beans for chemistry with him earlier, but seeing him now stirred a little something inside. Maybe it was the ambiance of Mudflats.

I took a sip of the Tipsy Tidal Wave, and my tongue, nose, ears, and eyeballs immediately caught on fire.

"Eeep." I clenched my eyes shut while my nose ran and my ears popped. My palm automatically slammed the table to the sound of chiming silverware.

"Can you get this woman some water?" A man's voice commanded from across the room.

Please don't let it be the GQ model-slash-grocery delivery driver.

Otherwise known as Max.

With my eyes still shut, I felt a pile of paper napkins being shoved into my hands. As I tried to open my eyes, snot rolled down my chin, and I did a quick wipe, wishing I could lick the table, or anything, really, to get the spice to go away.

"Here's the water," the bartender said as I attempted to wrench open each lid to focus on the glass. "I'm so sorry. I only made it slightly spicier than usual to help with your bad candle issue."

I gulped down the water, wishing it were a fire hose, and nodded as my eyes landed on the man next to the bartender.

It was Max.

"What candle issue?" he asked the bartender.

Which baffled me out of my stupor. He'd heard about the candle issue from my very lips less than an hour ago.

The bartender glanced at me. "She told me she ate

some candles before she got here and needed to get the taste out of her mouth."

I wiped my eyes with the napkins and nodded. "It's true. I can usually handle my spice. Must be a reaction between the chemicals in the candle and the cayenne."

Mr. Sexy kept his eyes on mine while I kept looking at the bartender, and for some reason, a wave of tingles washed over me. This was not the reaction Max had drilled through me back at the house. Had the gin and cayenne gotten to me in a matter of seconds?

"It's a good drink, though." I didn't want the bartender to feel bad.

The bartender laughed and shook his head. "How about we go with something gentler?"

I chuckled and dabbed my eyes again, still feeling the pull to look at Max. "Good idea."

When the bartender left, Max stayed.

At least that was consistent.

"Why did you eat a candle?" he asked, arching his dark brows.

"I thought it was a cookie." I turned my attention to him, which was a big mistake. "And haven't we gone over this before?"

His gorgeous hazel eyes locked on mine, and the

intensity behind them was enough to start another kind of fire. The man's dark hair had a bit of wave to it, so his strands looked a bit unruly, which kind of matched the red buffalo plaid flannel shirt and dark, worn jeans he was wearing. He looked like he'd been out collecting firewood all day.

In a sexy and intriguing kind of way.

Except . . . how did he change his shirt so fast? I was sure Max's flannel was solid red. I was a graphic designer. I remembered these kinds of details.

Max still didn't say anything but shook his head.

"It was back at the rental, remember?" I reminded him, seriously worried about his cognitive state.

He smirked. "I see."

"Do you find other people's misery funny, or is that only around the holidays?" I chided, noticing I had dried drool on my chin.

Max laughed, shook his head, and walked out of the bar as he wished me a good night while I was left wondering if coming to Fireweed was a bad idea.

Chapter Two

Levi

My brother had struck again. Max had a real way with the ladies, and I couldn't understand it. We were identical twins, yet everywhere he went, he burned bridges for both of us.

But last night.

That was brutal.

As the woman with big blue eyes and long, dark hair looked up at me in between her near medical emergency, I wanted to kick my brother where it counted. I could see that he'd already screwed up my chances with her. But I'd called Mudflats after I left and paid for her order anyway to make up for whatever my brother did or said to her before I bumped into her.

Neither my brother nor I were full of sunshine and

butterflies, but there was something about him that made it even worse, and since I looked like him and he looked like me, if he struck out, I struck out.

And last night, I definitely didn't want to strike out. The woman oozed sex appeal and intelligence and . . . God, those lips.

I shoved my hands through my hair and let out a groan of utter annoyance. I had to get over it. This was the burden I had to carry in life.

My brother.

I laughed to myself and turned on my laptop as my devoted assistant popped her head into my office. Surprise filled me. She'd been stuck on a vacation in Vermont with her family and flight delays since Thanksgiving.

"Hello, stranger," she gushed, tapping on the door frame while holding a cup of coffee. "Our new temp will be here any minute. Try not to scare her off, okay?"

My brows rose. "Have I ever?"

She delivered the iced Americano from my favorite coffee shop by the ferry terminal. "Why do you think we only hire temps for that role now?"

I cocked my head and rolled my eyes. "Come on. You're overexaggerating."

"Am I?"

Maybe not.

"How'd you get back so early?" I asked, taking a sip of the Americano. Boy, I loved Gabby's Goodies and Espresso. "And thanks for this. But I'm fully capable of getting coffee."

"Well, as luck would have it, I caught a red-eye that became available. There was one seat left, so I snagged it, and I thought I'd spoil my boss on the way here with his favorite beverage to make him nicer to our new hire and try not to banish the Christmas season from the office like you do every year."

"Wait. You left your boyfriend on vacation with your family in Vermont?"

She laughed. "You say it like they'd eat him or something."

I shrugged and logged onto my laptop.

"If I didn't take the ticket, I wouldn't get back here until Wednesday, and I was afraid you'd chase her away before I got back. And we need this one."

"Fine," I grumbled with a smile. "I'll play nice."

Marcy rolled her eyes this time and grinned. "I didn't ask you to do the impossible. Just don't freak her out. And don't forget on Thursday, you're meeting with the warehouse chain to get our bestseller in under their private label. We at least need her until then to make the label mockups."

"Duly noted." I opened my inbox, and Marcy closed my door.

The moment it clicked, my mind whizzed back to the woman from last night.

Chances were I'd never see her again, which was what would have made it perfect last night. I could have bought her a couple of drinks, and maybe she'd be into some holiday cheer and . . .

Oh. My. God. I sounded like my brother.

I needed to quit spending so much time with him.

Speaking of my brother, how and why did he run into her? I shook my head and let out a deep breath as I glanced outside to see the snow piling up. We had about six inches on the ground, which in Island language meant we were nearly snowed in. But the views of Puget Sound from the office were beautiful, especially with the snow on the cliffs.

I reached for my phone and texted my brother a quick question.

Did you meet a woman last night?

My brother texted back.

I am still sleeping, and what the hell kind of question is that?

I shook my head. Of course, he was still sleeping. It was why Dad left me the business and my brother the money.

Lucky me.

I was the responsible one. While my brother was busy spending his life traveling the world, rock climbing, and jumping out of planes, I was going to college, learning about our family wine business, and promising to continue the legacy of Shantos wines.

I should be flattered.

Whatever. Didn't matter.

I didn't bother responding to my brother, but I did feel a little gleeful that I'd woken him up.

I had to get my holiday cheer from somewhere.

My calendar dinged, and I glanced at the message and couldn't help but smile. My assistant was determined to make the interior of the office look like Santa threw up his cookies. A few years back, I'd banned Christmas décor, parties, and the Secret Santa exchange because good things never came of any of it.

Ever.

But Marcy had a way of wiggling the décor back in

as a team-building exercise, and now we had one holiday party.

As I opened the invite, my calendar filled with office festivities from cookie decorating to tree trimming and hanging mistletoe. I wasn't sure how appropriate the last item was, but I was already known as Scrooge around here. Or was it the Grinch? And here Marcy was trying to wiggle even more holiday to-do items. I'd have to chat with her later.

My office phone rang, and I put on my headset before answering Marcy's call. Her cheery grin showed up on my laptop.

"The new hire is here." She waited for me to respond, but I didn't know what to say since I had never dealt with them. Marcy wouldn't let me, so why that had changed this morning, I hadn't a clue.

"Okay." I glanced at the screen and saw the back of a female's head. "And?"

Marcy smirked as the woman turned around, and I realized the last twenty-four hours of my life had been orchestrated by a twisted sense of reality.

"Marcy, take me off video."

Her smirk only grew.

"You sent my brother to our rental last night? What on earth did you do that for?"

"I thought it would be nice if we delivered groceries to her so she had one less thing to think about."

I glared at my assistant. "You're lying."

"I would never lie to you." She smiled. "I might leave out a few details, but . . ."

My jaw clenched as the woman from the bar patiently waited for my assistant to finish with this call.

She was even more beautiful than I remembered. I quickly clicked through my inbox, looking for the message from Marcy with the new hire's information. When I'd found it, I let out a slow breath.

Skye Lenox.

Lives in Maine. Last temp job was in Manhattan at some fashion magazine. Highly qualified.

Judging by her credentials, we were lucky to have her.

"I'll send her in," Marcy chimed in.

"No. Wait—"

But she hung up on me.

I was the boss. Since when did my employees hang up on me?

In less than a minute, Marcy was tapping on my door and pushing it wide open.

I glimpsed Skye behind Marcy, and my breathing stopped. She was even more beautiful in regular lighting.

Not that it mattered.

I didn't date employees.

And I certainly didn't date people my brother met first because they could never get the bad taste out of their mouths.

It happened often enough for me to know.

And woefully accept.

"This is Skye Lennox," Marcy said as our new hire stepped forward. "She has glowing recommendations, and her portfolio is out of this world. I'll leave you two to go over her first assignment." Marcy stepped aside as Skye's gaze met mine.

She looked stunned.

And embarrassed.

But why?

She didn't do anything wrong.

"It's nice to meet you, Skye. I looked over your resumé, and it's quite impressive."

Skye blushed and tipped her head down. "Thank you. I've been lucky enough to work at some incredible companies. I'm really excited to work for a company where I finally love the product."

I laughed, and her gaze met mine. "So, you're a fan of wine?"

Marcy shut the door, leaving Skye and me alone. I

motioned for her to take a seat, which she quickly did.

We were a casual office, but seeing Skye's wardrobe choice made me want to change that. When she sat, her pencil skirt lifted slightly, and her pink satin blouse shimmered over her breasts from the lighting overhead.

"I think you kind of know I'm a fan of most alcoholic beverages after last night." She cocked her head and narrowed her eyes. "Or do you not remember that either?"

I cleared my throat and considered whether I should clear up the situation.

"I'm sorry. I shouldn't have—"

I smiled and shook my head. "No. I completely understand."

Her dark brows rose, and her blue eyes filled with relief. "You do?"

Closing my laptop, I studied her as she glanced out the window.

"I have never worked somewhere with such a beautiful view, and the home that I'm in is absolutely amazing."

"I'm glad you approve."

"Approve?" She laughed. "I may never leave."

"Did you manage to get the candle taste out of your mouth?" I asked, genuinely curious.

She laughed and nodded. "Between the blue cheese cheeseburger and whatever drink the bartender served the second time, they wiped it away." She cupped her hands in her lap and brought her eyes to mine, which sent a thrill through me that should never have happened. "And thank you."

"For what?" I shook my head. "You're more than qualified for this position. I should be the one thanking you."

The words made her smile wider. "Thank you for picking up my meal last night. I didn't expect that."

I laughed and nodded. "Well, I didn't expect you to be my new hire. So, I'm sorry if it was inappropriate."

She narrowed her eyes at me in confusion. "Marcy sent you to deliver groceries. You knew I was your new temp."

I let out a deep sigh and looked out the window to see the snow really coming down now. "Marcy sent my twin brother to deliver your groceries."

Her hands flew up to her mouth as her eyes widened. "There are two of you?"

I chuckled. "I assure you, there is only one of me."

Skye's cheeks reddened. "So that's why you had no idea my appetizer was a candle. Why didn't you say something?"

"I honestly had no idea that I'd see you again or that it mattered." I picked up my Americano. "I'm Levi Adams, and apart from how Max and I look, we are nothing alike."

She nodded, giggling, and the sound filled me up with something unexpected, but I was quick to push the feeling away.

"He's a weird duck," she added.

I almost spat out my coffee as our eyes met, and I nodded in agreement.

"Sorry. I shouldn't have said that." She grimaced. "It will soon become really apparent why I like temp work. I might be a stellar graphic designer, but I suck at keeping my mouth shut."

This was an interesting development.

"Is that so?"

"Yup. For instance, at the magazine I left, there was a photographer there who was extremely popular. He was a freelance photographer, but the magazine had recently hired him to shoot the next six issues."

I cocked my head, unsure of where this was going.

"Anyway, I had to work with him on layouts and everything, and he was a complete creep." She shrugged. Her eyes widened when she realized where her conversation was headed, and I did my best to keep in a chuckle. I couldn't resist the twinkle in her eyes as she was relaying her story, so when she looked away, my heart dropped a little.

Which was a problem of its own.

I was the owner of a company.

She was a temp.

Relaying a sexual harassment story to me.

My heart shouldn't be involved in anything other than terror.

No flutters. Nothing.

"And then what happened?" I prompted.

"Well, I'm all for work-related relationships because, let's be honest, we spend at least eight hours a day at the office, so where else would you find someone? But if the woman says no, then . . ."

I tried not to stumble over her reaction to dating coworkers.

"Absolutely." I nodded in complete agreement. "It doesn't matter how two people meet. They both need to be consenting adults."

"Yup." She smiled and straightened in her seat. "So, one day, I walked in to see the photographer trying to get handsy, and the model clearly didn't want it."

"Then what happened?"

"I knocked him out." She cleared her throat. "And the

camera shattered."

I loved the fiery sound of her voice and couldn't help but chuckle. "Nice one."

"I thought so. The magazine wasn't as thrilled."

"Seriously?"

"He's all the rage right now for photos." She rolled her eyes. "Needless to say, they bought him a new camera, and here I am, telling you something I should never have uttered to another soul, especially you."

"I don't mind." And I really didn't. "What happened to the model?"

"She thanked me and filed a police report."

"Well, other than Marcy getting a little handsy with the sugar cookies, I can't imagine you have to worry about clocking any of your fellow workers here."

"Sounds like my kind of workplace."

Chapter Three

Skye

Why, oh why, did I think it was okay to tell the man sitting in front of me about my vigilante moves in Manhattan? Bringing up groping? Thank God I didn't walk in on anything more graphic, or I would have word-vomited that to him too.

But he didn't seem to mind that my mouth ran wild.

And how could he be Max's twin?

It was like if you took Max's brain and reprogrammed it to be the exact opposite of awkward and annoying, you'd get Levi.

And how could my reaction to him be so very different?

It was near impossible not to drool on myself as he spoke. His perfect lips and chiseled jaw made him the perfect candidate for his own cover shoot.

The intensity behind his hazel eyes made me nearly stick to the seat with sweat, and every time he smiled at me, I felt like I'd just reached the tippy top of a rollercoaster.

Not a good sign

"My sales team is meeting with the biggest club warehouse chain in a few days, so I know this is short notice, but we were hoping you could do some quick mockups for the team to take in showcasing our Pinot Grigio."

I nodded, forcing the flutter away.

"We have to sell them on the fact that our Pinot is the rising star of retail and that if we produce it private label for them, they'll knock out the competition at their club."

Levi slid his laptop between us so that I could see it. "I did some quick sketches so you can see the direction I wanted to take with it. I figured we could either go in and sell them on a quirky brand or a refined brand. I went with refined."

I nodded. "Good choice. I like where you're going with this."

He scrolled the page up, and I saw a few boards he had put together.

"I'm surprised the CEO is putting together a mood board instead of his marketing team." My eyes met his, and he pulled his laptop back. "That is what you are, correct?"

He smiled and sat back, studying me with his cool gaze. "This is important. I want to make sure that if we don't win the bid, I can only blame myself."

I bit my lip, deciding whether I should say what was on my mind.

Nope. Shouldn't say it.

"And if you get in, you can congratulate yourself." The words flew out of my mouth before I could stop them.

I. Was. Fired.

Levi's gaze sharpened, which only made him sexier. He closed his laptop.

"That is certainly one way of looking at it," he said evenly without taking his eyes off me.

A charge ran between us, and I felt the air get sucked right out of the room.

I'd done it again. My only saving grace might be that they needed some art in less than seventy-two hours.

"You think you can handle it?" he asked with a smile resting behind his gaze even though it didn't reach his lips.

Laughter erupted from the nervous ball of emotions deep in my belly.

"Of course, I can get this finished. I'd work day and night if I thought it was a problem." I let out a slow breath as my pulse pounded in my ears. I didn't know if the reaction was from sticking my foot in my mouth again or the way he was looking at me. "I never miss a deadline."

He ran his palm across his chin and finally smiled. "Welcome aboard, Miss Skye Lenox. I think you'll be a good fit for our company."

I stood, noticing my knees wanted to knock together for no good reason, and gave a quick nod.

"Thanks." I spun around and stopped at the door and looked over my shoulder, catching his gaze roaming the back of me. "And thanks again for dinner."

Levi dropped his gaze to his closed laptop and nodded as I walked out of his office, wondering what would be in store for me for the next several weeks.

Marcy saw me and sprang to action. She walked over and grinned. "Well, you haven't run away so far. He's the ultimate test."

I chuckled until I realized she wasn't kidding.

"I've got your desk set up over here. There's a beautiful view of the water, and you're only a few steps from the sales gurus who are rarely ever in the office, but as you can see, they printed out giant heads and taped them to their chairs."

I laughed and nodded, noticing the giant cardboard heads staring at me. "Clever."

"They'll love to hear you say that." She smiled. "And the marketing team is tucked in that corner. I would have sat you over there, but the only desk left is staring at a blank wall, and I didn't think that would be very nice. Plus, you're close to the breakroom here."

"A woman after my own heart." I glanced at Marcy and wondered how old she was. She didn't seem like she was my age, but she didn't really seem like she was older than me, either. My gaze dropped to her ring finger. Not married. Her red hair was swept into a bun, and she seemed like an upbeat person.

Maybe she and Levi were an item. They seemed awfully close when she introduced me.

"I.T. has your Mac Studio all set up and a MacBook if you prefer." She touched the brand-new machines, and my jaw almost fell open. This was what graphic artists dreamed about.

"Wow. This is great," I said, running my hand over the cold metal. "Thanks."

"Of course. And they left your username and password in your drawer. Just make sure to change your password once you log in, but I'm sure you know the drill. If you need anything, I'm at the desk right outside Levi's. But first, I need to run to the hardware store to pick up some

Christmas decorations. Levi hates Christmas, and I absolutely get my jollies from making his life miserable. He banned the Secret Santa gift exchange years ago, but now we just do the Secret-*Secret* Santa exchange."

I laughed and nodded, realizing how much I liked Marcy. "Thank you for the groceries, by the way. I had the oatmeal this morning."

"Absolutely." She winked at me. "It's the least I could do, considering we've pulled you clear across the country for the holidays."

"It's my pleasure."

She flashed a smile before turning around and heading toward Levi's office.

The first thing I needed to do was focus on the task at hand. I turned on my Mac and watched the little apple appear before typing in my credentials and quickly changing my password.

"How's it going? You must be Skye," a male voice sang out.

I glanced in the direction of the noise and saw a guy sauntering over to me. He looked like he'd already had one too many glasses of wine this morning, but he seemed nice enough. He certainly was no Levi.

Oh, no. Why did that thought pop into my head?

Of course, he was no Levi.

Levi was sexy and knew how to dress and owned this freaking company, so I should just stop with it and do my job.

I raised my hand and gave a little wave. "Hi. That's me."

"This is completely unprofessional . . ."

Not a date. Not a date.

"But we have a little bet going on how long you'll last here before you quit, and I was hoping to have a little bonus stashed for the holidays."

I snickered and shook my head. "I'm sorry to disappoint you, but I'm not going anywhere."

His brows rose. "Have you met Levi yet?"

I nodded and smiled. "We had a lovely discussion this morning."

Shock flew across the guy's features. "As in Levi Adams?"

"I've met both Levi and Max. Lovely people."

The man's brows furrowed. "Are you related to them?"

I shook my head, trying to hold in my laughter. "Nope. Is there something I should know?"

He walked closer to me and leaned his elbow on an elevated drafting table. "Levi fancies himself an artist, so he is extremely hard on any male or female who plants their bum in that seat."

I nodded, thinking back to his sketches. They were beautiful for what they were.

"Thanks for the heads up, but I should probably get to work. We're on a tight deadline."

He straightened and nodded. "Indeed. Well, if you need anything, I sit just over there, and my name is Stan."

"Thanks, Stan. I appreciate it, but don't count on winning any money. I'm here until January of next year."

He smiled and nodded. "I hope so. You seem great."

"As do you."

I watched him wander off to his desk and stare at his laptop while I opened my inbox, surprised to see several emails from Levi since I'd left his office.

"Stan," Levi barked, and I nearly hopped out of the chair.

Stan laughed. "Levi."

"Can you come into my office?"

I kept my eyes on Illustrator in front of me as I heard the door close. A woman chuckled across the way, and I looked over to see her watching me. She gave me a big smile and a wave.

"I'd come say hi, but I don't want Scrooge to come

unglued after he's through with Stan."

I laughed and nodded. "Gotcha."

Thinking back to the sketches that Levi had captured for this presentation, I began my work and got lost in my happy place. There was very little I loved more than watching edges, corners, and circles of design come to life in a meaningful and beautiful way.

I heard a few murmurs and looked over to see Stan sitting at his desk, looking a little pale.

I was guessing his conversation with Levi didn't go as well as he'd hoped.

"Skye." Levi came up behind me as I glanced over my shoulder. "Would you like to go to the meeting with us on Thursday?"

Seeing him standing next to me was an entirely different experience than seeing him wedged behind his desk. His long, lean legs filled out his jeans, and the charcoal wool sweater clung to his chest. I hid a smile, realizing he looked like the epitome of the NW male, but the NW male who left other men quivering in their boots.

"Umm." I looked in the direction of Stan and realized several of the coworkers were eyeing us. "Whatever you think would help or . . . I mean, I don't want to be a bother."

Levi smiled but noticed my gaze and looked over to

see my coworkers pretending not to be listening. He let out a disgruntled sigh and shook his head.

"I'm sorry for Stan's behavior. He assures me that it won't happen again."

I didn't know whether to plead ignorance or agree, but I never did well at lying.

"Your silence says it all."

I glanced at Stan, knowing he'd be here long after I left. "It's just a harmless prank to keep themselves amused."

He tilted his chin. "But I'm not paying them to keep themselves amused."

I smirked, looking up into his gorgeous eyes. "That's one way of looking at it."

Levi watched me carefully, and the electricity running through us was incredible. "And what's the other way?"

"Maybe the office is a little tense, and their way to blow off steam is to form comradery to survive?" I shrugged. "Just a guess. I mean, I know how unsettled I'd feel working somewhere that had high turnover."

"We don't have high turnover. All of our employees have been here for years, a decade in some instances." He smiled. "Except for your position."

"Well, maybe this one position represents to them that

their head could be on the chopping block next. You know, off with their heads and all that."

He scowled. "Never. They're like family."

My brows rose. "Do they know it?"

He ignored my question and glanced around. "I wonder where Marcy went."

I chuckled, knowing full well where she went, and at the moment, I was completely on board with her doing anything she wanted to annoy her grumpy boss. I'd been in the workforce long enough to know that it was only a matter of time before Levi set his sights on me. He might be polite now, but that was because he needed me to stick around until Thursday.

After that, it was anyone's best guess.

"I just don't think it's appropriate for a current employee to make a new employee feel less than or as if their time here might be limited."

"I see." I let out a steady breath and kept my gaze on his before lowering my voice. "While I appreciate that, it's probably not great to intimidate a current employee who's been loyal. No need to talk to your employees on my behalf. I can take care of myself."

He smiled, and his gaze became unexpectedly heated. "Is that so?"

"Completely."

Chapter Four

Levi

We'd barely hit noon the Monday after Thanksgiving, and Marcy had managed to make the entire office look like Santa Claus and his elves had nothing better to do than fill my office with knickknacks, doodads, lights, and enough sweets to make anyone sick.

But she knew what the employees loved.

Which was a good thing because I didn't have a clue.

I looked at Stan, munching on one of the sprinkle cookies, and felt marginally bad about calling him into my office, but it wasn't appropriate. A person didn't go over to a new employee and tell her the team was placing bets against her.

Skye was chuckling with some of her coworkers as she carefully inspected her sugar cookie with her glasses on, and I laughed, thinking back to her debacle at Mudflats last night.

I still couldn't get over it being the same woman we'd hired to save this deal. We'd already missed one opportunity to sell ourselves, and I wasn't going to miss this one. Too much depended on it. All of the employees' well-being depended on it, though they didn't know it.

Sales had taken a downward turn last year in the adult beverage industry, but our portfolio was hit even harder. I knew what was on the line if we didn't get this deal.

"Hey, Mr. Scrooge." Marcy wandered over to me with a plate full of cookies. "I special ordered everything from Gabby's Goodies." She waved the plate under my nose just when I caught Skye looking in my direction. I pretended not to notice as Marcy continued, "You know you want some, especially the ones with powdered sugar."

"Fine, Marcy. Will that make you stop bugging me about them?" I grabbed a cookie and took a bite.

She laughed and grinned. "Nope. Just wait until when we have the cookie decorating party."

"I can't wait." I took another bite. "These are good, though."

"Of course they are." She flashed a wicked smile. "But it seems like your mood has slightly improved since last week. I wonder why."

"I have absolutely no idea what you're talking about." I pulled my eyes away from Skye and glared at Marcy.

"Sure, you don't. I heard you invited Skye to Thursday's meeting. That's kind of a brazen move."

"She should be involved."

"Interesting. I heard you had a little chat with Stan."

"How can you possibly be everywhere and nowhere at the same time while finding out everything?" I laughed and shook my head.

"It's my job. I'm your eyes and ears."

"Well, he told Skye they were all placing bets on how long she'd last."

She nodded in agreement. "Yeah. That was tasteless."

"And we don't have time for any more issues."

Marcy pressed her lips into a thin line and nodded. She was one of the few who knew our predicament.

"How did she take the teasing?"

I smiled. "She told me she could handle herself."

Marcy chuckled. "And I think she means it."

"I have no doubt."

She took a bite of the cookie before setting the plate down. She clapped her hands, and everyone stopped talking and looked over at her.

"Okay, folks. I've got plenty of green and red sparkly garland, ornaments, fake snow, and whatever else I could find that I need you to help me hang on every single piece of naked cubicle, all the doorways, and the reception desk. There's a prize in it for the person who can decorate their desk with the most decorations and a prize for the one who can convince Mr. Scrooge here to allow decorations in his office."

Most of the employees laughed, but I noticed Skye didn't. Instead, she looked at me expressionlessly. I stared back at her, which left her to raise her brows, but she didn't move as everyone else scurried away.

Marcy turned her attention back to me. "It's funny. I didn't even have to tell them what the prize was. Remember that. Employees respond really well to positive affirmation, Levi."

I tore my gaze away from Skye and took a deep breath. "I get it, Marcy. But I have a lot on my mind, as you well know."

Marcy nodded and patted my back. "I hear ya. Just be nice to the new one, okay?"

Skye reached for another cookie as Marcy blasted Christmas music over the speakers, and I made my way over.

"Mr. Scrooge, huh?" she asked, taking a bite of a sugar cookie.

"I see you trust that these are actual cookies."

She laughed and slid her reading glasses from atop her head. "Glasses and no wick mean it's okay to eat."

"So, what's the deal with your title?"

"CEO?" I asked.

"No. Scrooge."

I laughed and shook my head. "I'm not exactly into Christmas."

She smiled and took another bite. "Ah, right. Holidays are a waste. I got that message loud and clear from Max. He seemed a little perturbed that he had to deliver groceries to me since Marcy was stuck in Vermont."

Of course, Max did. He was born without one polite bone in his body.

"Speaking of . . ." Skye glanced around the bustling office with employees hollering over Christmas music and diving for ornaments. "Where is your other half?"

"He's not my other half."

She laughed. "You know what I mean."

"He doesn't work here. My father gave our wine business to me."

"So, what does he do?" she asked, genuinely curious.

"When he's on the island, not much of anything. He might spend his days kayaking or kicking back and playing video games. He does enjoy the occasional cliff dive."

She looked surprised. "Do I detect a hint of bitterness?"

"Hah." I laughed and shook my head. "I wouldn't want his life. He has no sense of purpose or direction."

"And that's important to you?"

"It's helpful to wake up in the morning." I glanced around the office. "Shouldn't you be decorating?"

She looked over at my office, and my chest tightened. "How about I start with yours?"

"You wouldn't dare."

"Try me." She flashed a wicked grin before digging out the remaining red garland from the bag and several polar bear ornaments wearing striped beanie hats.

Marcy handed her the tape, and Skye marched into my office, looking over her shoulder. "I'm sure you won't mind. Hey, Stan. Can you lend me a hand?"

Stan's eyes snapped to hers and then nervously to mine while I stood frozen.

"No problem, Skye."

He left his desk and followed Skye into my office while Marcy attempted not to laugh. I put my finger up to warn her, and that only made her burst into fits of maniacal giggles.

My office was out of control, and it all started once Skye arrived.

"Ready for lunch?" The familiar voice of stability echoed into the office as Marcy turned around to see Maddie. She gave her a quick hug and spun around and winked at me.

"Please take him off our hands. He's a bit crotchety right now."

"I am not," I assured Maddie, who smiled in response.

Maddie ran the local tea store and agreed to meet me to go over some brainstorming ideas. She spent most of her time on Hound Island since she'd married and had children, so I was lucky to meet with her.

"I'll be right back." I motioned to my office. Grabbing my coat, I avoided eye contact with Stan or Skye and made my way out of my office and over to Maddie.

"I am so starving," Maddie told me. "I need food like stat. Chance has a huge catering event he's working on, so I didn't want to bug him with my incessant begging for eggs Benedict."

I laughed and shook my head as we wandered out the door. "It must be nice to be married to a gourmet chef."

Maddie grinned and rubbed her belly. "Especially when you're expecting."

My eyes widened in surprise. "Are you serious? Does

that make this eight or nine kids?"

She chuckled and shrugged. "I think I'm up to three or four. I don't remember."

The snow was quickly piling up, and I took Maddie's hand in mine to make sure she didn't slip as we walked across the street to the diner.

"Is Chance excited?" I asked. He'd become a good friend years ago, and I knew he loved his family more than anything.

"He's absolutely terrified but equally excited. Chance gets like this with each pregnancy. He worries to death and then can't help himself."

"What does he worry about?"

We both checked for oncoming cars and walked along the crosswalk to the flashing open sign at the Dancing Griddle Café. Ever since Claire Swanson took over the café, it quickly became one of my favorite lunch spots, and it didn't hurt that her husband, Dwayne, was one of my good friends and also the town sheriff.

"He worries that we'll screw them up, I think." Maddie smiled at me as I opened the door and she went inside.

"You two are the best parents ever."

Maddie elbowed me as Claire spotted us and pointed to the corner booth, my favorite.

"So, have you thought more about what I mentioned?" She sat down in the booth, and I scooted across from her.

"You mean selling the winery?" I shook my head. "I can't do it."

"Your father didn't mean to make you miserable by handing it over."

I laughed and glanced around the familiar café that was fully entrenched in Christmas decor. "No, he didn't."

"When's your meeting to go private label?" she asked.

"Thursday. I think we have a great shot at getting into their warehouses."

She grinned. "Well, I always buy bulk, and that includes wine."

I laughed as Claire came over.

"Your usual?" Claire asked me, and I nodded as she turned over the cup and poured me fresh coffee.

"And I'm going to change it up today and order a bowl of today's soup and the ham and grilled cheese sandwich," Maddie told her.

Claire smiled and studied Maddie for a brief second. "Not your usual tuna on rye?"

Maddie grinned and shrugged. "What can I say? I

have to watch my mercury levels for a few months."

Claire hopped on her toes and almost knocked over my coffee as she bent over the table to hug Maddie. "Oh, congratulations."

I heard Maddie say a muffled thank you before Claire stood back up, straightened her outfit, and headed toward the kitchen.

"Chance said his buddy, who's the marketing director for an IPA brand, tanked this year too."

I shook my head and sighed. "Things were going so well. In the last five years, we grew so much, and I scaled up to match, but it's been brutal. I'm afraid I'm going to have to cut some jobs."

"But this deal would stop that from happening," she said flatly.

"Sure would." I tapped my finger on the table. "And I think one of the things that will sell us is our willingness to have vision and partner with them."

Maddie nodded in agreement.

"And our new graphic designer is really talented. She's amazing, actually."

Maddie cocked her head quickly. "Amazing? Talented?"

I nodded. "Yeah. She's amazing and currently

decorating my office to look like an elf clan stampeded through it."

Maddie chuckled. "You really do hate Christmas, don't you?"

I grinned and took a sip of coffee, looking over the rim to see Maddie eyeing me suspiciously. I set my cup down.

"I don't hate Christmas. I just prefer the other three hundred and sixty-four days of the year."

And I wish I could do what I truly wanted to do ever since I was a child. But doing it on the weekend and after work would have to do.

When I wasn't so stressed about running this company.

She laughed. "Fine. Now, let's get down to business."

Chapter Five

Skye

I'd tried extremely hard to pretend that I wasn't curious about who Levi went to lunch with. She was beautiful and had a smile that made me want to be BFFs with her. All the while, this odd little feeling in the pit of my stomach surfaced. But they'd been gone an extremely long time. So long, in fact, that I managed to finish two layouts for his approval. Marcy had come by and loved them, so that made me feel a little calmer, but I had no idea what Levi would think.

Or if he planned on returning.

And by the sounds of it, I needed his approval more than anyone's if I planned on staying on the island longer than a week.

"Hey, Marcy."

He was back.

I spun around in my seat to see the wrong twin coming into the office. Without realizing it, I scowled and turned back to start my next project.

"Ah, if it isn't candle girl," Max said, coming up behind me. "Have the groceries come in handy?"

"Actually, they did." I didn't drag my eyes from the screen. I was hoping it would be a quick visit.

He stood next to my desk and played with the silver tinsel that dangled from my pencil holder. I'd covered pretty much anything I could with the glittery stuff, and now it was attracting Max like a kid to a carnival ride.

Unlike my boss, I loved anything and everything to do with Christmas. It didn't matter if it were the simple acts of making hot chocolate and sticking a candy cane in the mug or spending an afternoon sledding. I loved the holiday and made it stretch for as long as it could.

"I didn't think you worked here?" I asked, glancing up at Max as he toyed with the tinsel.

It was nearly impossible to believe these two were related, except for the small fact that they were identical twins. And I don't know why it was bothering me so much that he was fondling my tinsel.

He cleared his throat, and I finally looked up at him.

"I thought that maybe I could show you around Fireweed Island this week. Unless my brother has you buried to the eyeballs in work."

The shock of his invitation made me speechless as Stan glanced at me across the room and waggled his brows at me.

Max tapped my desk to get my attention again. "How about it? Is it a yes?"

"Actually, I appreciate the invitation, but I have a lot of work to do before Thursday's meeting. I'm sure my nights will be taken up with prep work."

My reply didn't seem to faze him. "How about Friday, then?"

Max glanced behind me, and his expression fell.

"What about Friday?" my boss barked.

Oh, thank goodness. The perfect twin had arrived.

I spun in my chair to see Levi glaring at his brother.

"I was letting Skye know that I would love to show her around Fireweed Island. She said she wasn't available until Friday."

My gaze flicked to Max's. "Actually, I didn't say I was available on Friday. I said that I have a lot of work to do before Thursday's big meeting."

"Which means Friday, you're free," Max tried again.

I shook my head. "No. It doesn't really mean that."

"Max, what do you think you're doing?" Levi asked. His voice was slow and steady. I noticed a couple of other employees huddled around Stan's desk for an optimum view.

"She's a single lady who's new to the island. I won't be around much longer before my next trip, so I assumed she might like to take me up on my offer of a grand tour of Fireweed."

"I never said I was single," I muttered under my breath.

Max and Levi both looked surprised.

"Oh, well, then," Max said, taking a step back. "I didn't know you were in a relationship."

I glanced at Levi and then at Max. "I didn't say I was in a relationship either."

Max's hands flew up. "Well, which is it?"

"Which is what?"

"Are you available or not?"

"No. I'm not available."

Max scowled and glanced at his brother before stalking off to a conference room.

I noticed Stan and the group of nosy coworkers all went back to their desks.

"I'm sorry about my brother." He leaned against my

desk and glanced at the tangled mess of tinsel. "What happened to this?"

"Your brother. He kept fondling my tinsel, and now it's in a knot." I glanced up at Levi, and my heart did a little somersault. How could two identical men give me such stark contrast?

"Again, I apologize for his behavior. Soon, he'll be jumping off cliffs in the Maldives or something."

"Are there cliffs there?"

Levi smiled and shrugged.

"So, he won't be spending holidays with family?" I asked.

"I'm his family, and no."

"Oh." I did a horrible job of hiding my surprise.

I pulled my gaze from Levi's and stared at my laptop.

"Marcy told me your first two designs were out of this world."

My eyes snapped back to his. "Really?"

He nodded and pointed. "Let's see them."

A wave of nervousness rolled through my body. I'd always been confident with my designs, but for some strange reason, I was suddenly concerned about impressing him.

Maybe it was an ego thing since he'd let so many other graphic designers go.

Or maybe I just cared what he thought.

I quickly pulled up Illustrator, and he bent down to look closely at the first design. His shoulder was nearly touching mine, and heat rolled up my body, inch by inch, the longer he stayed near.

"Skye." His voice was low and rumbly.

"Yes?" My breath hitched in the back of my throat.

Did he hate it?

Levi was still hovering close, looking at the screen.

"This is brilliant." He straightened. "Beautiful."

It felt like I could finally breathe again.

"You've captured exactly what I want to get across. We're going to nail this meeting."

And that was it. He didn't ask to see the second image. He didn't offer critique. He didn't fire me. He just left.

Stan started clapping as he walked over, laughing. "That has never happened before. Can I get a look?"

I nodded as Stan glanced at my computer. "Wow. That really is fantastic, Skye."

"Thanks. I—"

"What the hell happened to my office?" Levi's voice boomed into the entire office, and Stan's eyes grew twice their size.

"I forgot that we decorated his office while he was

gone at lunch." I chuckled. "Think he likes it?"

"Who sprinkled glitter on my desk?"

Stan spun around and headed back to his desk as I sprang from my seat and darted toward Levi's office.

Just as he was storming out, I crashed into his chest.

He hissed a deep breath and looked down at me while motioning for me to step inside.

I glanced at Marcy, who looked more amused than worried, before I stepped into the CEO's office and he closed the door.

The silver and red glitter had been mostly swept to the floor, but I didn't have the heart to tell him he had plenty more stuck to his chin.

"Have a seat, please, Skye." He pointed at the chair.

"But there's glitter in it," I objected.

"My point exactly." He watched me carefully as I walked over and took a seat without bothering to dust it off.

I crossed my right leg over my left, cupped my hands on my knee, and waited until he sat at his desk to say something.

I wasn't going to apologize because this situation was an office-sponsored event.

His brows rose as he waited for me to say something while I admired Stan's and my handiwork. We'd managed to frame the beautiful sparkly garland around his window, along with hanging a few felt stockings from the window frame. There was a mountain of fluffy, fake snow in the corner where we'd also put a *North Pole* sign and Santa's sled to clear up any confusion that we were indeed in the middle of a magical winter landscape.

"I like to win," I stated.

I caught a glimpse of surprise behind his gaze before he clasped his hands together and leaned toward the desk.

"You like to win?" he repeated, but I knew this might be my only chance to make him forget about the glitter fairies and focus on my work.

"Yes. It's what makes me good at what I do. You want to win over the private label bid on Thursday. I can help you do that." My eyes stayed focused on his, but it was impossible not to see the alarm from my response.

"And what do you have to say about this?" He unlocked his hands and waved them around the office.

"We won."

Levi scowled. "How do you figure? It looks like a herd of elves had a drunken escapade around my desk."

He found some glitter he'd missed wiping away, stuck it to his index finger, and held it up.

"The challenge was to make you love the décor in

your office, and that is what I set out to do." I smiled. "Give it a few days, and it will grow on you. First, you might start singing a Christmas carol under your breath. Second, you might crave a gingerbread cookie. Third, you might realize that a little Christmas garland never hurt nobody. And finally, you might even give your employees Christmas Eve off."

He cocked his head. "They get Christmas Day off."

This might be harder than I thought.

"If you don't like what Stan and I did, I can clean it up for you after you leave."

Levi was quiet for a second or two. "It's fine. It would take more time than it's worth to clean it up."

I nodded.

"You like to win . . ." He looked around his office just as his brother knocked on the door and barged in without waiting for Levi to answer.

He was standing next to me in a flash. "Man, you hate Christmas. What happened in here?"

Levi looked at his brother and glanced at me. "We had an office competition."

"You do every year. It's not like you ever participate." He walked over to the *North Pole* sign and bent down to get a better look. "This is really corny. Who thinks ice skating penguins are cute?"

I frowned and felt my spine straighten instantly. "I do. I think penguins doing just about anything is adorable. In fact, someone who doesn't find them cute is suspect on my list. Kind of like people who hate dogs."

Max spun around and slid his hands into his back pockets. "Dogs are inferior to cats. Everyone knows it."

"On whose planet?" I countered, feeling the heat rise in my cheeks.

His eyes narrowed. "Well, let's be honest. Any animal is preferable to a dog."

I gulped in my hiss and flinched before looking at Levi to see where he stood on the matter.

"If it makes you feel better, I have a rescue dog," Levi assured me.

My shoulders relaxed a little, but I noticed Levi didn't take his attention from me.

"And I like penguins," he added.

"I stopped by to see if I can borrow your bike?"

Why would Max want to borrow a bicycle in the snow?

Levi looked out the window before turning his attention to Max. "When?"

"Uh, now."

"It's snowing, and there's like six inches on the

ground." Levi shook his head. "No."

"I read there's this wicked way to do pump wheelies in the snow." Max kicked some of the fake snow on the ground, and I got personally offended.

"You can't handle my motorcycle on a good day. Why would you think I'd give you the keys in the dead of winter?"

Ooh, a motorcycle? Now that was a vision of Levi I could get behind.

Max rolled his eyes. "Fine. Whatever. Are we still having dinner tonight?"

Levi's jaw clenched.

"Actually, Levi and I are working on the big project tonight. Possibly tomorrow, too," I blurted out.

The tension in Levi's expression magically disappeared, and Max nodded. "Okay. That works better for me, anyway. Seattle is calling my name."

"Enjoy working your life away, Brother," Max said over his shoulder before closing the door behind him.

Chapter Six

Levi

Charming didn't even begin to describe Skye. Neither did refreshing nor brilliant. Sure, she was all those things, but there was something even bigger than that guiding her life. How she picked up on my not wanting to hang out with my brother was beyond me.

But I was grateful.

And she was right. Even though my office looked like a band of elves threw up inside, I didn't mind the glitter.

Maybe it was because Skye did it, but I didn't hate it.

Skye popped her head into my office a little after five o'clock. Most of the employees had headed home and coming into the office tomorrow looked less likely with the amount of snow accumulation.

"Hey, Boss," she sang. "I have a few more things to

show you. Hopefully, you don't think I overstepped my bounds."

I wasn't exactly sure how or why she'd think that, but I pulled my eyes away from my screen and saw her standing in my doorway.

She was adorable.

And sexy.

And taken.

She said so herself.

Just the thought put a damper on my spirit, which didn't make any sense considering I was her boss and she lived across the country.

"Wanna follow me?" She motioned with her index finger, and I nodded like a lost puppy dog.

"I'll be there in a sec."

She grinned and nodded. "Sounds good, Boss."

No one called me Boss. I had no idea why, but when she said it, I liked it. I opened a drawer and saw the stack of company holiday cards that I was supposed to sign so Marcy could send them out to all our vendors, distributors, and customers.

Another day. Maybe after Thursday's meeting.

I stood and rolled my shoulders a few times to lessen the tension, but it was only stronger. Walking to the window that overlooked the water, I thought back to my dad. Had I let him down? Would he be disappointed in me?

A heavy sigh escaped as I turned around and headed out to see Skye. Just the thought turned my mood right around.

Some of the office lights had been turned off in the far corner, and the entire office had either tinsel, garland, or ornaments dangling from anything within arm's reach. I wanted to be indifferent like I'd always been toward this time of year, but for some reason, it felt different today.

Skye heard me coming over and spun in her chair. She had a gleam in her eyes and had already pulled up a chair next to her desk.

When I sat, the sweet smell of her perfume drifted over. The same incredible scent I smelled earlier when I was leaning over to look at her work.

Was there not one repulsive thing about her?

Why did it matter?

It didn't.

"I hope you like what you see."

You have no idea. I bit back a smile and gave a quick nod. "Show me what you've got."

"I'm thinking we focus on the blind taste tests right away. I've created graphics that I think get the point across. This brand always comes out as stellar. Why would a club store want to go with an inferior product when they have at their fingertips the finest Pinot Grigio that they have first dibs at?" She watched me study the graphics. "They should know they aren't the only game in town, and the other club chain is more than willing to pick you up."

I glanced at her. "We haven't offered it to the other one."

She shrugged. "They don't need to know that. As far as I'm concerned, if you did, they'd jump at the chance."

I nodded as a smile crept on my lips. She had a series of illustrations that read like a story. By the time I reached the last one, I was ready to buy my own wine.

"Where'd you come up with these facts and figures?" I asked.

"I dug around on your server, and I asked Marcy."

I laughed and shook my head. "You're nothing if not honest."

She grinned. "So, what do you think? I saw an email earlier about leading off the meeting in a different direction, but sometimes, a picture is worth a thousand words."

"I like it. Your idea is actually phenomenal. It doesn't give them much room to object. If their entire goal is to give their customers the best product and value, then what you've shown them makes the choice obvious."

Skye grinned. "I'm glad you agree."

"Absolutely."

She reached for a Post-it note, and her fingers grazed mine. A bolt of electricity shot through me, and I saw her pull back.

"You okay?" I asked.

Skye bit her bottom lip and nodded, grabbing the Post-it. "Totally."

She started scribbling some notes on the small piece of hot pink paper and stuck the first on the screen, followed by several others.

The last of the employees headed out, waving as they left, and I turned my attention back to Skye.

"Hey, I wanted to tell you thanks," I said softly as if my brother was about to jump out from nowhere.

"It's what you hired me to do." She grinned and shoved a few strands of stray hair from her face.

"No. I meant with my brother. Telling him that we needed to get work done."

Her smile only widened. "Well, it was true."

I laughed and shook my head. "You know what I mean."

"I do, and you're welcome. I know what it's like to have a sibling you sometimes just need a little break from."

My brow arched. "You do?"

Skye turned in her chair to face me. "Totally. Don't get me wrong. I love my entire family. We talk all the time. They're even coming out for Christmas."

"Wow."

She nodded. "But the endless questions about my dating life, or the lack thereof, along with the arrival dates of the imaginary offspring they're dreaming up, get to be a little much."

Smiling, I looked around the empty office. "So, your dating life? I thought you had a significant other."

She looked surprised. "Why would you think that?"

My gaze locked on hers. "You told my brother you weren't available."

"I'm not."

"Because you're in a relationship?"

She shook her head and shuddered. "No way. I've learned my lesson on that front."

"You're not seeing anyone?" I couldn't hide my surprise.

"Not a soul." She chuckled. "And especially not your brother."

"Burn," I said, grinning.

A few seconds of silence sat between us, and before I

knew what was happening, I did the unthinkable.

"Are you free tonight?"

She looked at me. "For what?"

"Dinner? We can discuss all your ideas over some amazing French fries at Mudflats."

Skye looked genuinely happy. "I would love that. I've been craving them since last night. But there's one condition."

"What's that?"

"Honesty."

I nodded. Of course, I'd be honest with Skye. I had nothing to lie about.

"I don't mean to intrude or put my nose where it doesn't belong." She stopped herself.

Oh, no. Here we go. She wanted to know about my family, my brother.

"I can tell there is more than you're letting on about this meeting on Thursday."

I glanced around the office and squeezed the back of my neck. "How?"

"My dad owned his own business. There were a lot of ups and downs that came with it. I recognize hidden stress."

"I'm beginning to think you're also a mind reader." I smiled as she stretched her arms toward the ceiling. Her pink blouse tugged slightly across her chest, and I stood to give her space.

"Just perceptive. It's almost a character flaw," she said, bringing her arms back to her sides as she stood. "I'm starving, so if it's okay with you . . ."

"Totally."

She bent down and pulled giant snow boots out from under her desk, kicked off her heels, and slid on the boots.

I grinned, laughing. "You're perceptive and prepared."

"I came from Maine. What can I say?" She slipped her goose-down parka on and looked at me. "It can't be a far walk."

"It's not, but I'll drive. I don't need my good luck charm getting frostbitten before the big meeting."

She nodded and put her purse over her shoulder before slipping her hands in the pockets of her coat while I went to my office to pick up my keys, wallet, and jacket.

When I looked up, she was in the doorway, and her gaze caught mine.

"You have a lot riding on this meeting."

I nodded silently. "Everything."

Her eyes narrowed as she cocked her head. "What do you mean, *everything*?"

I'd been bottling it all up for so long that the thought

of having someone to talk to was nearly exhilarating. Sure, I'd gone pretty deep with Maddie today at lunch, but I still held back.

"I'll explain over dinner."

She nodded and smiled, not taking her eyes off mine. "I'm counting on it."

Chapter Seven

Skye

What was I thinking?

I'll be Home for Christmas played through the restaurant, and a beautiful Christmas parade of boats chugged along outside. Blinking red and green lights lit up the night sky as the boats circled the island. Of course, we had a window seat to see the entire thing, and all I could think about was how amazing it would be to share it with someone.

It was one of the most romantic settings ever, and I was sitting across from my insanely good-looking boss.

But luckily for me, all I had to do was think of his twin, and any crazy Christmas urge to shove Levi under the mistletoe suddenly disappeared.

I glanced at Levi and noticed he was watching me.

"It's beautiful, isn't it?" he asked, his lip curling

slightly.

"Amazing, actually." I took a deep breath in, feeling something change between us.

"Tell me, Skye. Why are you here for the holidays?" he asked as the server came over.

I was relieved by the distraction.

"Would you like a cocktail or a bottle of wine?" Levi asked me.

I looked up at the server. "I would love a Dirty Pickle martini with Cîroc vodka."

"Absolutely. And you, sir?" the server asked.

"I'll take a Bombay Sapphire martini." He laughed. "You know to call me Levi."

The server grinned. "I thought you might want to impress your date, but I'll get the order placed."

"I'm not a date," I blurted, and the server grinned before walking away.

"A Dirty Pickle martini with Cîroc vodka?" Levi's brows rose.

"I love pickles." I chuckled. "In all forms."

"I didn't know there was a drink form." He smiled wider.

"Take a dirty martini, and instead of olive juice, replace it with pickle juice." Just the thought made me happy.

"I'll have to give it a try sometime."

"Totally." I nodded in agreement, noticing how easy it was to be myself with Levi.

His eyes stayed on mine. "So, back to my question."

I grumbled a smile and rolled my eyes before looking at the menu. "No reason."

"You obviously love the holidays, and it sounded like, apart from the usual family annoyances, you love your family. Washington is a heck of a long way away from Maine."

"They're coming for Christmas."

He nodded and took a breath. "But isn't it about the whole season with you people?"

I laughed as the server brought our drinks. "Us people?"

Levi chuckled and took a sip of his martini.

We both placed our orders, and I turned my attention back to Levi, but his attention had never left me.

"You talk about people who enjoy the holidays as if we're diseased or like we're a plague that will spread," I observed.

He shrugged and chuckled. "You might be onto something."

"Fine. I'll tell you why I'm here. I had a nasty breakup

with my boyfriend of three years, and I didn't particularly want to bump into him and his newly pregnant girlfriend around town."

"Ouch."

I laughed. "You could say that. But I wish them well."

He took another sip. "If anyone else had told me that, I wouldn't believe them. But with you, I do."

"That I wish them well?" I shrugged. "I won't lie. It hurt worse than an angry mob of wasps stinging every orifice of my body."

Levi laughed. "Well, that's quite the visual, if not a bit specific."

I smiled, feeling freer than I had in a long time. "I'm direct and descriptive. Lucky you."

"And I thought you were merely perceptive and prepared."

My brows rose in surprise. "You think I'm perceptive?"

"Scarily so."

"Well, thank you."

"For what?" he asked.

"For thinking I'm prepared." I took a sip of my martini and let the pickle juice settle onto my tongue before gulping it down. "And perceptive."

"You are. It's a fact."

My boyfriend always liked to tell me how I was always ill-prepared for life, so this was a bit refreshing, especially since it was my boss thinking that I had my act together.

"So that's my story, and I'm sticking to it. Maybe next year, I won't mind being back home, but right now is not that time. Thankfully, my family figured it out without my having to tell them."

"Which is why they're all coming out here."

I nodded, suddenly feeling sheepish. "I probably shouldn't be telling my boss these things. I'm pretty sure talking about my love life tops the list of Things Not to Do on Day One."

"I don't mind."

"Now that you got the dirty secret out of me, it's your turn?"

He smiled. "I don't have exes walking around pregnant, if that's what you mean."

"Nice try."

Levi nodded slowly, and a glimpse of sadness surfaced in his gaze. "Fine. A deal is a deal."

The server set the halibut I'd ordered in front of me and the filet in front of Levi.

"Anything else for you two?" he asked.

I shook my head and thanked him, as did Levi.

After we each took a bite, Levi nodded. "The business has been growing steadily over the last several years. Actually, that's putting it mildly. Sales were soaring, doubling year after year."

I nodded, feeling my stomach knot in anticipation. I knew where he was headed with this.

"And then last year, the entire alcohol segment started to take a turn, and to say we weren't spared would be putting it mildly."

I took another bite of halibut as he pushed his steak around. His eyes met mine again. "So, we had scaled appropriately. More employees. Larger facilities. And now, I'm facing a very stark reality of laying off people and scaling back our facilities or else . . ."

"You don't have to say it." I glanced around the restaurant, knowing how small towns worked. "But this deal with the warehouse chain would turn it all around?"

Levi let out a deep breath. "It would make all of my worries disappear. No layoffs. Increased output to sustain our new facility."

"You'll get the deal."

His eyes locked on mine. "You're certainly

confident."

"I like to win."

Levi smirked and nodded. "You've mentioned that."

"It's true. Another character flaw."

Levi laughed and shook his head before taking a bite of steak. "I'm really beginning to like all of your character flaws."

"Just wait. You'll be buying me a ticket back to Maine before you know it."

He didn't say anything. Instead, we quietly ate our meals for a couple of minutes. And it was strange. There wasn't anything awkward about it. No incessant need to fill the silence with babble or small talk, no uncomfortable fidgeting or weird glances.

I looked out the window and smiled as the trail of boats could barely be seen in the distance. "How many times does the parade happen?"

"I think it's nightly through the month of December. It used to be Monday nights and then Monday and Friday nights, and now it's whenever any of the residents want to fire up their boats."

"That's awesome. I enjoyed Manhattan during the holidays. Obviously, completely different from here. But this is calmer and cooler."

He glanced around the restaurant and turned his attention back to me. "It *is* cool. How's your martini?"

"Incredible. Best one ever." I clicked my tongue, and he smiled wider.

"What's going on in that head of yours?" he asked, and I'd be lying to myself if I didn't confess to liking the way he looked at me.

Like I was the most fascinating woman in the world.

"Do you ice skate?" I asked.

"I haven't since I played hockey."

"So, that's a yes?"

His laughter rolled through my body, and I knew I wanted to do anything to make sure that deal happened for him. There was a lot more going on inside him, and for some crazy reason, I wanted to find out what it was.

"It's not like back East or the Midwest. It's not cold enough to have outdoor ice rinks."

My brows rose. "What about indoor ice rinks?"

He laughed. "There's probably some around."

"Okay. How about when we get the deal on Thursday, you take me to an ice rink to skate?"

Levi finished his martini. "Fine."

"And the entire office," I added.

A twinkle of something I didn't recognize dashed

through his gaze. "Deal "

I nodded. "Perfect. You'd better dust off those old hockey skates. I wouldn't want you to blow out your knee or something."

Levi laughed and shook his head. "How old do you think I am?"

"Older than me by a long shot."

"Well, as your employer, I can't ask how old you are, but I didn't know I looked like death warmed over."

I smiled. "Not when you smile."

"Are you saying I don't do that?"

"You smile some, but you wear them well. You should try it more often."

"I'll have to remember that."

I nodded as the server came over and asked if we wanted another round, which we did. When the server left, I took my last bite of halibut.

"Especially remember it for Thursday."

"Will do."

And I could tell he meant it.

"My employees deserve this more than anything," he told me, lowering his voice. "I know I have a great team. They put up with me."

"Why do you say it that way?" I laughed. "I mean, I

can come up with some reasons, but . . ."

Levi glanced out the window and smiled. "Because recently, I've been stressed and probably haven't been the kindest."

"Your employees seem to love you. Even Stan after he got his butt handed to him." I laughed. "Probably because he knew what he did wasn't the smartest thing. From what I can tell, you're fair, direct, and honest."

He laughed. "Isn't that being decent?"

"As an official temp girl, I can tell you that most bosses are not like that. Some are flat-out mean for no reason. Others are on power trips. Some just don't even know what the heck they're doing." I shrugged. "I know I've only been here for a day, but the office mood is chill and very festive."

He chuckled. "Well, we can thank Marcy for that."

I grinned. "And I did."

The server came by to take our plates and ask about dessert. My chest tightened, thinking my night with Levi was suddenly over, so I ordered a cheesecake. Suddenly going back to my empty house across the country from my family seemed lonely.

"What makes you take temp work?"

I took deep breath in. "Do you want the professional reason or the personal reason?"

"How about both?"

"Fine. I think subconsciously, I knew my relationship was on the rocks, so I started to accept assignments out of town."

"Ah. So, instead of sticking around and fixing things, you decided to flee."

I chuckled. Hearing it out loud didn't make me sound any better than when I'd said it to myself.

"I think it was to protect myself. I'd caught a couple of flirty texts he'd sent to other women, and I just didn't know what to do."

"Did you confront him?" he asked.

I nodded. "And of course, I was told I was making a big deal out of nothing."

Levi folded his hands together. "And yet he's walking around with a woman who's not you and she's very pregnant."

"Exactly."

"I hate to ask . . ."

I clenched my eyes shut. "Go ahead. Get it out."

"Was she one of the women he was texting?"

I blinked my eyes open and let out a deep sigh. "She was. Turns out they'd been hooking up while we lived together."

"Then I take it back."

"Take what back?"

"That you were trying to flee. You were just being perceptive. Somehow, you knew what was going on and protected yourself."

"Hearing you say that makes me feel better, so thank you." I shifted in my seat. "So professionally, I want to start my own graphic design company. I'm probably fooling myself about my capabilities for running a business, but I'm still clinging to the dream, taking temp work while I figure out how to go about starting my own business."

Levi kept his gaze on mine, and my body flushed with heat. There was something about the look in his eyes that made my body buzz with excitement.

"Give yourself some credit. You've got a great mind, Skye. Don't give up on your dreams."

Chapter Eight

Levi

It was Wednesday morning, and the office bustled with happiness and vibrant energy. There was something about having Skye here that made things different. Her coworkers were always hovering around her, asking her for opinions and sucking up Skye's positivity.

And it had only been two and a half days since she'd arrived.

"How's it going?" Marcy asked, wandering over to me in the breakroom.

"Pretty good."

She nodded and smiled. "You seem calmer."

"Do I?"

"A million times over." She looked in the direction of Skye. "Does she have anything to do with it?"

I nodded. "Probably. Her designs make me believe we're going to win this bid."

"Is that all?" she prompted, putting a tea bag into her Santa mug.

My brows arched, knowing it was probably impossible to hide things from Marcy. "What do you mean?"

Her hand whipped to her hip. "You know exactly what I mean."

"We're keeping things completely professional," I said flatly.

"Then why'd your lip curl slightly on the left?"

I cocked my head and rolled my eyes. "Marcy, you're seeing things."

"I sure am. Do you know why I called Max to deliver the groceries instead of you?"

I shook my head. "I can't fathom why."

"Because I knew she'd be turned off by his behavior." She stepped closer. "If I sent you, who knows what would have happened that first night?"

"I'm not following."

She groaned. "You're hot. Your brother is too, obviously. But he has the personality of a vulture. You don't." She wiggled her finger in front of me. "And don't pretend like you don't know that."

I laughed and took a sip of my coffee. "One thing I know is that if my brother gets to a woman first, I don't have a chance in hell of dating her. He taints this look." I whipped my hand around my face, and Marcy chuckled.

"Taints what look?" Skye asked, coming into the breakroom. "Should I change something with the logo?"

Marcy burst into laughter as I spun around to see Skye's gaze filled with concern.

"No. Absolutely not," I assured her as Marcy patted her back.

"I was just talking to my boss about his lack of a love life. Unprofessional, I know." Marcy grinned. "But I think my boyfriend hopes Levi finds someone so he doesn't crash any other vacations or Sunday dinners at my mom's."

Skye's mouth dropped open. "You've gone on vacation with Marcy?"

I laughed. "In all fairness, we've been best friends since high school, and I introduced her to her boyfriend because he and I used to travel together."

She glanced at Marcy, who nodded in agreement. "Truthfully, we'd miss him at Sunday dinners."

Skye's gaze caught mine, and I felt an unexpected charge. The next month was going to be a delicate balancing act.

"I would too. He's good company if he gets out of his own head."

My heart stopped.

Marcy's brows rose. "Oh, yeah?"

Skye nodded. "Yup. We had dinner on Monday to talk about Thursday's meeting and to get him out of having to spend an evening with his brother."

I could feel Marcy's eyes on me, but I refused to look. I kept my focus on Skye, which wasn't hard to do.

"Interesting how that slipped your mind yesterday morning when I asked how the night before was, Levi?"

I cleared my throat, and Skye innocently looked at me.

"He did have a couple." Skye gave a flick of her wrist to indicate drinking and grimaced.

Why did every single thing this girl did turn me on? She could trade my deepest, darkest secret to a competitor, and I'd probably hug her for it.

"Oh, then I should probably tell you that when we get the deal on Thursday, he has to take the entire office to an ice skating rink."

Marcy laughed in surprise. "Seriously?"

I nodded reluctantly while Skye grinned from ear to ear. She'd worn her hair in a twist today, and a few pieces of her dark hair fell along her cheeks. She wore crimson lipstick to match her red wool sweater and dark slacks. She was stunning, and it was hard to pretend I didn't notice how attractive she was.

Marcy snickered. "Sounds fun. I'm sure the office will love it. I'll start calling places across the water to see about renting it."

My heart stalled, and I held up my hand. "Let's wait until the deal is done."

"Nonsense," Skye said, shaking her head. "Put as much good energy as you can out, telling the world it is already a done deal. We will be the face of the club store's new private-label wine, and you two will have something to celebrate at your next Sunday dinner."

Her determination made me smile.

"Well, speaking of Sunday dinner, Skye," Marcy said, barely glancing at me as I took a sip of coffee. "How about you join us? My mom loves meeting new people."

Skye bit her bottom lip and looked up to the ceiling as she thought about it before glancing in my direction. "Are you sure? You might get tired of me by the end of the week."

Without realizing it, my mouth started going. "I think that is pretty much impossible."

Her eyes shifted to mine. "Yeah?"

I nodded as Marcy held in a chuckle.

"I would love to come to dinner at your mom's. What can I bring?"

"Absolutely nothing," Marcy assured her.

"Okay. Well, I'd better get back at it." She spun on her heels with a small bag of potato chips and a glass of water.

After a few seconds of silence, Marcy slowly turned to eye me. "Dinner on day one?"

"It wasn't my idea."

She folded her arms. "We need her. Don't blow it."

I scowled. "What makes you think I'll blow it?"

"It's the holidays. You hate Christmas. With each day closer to the holiday, you become grumpier. You're annoyed with your brother, and you're stressed to the gills about your business. I could see the potential for a lot of blowups, and it wouldn't be the first time."

"I've never dated an employee."

Marcy leaned against the counter and took a sip of her tea. "No, but any relationship you've attempted in December has burned worse than a dry Christmas tree."

"I get it." I shook my head. "Believe me. I don't want to do anything to jeopardize tomorrow's deal or the future of my business."

For some reason, the thought of this business being

mine in the future left a sour taste. I knew I was fortunate beyond belief to inherit this company, but it left me drained every single day. And the wine was my father's passion. Not mine.

"Earth to Levi." She waved her hand in front of me.

"I didn't go anywhere," I muttered.

She winked at me. "You have it bad if you're daydreaming about her after she's barely left."

"Joke's on you. I was busy thinking about this company and tomorrow's meeting."

Marcy pressed her lips into a thin line and shook her head. "I'm sorry, Levi. I should have known. I understand a lot is riding on it. I shouldn't be teasing you."

"It's fine. In fact, I'm going to check with the sales team."

She gave a nod, and I left the breakroom and wandered over to Stan and the others.

He smiled and waved, glancing at Skye. Poor guy had it bad for her too.

Evie, who'd been working here since college, walked over and sat on Stan's desk. She was taking the lead for the numbers portion tomorrow.

"How do you feel about everything?" I asked.

She took her glasses off and nodded. "I have the deck

memorized frontward and backward. We're going to nail it. Skye has made it even prettier. I just feel good all around."

I glanced over my shoulder at Skye, who was staring hard at her monitor. How could she make that scream sex?

Shaking my head, I glanced back at my sales team. "I didn't know she fit that in as well."

Was this woman superwoman? She did more in three days than any of our other graphic artists had done in weeks.

"I just plan on going over the pitch once more, and I'm ready."

"Same," Stan said, nodding. "I think we've got this. I'll probably just stay late tonight to work on it without interruptions from my cat or something."

I laughed, leaning against Stan's desk. "Should I order in pizza, and we make a thing of it here?"

Stan smiled and nodded. "Sounds good to me."

"Ditto," Evie said, sliding off the desk. "Maybe see if Skye wants to stay too? She's such a doll."

My brows rose in surprise. Evie didn't like people.

And by people . . .

I meant people.

But for some reason, she knocked it out of the park when it came to sales. Part of me thought it might be because she didn't see the people she was pitching to as human, but she was a great employee and friend.

I nodded, dusting some fake snow from my pants. "Good idea."

"I'm full of them." She winked at me and wandered back to her desk as I made my way over to Skye.

"Hey," I said, coming up next to her. "Evie loves what you did to their presentation. Thanks for going above and beyond."

Skye spun in her chair, and my heart squeezed at the sight of her. She had a pencil sticking behind her ear to go along with the colorful assortment of Post-it notes everywhere.

"It's my pleasure." Her smile lit up my insides as her gaze scanned my body unexpectedly.

"Anyway, I'm ordering pizza for dinner for those who want to stay and prepare for tomorrow."

"Yeah?" She glanced at Stan and Evie before bringing her eyes back to mine. "Well, count me in. I don't have anything else to do tonight."

"Nice. Well, Stan hates pineapple, and Evie despises mushrooms. Is there anything you hate on your pizza?"

"Nope. I'll even eat anchovies." She reached for another Post-it note. "But it's a shame Stan doesn't like pineapples. It's the perfect balance between sweet and tangy.

That takes him right out of the dating pool here on the island."

"You have one?" I asked, surprised.

She smirked. "I was teasing."

"Right."

Her gaze fell below my waist before riding right back to mine. "Umm. I don't know how to say this other than . . ."

She stopped talking and smiled.

"Go ahead," I prompted.

"Well, your crotch is glittering."

I glanced down to see fake, glittering snow stuck to my pants, and I shook my head.

"This isn't helping me love the holiday," I joked as she chuckled, and I wandered off to my office to dust off the fluffy stuff.

As I was frantically wiping, Marcy walked in. "Should I come back?"

"Ha-ha."

"So, does the gang want pizza?"

"Yup. Let's do a Canadian bacon and pineapple pizza, a combo without mushrooms, and two pepperoni pizzas."

"Stan hates pineapple."

"But Skye loves it."

Marcy laughed. "I see how it is. Jay's flying in tonight, or I'd join you."

"He finally just now got a flight out from Vermont?"

She chuckled. "For your information, he could have come home yesterday, but he just happens to love my family that much."

I chuckled. The truth was that he was going to ask Marcy to marry him, and he was busy picking out a ring with the help of her mom while Marcy was back here. I'd gotten plenty of texts about it all week.

Skye walked up to Marcy and glanced at me in the office. "Hey, feel free to say it's a bad idea, but since I'm just down the street, and it's essentially a company house, maybe we should work there and have pizza? Might make people feel less like they're at work? I mentioned it to Evie, and she was totally on board."

Marcy couldn't contain her smile. "Sounds like a good idea to me. How about you, Levi?"

"Yeah. Sure. Why not?"

Marcy clapped her hands. "Okay, then. I'll order the pizzas to be delivered to Skye's house."

"And I'll let Evie and Stan know to let everyone else know to come on over. This should get us all pumped enough for tomorrow."

Skye nearly skipped out of my office, and I wondered if this was a bad idea.

Chapter Nine

Skye

I'd changed into a red sweatsuit with Santa on the sweatshirt, moved the cookie candles out of the kitchen so they didn't look like they were meant to be eaten, and turned on my tiny Christmas tree that I'd gotten at the hardware store yesterday after work. I even managed to put on Nat King Cole's Christmas music.

While the office had been decorated in enough Christmas décor for a stadium, it didn't feel quite as cozy as this house, and I thought Stan, Evie, and everyone else might enjoy it more.

The doorbell rang, and I dashed to open it, expecting the pizza man.

But I got Levi instead.

And the sight of him nearly took my breath away.

He'd changed into a pair of jeans and a dark grey sweater.

I grinned. "You're not the pizza guy."

"Not yet." He smiled, and I motioned for him to come inside.

"Enough of that talk," I told him, closing the door. "We're gonna nail this tomorrow."

Levi nodded as his gaze steadied on mine. "You know, I totally believe you. I'd be shocked if we didn't."

I smiled at my boss as he moved by me. His hand brushed up against mine, and my body shuddered unexpectedly.

Get it together, Skye.

He's just a man.

An incredibly perfect man with an incredibly imperfect twin.

Focus on the twin, Skye.

"I love what you've done with the place." His expression fell, and he laughed. "Sorry. That was so bad."

I chuckled, nodding. "Yeah. It was. But whoever did this place has excellent taste."

"Thanks."

"It was you?"

He nodded as the doorbell rang again. I opened the

door to see a gaggle of my coworkers. Instead of stepping inside, they pretended to be carolers and started to sing *Jingle Bells*.

I saw the pizza man park and ushered everyone inside as Levi came over to help with all the pizzas.

"Holy cow. How many pizzas did you order?" I asked.

"Seven."

I glanced over my shoulder. "That's like three-quarters of one pizza per person."

His brows arched. "And?"

"And you're a man after my own heart."

We thanked the delivery driver and carted in the huge pizza boxes as everyone congregated in the kitchen.

"Remember when most of us crashed here on New Year's Eve last year?" Evie asked.

Levi and everyone nodded.

"Well, that sounds fun." I smiled and helped to set the pizza boxes out, along with extra plates.

"The views of the fireworks from here are amazing," Evie explained. "And same at Levi's house, but you know, he's the boss. So, this is neutral partying ground."

I laughed. "Must be quite the parties."

"But he's kind enough to throw a party here," she

added, looking over at him. "Since he maybe shows up for ten minutes."

I glanced at Levi. "An entire ten minutes?"

He grinned. "What can I say? I suck at the holidays."

I nodded, opening the closest pizza box to see a pizza full of huge pineapple chunks.

Levi reached next to me for a slice of pepperoni.

"Did you do this for me?" I whispered.

"Sure did." Levi smiled, grabbing a slice of the Canadian bacon and pineapple for him as well.

"Well, thank you. That was very sweet of you."

He nodded and headed toward the living room, where some of the other employees were already camped out with their food and laptops.

By the time I'd made my way in, there weren't any spots left.

Evie's hand shot up. "Ooh. Over here. You can squish in between me and the armrest."

I laughed and glanced at the floor where several people were sitting. "I'll just take the fireplace stoop."

Levi stood. "No. You'll get too hot."

"No. I'm totally fine," I assured him.

He sat back down, but Evie nearly elbowed him off his seat.

Stan was setting up the projector as everyone else ate pizza and chatted, but I felt Levi looking in my direction, except that every time I tried to catch him, he was staring at his plate.

Which meant it was probably in my head like so many things were when it came to dating.

Whoops.

I wasn't dating him.

He was my boss.

Only my boss.

I looked over at him and finally caught his gaze on me. He smiled and held up a piece of pineapple and winked before tossing it in his mouth. For some reason, it made me feel giddy.

When Stan finished hooking up the projector, everyone quieted down and got to work immediately. Evie stood and went over her section, followed by Stan.

But they were leaving so much on the table with what Levi's wine company offered in terms of bottling a private-label wine. My fingers were getting twitchy with agitation, and I saw something stirring in Levi's gaze.

I was the new girl, and I didn't want to create enemies by stepping on seasoned salespeople's toes. But this was important. I had to say something. When the next lull happened, I stood and started relaying my experience of working with Shantos Wines.

I highlighted the people, the work ethic, and the passion to make people smile with wine. Shantos Wines was the only option on earth that merged two incredibly important factors when choosing a manufacturer for a private label. Buying loyalty by being cost-effective while achieving premium product was how Shantos had built its legacy so far, and there was no intention of stopping.

I glanced at Levi, and my cheeks flushed when I saw the look in his eyes.

Evie stood up, and Stan shook his head.

Shoot. I'd done it again.

Time to pack the bags.

I'd overstepped my bounds, dabbled in something I wasn't hired to worry about.

Levi slowly stood, and I braced myself for what was next.

But to my surprise, he and everyone else started clapping.

I looked around the crowded living room and felt my body start to relax, and the flush from my body left while my cheeks blushed for a different reason.

"Will you be able to remember that tomorrow?" Evie

whispered, and I chuckled. "Go, girl."

Levi's gaze connected with mine, and it felt like no one else in the room existed. My body trembled a little as his mouth opened, but he didn't say a word.

Instead, he mouthed two words.

Thank you.

And it made my entire heart swell with emotion.

As Stan swatted his back, Levi snapped out of it and went back to being the CEO of Shantos Wines, void of vulnerability but full of bite.

An hour later, my coworkers were mostly funneling out, taking a few stray slices of pizza with them until it was just Levi and me standing in the living room.

My little Christmas tree twinkled pathetically in the corner.

The tree hadn't felt minuscule until Levi stood next to it and made it look woefully inadequate in terms of size.

"Do you like my tree?" I asked.

His brows furrowed. "Tree?"

I laughed and nodded. "Yeah. It's next to you in the corner."

He turned to spot the ankle biter of a tree and smiled. "I didn't even see it."

I rolled my eyes. "Obviously."

"It's quite lovely."

"Thanks." I laughed nervously, suddenly feeling like anything could happen tonight.

And that scared me.

I'd had a plan for the next month, and I'd hoped to stick to it, especially since my family already bought tickets to come out here for Christmas.

"You were incredible tonight." He took a step closer, and I noticed I did the same.

I bent over and grabbed my water to disconnect myself from the feelings washing over me. But all I kept thinking about was the little mouthed *thank you* from earlier. There was so much riding on tomorrow, but that wasn't all I felt from him. There was so much more underneath his salty exterior than being the boss. It was like every single time our eyes connected, I could feel him in my soul. And that was why I always fell so hard.

I cleared my throat and looked up at him. "I just said a few sentences."

"That was more powerful than any of the slides we had. Between your imagery and your words, we might actually get this."

"You *will* get this." I whipped my finger up in the air and somehow brushed his lips with it.

Levi smiled and shook his head as I dropped my hand by my side. "Damn, if we didn't hire the one woman in the country who makes me want to drop to my knees."

I swallowed back the desire to close the gap between us. I didn't need another relationship that went nowhere. I specialized in devoting years of my life to men who were either emotionally unavailable or physically somewhere else, or should I say, physically *in* someone else.

"I'm sorry. I know I shouldn't say—"

I shook my head. "No. It's not that. I just . . . there's something about you that makes me want to know more."

"Same."

"And since you're my boss, I know better."

"As do I." He took a step back and glanced at my tree. "And I would never cross that boundary."

Levi's gaze came back to me but fell to my lips, and heat drilled through me. There was something so sensuous about his hazel eyes, the intensity lurking behind his expression.

"So, we wait thirty days when I'm no longer employed and see if this thing that's happening between us is . . ." I grinned and stopped myself.

"Real?"

I nodded in agreement. "Real."

My stomach knotted at the rules I had just laid out for us as if there were an us.

He gave me a nod. "I should get going."

"Sure. Right. Absolutely. Makes sense." I smiled and glanced at the door, but neither of us moved an inch. "Or I could quit right on the spot."

Levi smirked and shook his head as his arms looped around my waist. He pulled me into him, and my breath caught deep down as desire poured over me.

This was crazy.

Insane.

But as his eyes locked on mine, electricity zinged through me as if this was the sanest moment in my life. I sensed everything—his breath skating over my scalp, the lemony, spicy smell that made my knees quiver, his heart rate steady and bold, his fingers gently circling my back.

"We seriously can't go down this path," I said more breathlessly than I realized.

Levi nodded and took a deep breath. "You're right, but I just needed to know what it was like to hold you in my arms."

His words messed with my head, and he didn't let go. I didn't want him to let go.

The fire roared behind us. The room smelled heavenly

from the candles and pizza, oddly enough. But nothing felt more comfortable and right than the man standing in front of me, holding me.

"Christmas is a complicated time for me. Always." His gaze stayed on mine.

"I've kind of gathered that." I didn't budge from his arms.

It felt good.

"And apart from being your boss, Marcy did a good job of reminding me of just how screwed up I can make things in the month of December."

"Why's that?" I asked softly.

"Lots of things." He didn't say anything else, but he pulled me closer, and I rested my head on his chest, feeling the hard definition just under the wool of his sweater.

"If you weren't ending this before it began, I'd have you pull that sweater off because it's making my cheek itchy." I closed my eyes for a brief second. "And it kind of feels like you get your lift on underneath."

Levi's body shook slightly in a rumble of laughter. "You always make me feel so good when I'm around you, and it's only been three days."

His arms loosened, but I didn't want to step away. Instead, I looked into his eyes and nodded. "I feel the same way, but I blame Christmas. I'm a sap around the holidays."

"That must be it. Christmas is attempting to wear off on me too." He nodded as I took a step back and brought in a deep breath to steady my world.

"Thanks for not firing me for going off on a tangent about the presentation tomorrow."

His eyes never left mine. "Never."

I chuckled. "Never say never. I'm really good at proving people wrong."

Levi laughed and nodded. "Fair enough. Do you want a ride tomorrow?"

"Evie's going to pick me up in the morning, and then she said we'll just meet at their headquarters in Issaquah?"

"Correct." Levi smiled. "Thanks for all you've done for my team. You may not see it, but I do."

"Thank you for everything, including this." I motioned around the home.

Levi nodded and bent forward as if he were about to give me a kiss. I closed my eyes, but instead, his mouth butted up to my ear.

"You're an amazing woman, Skye. I'll see you tomorrow." He pulled away, and I blinked open my eyes to see him turn and walk out of the house.

And I was suddenly left wondering if I could handle

being around my boss as only my boss for the next month.

When the door shut, my body shook in an absolute mess of emotions. I sat on the couch and let out a deep sigh of regret, knowing I'd finally met a man who made me feel special, and he was untouchable.

Chapter Ten

Levi

I'd finished answering questions from the VP of Private Label Acquisitions, and she seemed pleased. But the shining moment was when Skye took over like last night and highlighted what Shantos Wines valued and why those principles lined up with the club store. Watching her smile at the executives while never missing a beat was a delicate dance that I'd never seen before. She spoke of loyalty, legacy, value, and determination.

When she sat down, everyone clapped, but I kept my focus on the VP.

After last night, I didn't want to do anything more to jeopardize Skye's time here. I'd already crossed a line. It didn't matter that Skye said she'd wanted it too. I was the boss. I held power.

I knew better.

So, I needed to stay focused on what mattered to the future of the company, not my personal life.

Max was the lucky one who could indulge in having a relationship. It was just too bad that he had a personality to rival most rodents.

As the meeting ended, my team and I headed out to the parking lot. We could feel the energy rolling off the club's executive team. Excitement lit up the cold winter air as we all got into our cars. I'd told them all to take the rest of the day off. We needed to enjoy this moment no matter the outcome.

Evie waved, and Skye smiled in my direction. I gave a quick nod and climbed into my Mercedes.

Skye's expression fell, and my gut twisted into a mess of regret. I didn't want to hurt her, but this wasn't right to do. We had to stop anything before feelings got in the way.

Pulling out of the parking lot, I decided to head to the one place where I could say anything and not have it come back to haunt me. The drive was only about twenty minutes from where we'd had our big meeting, and the wide-open gates welcomed me inside the expansive space.

The rolling hills with towering pines and maples made my chest tighten. Coming here had always been a mixture of peace and pain. Ever since that night so long ago.

I pulled up to where my parents were buried and stepped out of the driver's seat. I grabbed my coat from the backseat and zipped up before making my way to the shared memorial for the two most important people in my life.

They'd shaped everything about me, my life.

And on the same note, they took so much away by handing me something my brother didn't receive.

I let out a deep breath and knelt at the graves of Mr. and Mrs. Adams, my parents.

I dusted off some of the pine needles and traced my fingers over my parents' names.

Dorothy and Simon.

"We had a big meeting today, Dad. We won't know until sometime next week whether we got it. But we need the deal. We really need it." I smiled, thinking about my dad sitting in his office, kicking his feet up on the desk after a particularly grueling day. My mom would stand behind him and rub his shoulders as if she were readying him for another round in the boxing ring. In hindsight, she knew more about what was needed than either of us. "I miss you guys. There's not a day that goes by when you two aren't on my mind, especially now."

I stood, seeing two giant pinecones under the pine tree, and grabbed them, placing them on the top two corners of my parents' plaque.

"As you can probably guess, I'm still single, and so is Max. No surprise there, I'm sure." I laughed, thinking back to what Skye said about my brother. "But another Christmas is coming up, and I'm just as miserable as I was the first year. It doesn't get easier, but I'm grateful for Marcy and her family. Max is leaving for the Maldives, so he won't be around. Probably for the best." I let out another deep breath, but the tightening in my chest didn't diminish. "If you could sprinkle some of your otherworldly powers over the company and its direction, that would be helpful and a really great Christmas present, even though I'm not much for the big day."

I knelt down and kissed my fingers before touching the cold granite. "Love you both."

The breeze started to pick up, and the clouds had turned a purer shade of grey, which meant snow was probably coming later. It was time to get on the ferry before the snow hit and the roads came to a sudden halt on the mainland.

I climbed back in my car and started toward downtown Seattle to catch the next ferry. The tension started to roll out of my shoulders even though I was bogged down in traffic. It was amazing how Fireweed Island was only a short ferry trip out of Seattle, but it felt like a different world.

I made a turn toward the terminals where giant

Christmas décor had been anchored to the lamp posts and saw a very small crowd of cars waiting. I didn't see Evie's or any of the other team's vehicles, so they must have caught the earlier ferry or decided to go grab lunch.

As I pulled up to the ferry booth, the woman smiled and directed me to the proper lane that had already started to move onto the ferry. By the time I pulled where I was pointed, I turned off the car, turned on some music, and leaned my seat back.

And immediately, my mind drifted to Skye.

What was I going to do?

She was like the perfect ball of energy, smarts, and fun rolled up into a giant Christmas present that I couldn't have. Skye absolutely killed it for us today. The entire team did a tremendous job, and if we didn't win this bid, then at least I knew we did our best.

But Skye.

I closed my eyes as the ferry took off toward the island and her smile and her laugh rushed into my thoughts.

Her touch.

The way she felt last night.

The look in her eyes when I almost kissed her.

Damn. My body was responding to her just from memories.

I shoved my hands through my hair and let out a groan of frustration.

I knew the best thing to do was to stay away. Work with her from a distance. Maybe work with her through Stan, Marcy, or Evie.

But I didn't want to hurt her feelings.

First things first. I just needed to get through tomorrow's workday back in the office to see if the feelings were still as hot as they were last night and this morning in the meeting. I literally had to keep my focus on the presentation while Skye spoke, or my entire body would have given me away.

Maybe it was just me. Maybe I imagined the feelings between us, but I swore every time I was around her, I wanted more.

As Fireweed Island came into view, I put my seat up and cranked the music down. Maybe I just needed some food and to download with Maddie. She was at her tea shop today while Chance took the kids to the zoo in Seattle.

The ferry docked, and I drove off toward the tea shop. The island bustled with tourists. Fireweed prided itself in having the most Christmas decorations out of the chain of islands. It was like a winter wonderland if a person was into that sort of thing.

Which I wasn't.

A car pulled away from in front of the tea shop, and I quickly nabbed the space, turning off my car as the first flake fell.

"Great," I grumbled. "Just what we needed."

I made my way to the store and pushed the door open to the little tinkle of the bell. Maddie looked up from behind the counter with her sister Holly standing next to her. Holly grinned and waved as her eyes went over to a group of women at one of the tables.

My gaze stumbled toward Evie, and then Skye, and I froze, glancing back at Maddie.

She hid a smile. "So, what can I get for you, Levi?"

The table of women fell silent, and I charged toward the counter. "Just a black tea."

Before I knew it, Skye was standing behind me. Her eyes were still twinkling from the high of success back at the meeting.

"So, you're standing in a shop full of special holiday teas and you order a plain, black tea," she stated, folding her arms over her chest.

"What can I say?"

Skye leaned over and lowered her voice. "You really are like Scrooge, except good-looking." She straightened and winked at me as Maddie slid over the cup of tea.

"Why don't you live a little and try the candy cane tea? It's what I'm having, and I'm addicted. Although my first cup was the Gingerbread Man tea, and lemme tell ya, it makes me think I have a crush on him."

Evie glanced over at us and smiled.

"Well, I'll remember that for next time." I gave a short nod. "And great job today. You and the rest of the team were incredible. I can't thank you enough."

Skye narrowed her eyes at me. "That's it?"

I nodded slowly. "Pretty much. I'm gonna go grab a burger to take back to the office."

"You're going back in?" Evie asked, standing. "Should we—"

I held up my hand. "No. Not at all. Enjoy the afternoon. I just have some stuff to catch up on."

Skye's eyes were still on me when I returned my attention to her.

"How about I come with you?" she offered. "I have a couple of things I'd like to get done before tomorrow."

Evie sat down and took a sip of tea as she watched us.

"Uh, yeah. Sure. I can give you a lift." I held my tea tightly as Skye smiled.

"Thanks. I just want to grab a few holiday teas for

home." She spun around and started talking to Maddie as I wandered over to the window and watched the snow fall harder.

If it weren't for the fact that I despised the month of December, the snow might actually be pretty. I glanced behind me to see Skye whispering to Maddie, who was laughing, and Holly glanced in my direction.

I scowled. I'd never experienced a positive outcome when a group of ladies was whispering and staring in my direction.

Holly quickly dropped her gaze to the bag she was helping her sister with for Skye, and I looked up toward the ceiling impatiently.

When Skye was finally done, she had a bag looped around her wrist and was holding two cups of tea.

"Were you worried you'd run out by the time we got to the office?"

Skye chuckled. "No, Mr. Scrooge. This is the Gingerbread Man tea that I thought you'd like. It's got a bit of a spicy kick and then turns calming."

I laughed, shaking my head as I polished off my black tea and tossed the paper cup in the garbage. "Are you saying I'm not calm?"

She chuckled and walked through the door I was

holding open for her. "I don't know what I'm saying."

I reached for the cup she extended as she looked up at me. "I hope I'm not intruding."

"With what?" I asked, noticing it was slipperier than when I'd gone inside. I reached for her arm to steady her as we neared my car.

"Thanks." She looked up at me. "With your work."

I opened the door for her as she climbed in and shook my head.

"Nope. Not at all."

I closed the door and walked around the front of the car and slid into the driver's seat.

"Well?" she asked, turning in her seat.

"Well, what?"

"The tea. Are you going to drink it or use it as a hand warmer?"

I smiled and took a sip. Clove and nutmeg numbed my tongue as sweetness came next. "It's good."

"I told ya." She buckled in as I slipped my drink into the cup holder. Our fingers brushed, and Skye's breath hitched. A tingle ran through my arm from just bumping into her. How was I going to get through the next thirty days?

I pulled onto the street and glanced at her. "You doing okay?"

"Yeah. I'm fine, but you're not acting the same way."

I cleared my throat and turned toward the office building. "I'm not sure I'm following."

She shrugged, and the office came into view.

"Marcy's been at it again," I grumbled, seeing twinkling white lights framing all the office windows.

"And it looks fantastic," Skye declared.

I parked, and Skye didn't move for a second, and then she shifted in her seat to stare at me. "You know, I was relieved to meet Maddie."

My brows. "Yeah? Why?"

"She's the gal you met for lunch, right?"

I nodded. "Maddie and her husband are really good friends."

Skye smiled and nodded.

I frowned. "What?"

Skye didn't answer. She grabbed her drink and got out of the car and headed toward the office.

By the time I'd made it inside, she was already telling Marcy how amazing the lights were, and I slid into my office and shut the door.

Chapter Eleven

Skye

It was late Friday afternoon, and I'd made it through the first week at my new temp job. I was relieved and perplexed. Ever since the night at my house, Levi had been doing an incredible job of either staying away from me or limiting his sentences to three or four words.

I thought back to the meeting and how little attention he'd paid to me while I was speaking. He either kept his gaze on the presentation or the female VP, which made me think he had a thing for her.

And that was completely fine because he was my boss, and I had absolutely no skin in the game. He could date or mess around with whomever he wanted.

Although choosing a female who can make or break your business might not be the best selection. Maybe Levi was a masochist. He already didn't like Christmas.

But at least he was a fan of canines. That was in his favor.

I stared at my monitor and shaded in some lettering as Marcy wandered over with a big smile.

"I hope you're hungry. My mom is so excited to meet you on Sunday. She's invited some other folks from around the island too. She doesn't like the idea of you not having any friends while you're here."

I grinned, noticing Levi finally opening his office door and stepping out. "I hope she didn't go to too much trouble."

"She lives for this," Marcy assured me. "So, how's everything going? You've had your first official week here."

"I love it. I'm just on pins and needles to find out whether we pulled it off yesterday."

Marcy smiled and nodded. "You and everyone else."

"How's Levi?" I asked. "He's been in his office a lot more than earlier in the week."

Marcy nodded, and I watched Levi head out the front entrance. I guess he was starting his weekend early.

Yesterday, after he'd dropped me off, he left after about forty minutes, which made me wonder if he really did need to come in.

Marcy clasped her hands together. "I think he's just got a lot on his mind."

"I'm sure."

Marcy bit her bottom lip and looked like she was debating whether to tell me something. "Don't take things personally if he's a little distracted. This time of year is always hard on him."

I nodded. "Absolutely not. I'm just here to do the best job I can. Are you sure I can't bring anything to dinner on Sunday?"

"I'm completely positive. Just your smiling and happy self."

I grinned and watched her walk away as my phone buzzed. I picked it up to see my sister texted me.

How'd the meeting go yesterday?

I smiled, missing my sister a little sooner than I'd expected. Usually, it took a couple of weeks away, but maybe it was because of the holidays. Or the fact that I'd suddenly gotten the cold shoulder from my boss.

It went incredibly well. Just waiting to find out if they got the bid.

Another text slid over.

We can't wait to come to see you for Christmas.

I smiled and texted back.

Same.

Another text popped on my screen.

Is your boss still bang-worthy?

"Okay, Gingerbread Man tea for everyone," Levi called out behind me.

My phone tumbled out of my hands and onto my desk as I spun around to see him and Maggie standing there with four stacks of cup trays. Evie glanced over at me, and I shrugged as the office swarmed my boss and Maggie for the special tea.

Levi's eyes locked on mine as I stood from my desk and slowly made my way over. Maddie had gone back out the door she'd come in through, and Levi only had a few teas left.

I smiled. "Gingerbread Man tea for the crew? That

doesn't seem very bah-humbug to me."

"It's my new favorite." He kept a straight face.

"Really, and is that all you have to say for yourself?"

"I thought everyone here would love it too." His brow arched. "Would you like a cup?"

"Don't mind if I do." I snatched one off his tray and took a sip, keeping my eyes on his. "You've kept to yourself today."

He set the tray down and nodded. "Been busy."

"I assumed."

The awkwardness between us wasn't natural. It was forced, like he was trying to make things between us . . . weird.

I paused on that last thought and turned around.

Why would he want to do that?

Whatever. Two could play that game. If he regretted Wednesday night, so be it.

"Hey, Skye," Stan said, walking over to my desk the moment my bum hit the seat. "Would you like to come out with a bunch of us for drinks?"

I glanced over my shoulder and noticed Levi watching us. Smiling, I turned to Stan and nodded. "That would be great. Thanks."

"We're just walking down the street to the new

place." He laughed. "Right. You wouldn't know if it was new or old. Anyway, we're headed out in about twenty minutes."

"Okay. Awesome." I nodded, looking at the clock. I didn't understand how it was so close to four o'clock.

As I turned my attention back to my computer, I felt a breeze come up behind me, followed by the sexy voice I'd sworn off minutes ago.

"You headed out for drinks tonight?"

I looked up at my boss.

Very much my boss.

It didn't matter that he had hazel eyes that reflected gold in the sunshine, something I'd only recently learned when he was on the sidewalk in front of the tea store yesterday, or the way the left side of his mouth curled up slightly more than the right when he smiled.

None of it mattered because he was my boss.

"Yup. Sounds like it." I tucked one of my legs under my bum and scooted into the desk.

"Fun."

"Probably not." I looked up at Levi, and he was smiling. "But it's the holidays, and I shouldn't be spending them by myself if another offer is on the table."

"I see." He rocked back on his boots and nodded. "Have fun."

Levi walked back to his office and closed the door. I wasn't sure if I was supposed to feel guilty that he wasn't invited or annoyed that he cared but didn't care. The whole thing was more than my mind could handle. Did he want to come? Not want to come? Was it inappropriate?

By the time four rolled around, I was all worked up. Stan popped by my desk, but I let out a grunt and looked at my screen. "Do you mind scribbling down the address, and I'll just walk over there when I finish? I don't want to get out of the groove."

"Uh . . . sure." Stan frowned and reached for the Post-it note I'd smacked in front of him.

He wrote down the name and address as Evie hopped over.

"It's just right down the street from Mudflats. You can't miss it," she explained.

"Thanks. I promise I won't be too long."

"I'll save you a seat." Evie gave a wave, and the group including Marcy walked out the door.

The office was empty, Levi's door was still closed, and I was more confused than ever. For whatever reason, there was some magnetic thing in the universe that just kept pulling me to Levi. Maybe I was a glutton for punishment, but I wanted to talk to him before I went to the bar. I wanted to know why he'd essentially ignored me yesterday and barely acknowledged me today.

As I shoved myself back from the desk, Levi's door opened.

I looked up to see him coming out. Surprise washed over his features.

"Oh, you're here still. I thought I heard the group go."

I smiled, studying the man who made my heart speed up a million beats too fast.

"Do you just lurk in your office until the coast is clear?" I asked, folding my arms over my chest.

Levi smiled, and the same insane pull to him pummeled through me. It was like the night he was in my living room, and I suddenly wanted to be kissed.

"Something like that." Levi scanned the office. "Why didn't you go with them?"

I shrugged. "I wanted to talk to you about some stuff."

He took a few steps in my direction, and my body stilled. Marcy had turned off most of the lights on the way out, and only a dim glow from the ones in the reception area lit the room.

Watching him make his way to my desk made it very difficult to concentrate on much of anything of substance. Instead, I was stuck on how good he looked in his worn jeans, black sweater, and leather hiking boots. He'd pushed up the sleeves on his sweater just enough to highlight his muscular forearms.

Ugh. The things I noticed.

"Are you quitting?" he asked only a foot or two away.

"Did you want me to?"

"Absolutely not. You're my good luck charm."

I cocked my head slightly as I looked at him. "Then why the cold shoulder?"

He drew a deep breath and ran his fingers along his chin. "I'm doing my best at keeping it professional. The night at your rental was a mistake."

His words stung.

They were the right words for this situation, the responsible and mature words that a boss needed to tell an employee. I knew it in my heart. My mind understood it completely, and yet I was left standing by my desk, wishing he'd suddenly scoop me into his arms and kiss me.

Which was my problem. I was a hopeless romantic, constantly thrown into utterly unromantic situations.

Take, for instance, my ex. I thought the night he came home to tell me he'd knocked up another woman was actually going to be the night he proposed to me.

My phone lit up with a grocery order, and Levi

glanced down as I remembered my sister's text that I hadn't wiped off the screen yet. I lunged to grab my phone, but Levi's brows furrowed before a huge grin spread across his face.

"Am I the boss in question?"

I slid the text off the screen and cleared my throat. "I don't know what you're talking about. There's no question. I just got a message that my groceries are ready for pickup."

"No, I'm pretty sure I know what I saw in the other message."

"Psh." I waved my hands in the air and rolled my eyes. "I really think you're getting ahead of yourself."

He took a step forward. "But I'm not the one who wrote the message."

I chuckled. "And neither am I. My sister is overly dramatic."

"What was the phrase?" He bit his bottom lip as he pretended to remember. "Bang worthy?"

I turned my phone over so my sister didn't send any other surprises and folded my arms over my chest.

"I don't even know what that means." I stared at him, trying to keep in my giggles. "You're my boss, which you've done a great job of reminding me."

Levi took another step closer, and I swallowed down the big ball of anxiety building in my belly. It wasn't just about wanting a kiss. It was about learning little bits about this man here and there and wanting to know so much more.

Like what happened between him and his brother? Where's his family? Has he ever been in love? Why does he hate December and Christmas? Why won't he just kiss me?

"I didn't mean to give you the cold shoulder." His voice was gruff but tender as I stood from my chair. "I'm not good at pretending I don't think about you twenty-four hours a day."

My eyes flicked to his, but I didn't know what to say. I slid over to my desk and sat, keeping both hands by my knees.

Levi moved closer, and my heart pounded in my chest as his eyes fell to my mouth.

"If you can't date me while I'm here, can you just be nice to me?" I asked, finding my voice. "Not ignore me?"

"I wasn't trying to ignore you. I just thought it was best if we kept our distance." He was standing directly in front of me.

"That won't work for me," I said, staring into his stormy eyes.

My entire body swelled with desire. He was inches away from me.

"I wasn't kidding when I said I'd quit," I whispered.

He smiled and shook his head. "I wouldn't make you do that."

"No. You'd just ignore me over the holidays." My throat was dry, and I licked my lips to regain some sort of moisture so I didn't choke to death in front of my hot boss.

Levi caged me in. "Is this what you want?"

My knees went in between his thighs as he closed the gap. I felt so small as he rested a hand on each side of me. One heavy breath, and our lips would be touching.

"Skye, I've never dated an employee," he said with a low, gravelly voice.

"I'm not exactly an employee."

He smiled wider but didn't move in.

"I thought maybe you didn't think I did a good job at the meeting. You never once looked at me. You were staring at the presentation or the VP the entire time."

Levi brought his hand to my chin and cupped it gently. "If I looked at you, I knew the entire room would know what I was thinking."

"And what was that?" My pulse raced as heat pooled lower and lower.

"That I wanted to push you up against the wall and taste you."

Chapter Twelve

Levi

"Well, Merry Christmas to me," Skye muttered, her cheeks blushing.

Within an instant, my hand fell from her chin, and I couldn't stop laughing.

"What?" She pouted as I stepped away to regroup.

"You kill me, Skye. I never know what's going to come out of your mouth."

She smiled that smile that instantly made me hard. It was like a sexy mixture of mischief and innocence. I moved back toward her so she wouldn't notice.

"What did you expect me to say?"

"I don't know, but not that."

She rested her arms on my shoulders, and our faces were so close I could smell the gingerbread tea on her breath.

"So, you weren't annoyed at me?" she asked, and my heart squeezed in disappointment. Had I really been that distant?

"Not at all, Skye. Every second I spend with you makes me imagine things I shouldn't be thinking about."

She wiggled her body closer to me, and I stepped forward, boxing her in on the desk. "You're smart and sexy, and you deserve more than what I can give you."

"But here you are," she said, resting her forehead on mine.

"Because I can't stay away. I've tried."

"And I don't like it." She dropped her arms from my shoulders and leaned back on them on the desk.

The curves of her body left little to the imagination as she watched me.

"And to think I almost got a kiss," she said wistfully.

I leaned over and brought my mouth close to her ear. I slowly ran my lips along her neck, and she shivered with a little moan.

A little moan.

And I hadn't even kissed her yet.

She lolled her head backward, exposing more of her neck.

This woman was so irresistible it was physically

painful.

I softly kissed her exposed skin and felt her body move toward me.

I straightened and let out a deep breath as she kept her eyes on mine.

"I want a real kiss," she whispered.

So. Did. I.

Shit.

I'd already broken every rule.

I did exactly what I said I wasn't going to do, and yet I couldn't leave. I couldn't turn away.

My fingers coiled through her hair, and my mouth found hers.

It was like my body was on fire with need for this woman. I'd never felt anything like it in my life. She parted her lips and wrapped her legs around my waist as I pulled her in.

Skye tasted spicy and sweet, just like I'd craved. Her fingers moved through my hair as she moved her tongue against mine and let out a sexy little noise.

There was no turning back.

We kissed and kissed until our mouths were numb and our bodies hot. She giggled as our lips parted and opened her eyes, looking as delirious as I felt. If I didn't have the desk to lean against, I didn't know what I'd do.

"Wow." She closed her eyes and inhaled. "I didn't know that a kiss could be like that."

My eyes fell along her body as she sat on her desk, her feet dangling over the edge, and all I could think about was having all of her.

Skye opened her eyes and smiled dopily, straightening on the desk. "I should probably get going to meet everyone for drinks, or they might wonder what happened to me."

I smiled and nodded. "God forbid they think you're sleeping with the boss."

She narrowed her eyes at me and laughed. "There could be worse things."

She sucked on her bottom lip and hopped off her desk. "Do you want to come with me?"

I shook my head. "Nah. I shouldn't."

"You're not doing very good on your list of should nots." She grinned. "Live a little and come out with us."

"Only for you," I said, knowing I meant it.

She grinned and picked up her phone. "Hold on. I just need to text back my sister."

I chuckled and shook my head. "Are you telling her I'm still bang-worthy?"

"Oh, yeah." Skye smiled as she dropped her phone into her purse and pulled on a coat. "See? Kissing me wasn't so bad, was it?"

"It never was about that, Skye." I shook my head. "I just . . ."

"You're just the responsible twin, the responsible son. You'd never do anything that would jeopardize anything for anyone, even if that means making yourself miserable."

I smiled slowly. "Something like that."

She let out a deep breath. "Our secret is safe with me, but if you're not tired of me come January third, I might not be able to keep it quiet any longer."

I had the date memorized the moment I'd met Skye. "The day your contract is up."

"Yup." She looped her hands through mine, and I didn't want to let go.

I pulled her into me and looked into her beautiful eyes. "I don't know if I can wait that long."

"It's the holidays. The days'll be gone in a flash."

I shook my head and let out a deep breath. That was the problem. December dragged on as if it were four years stretched into thirty days.

Endless cheer, reminiscing, and bloated parties.

And then came December 26th when everyone went

back to their normal lives as if none of the goodwill and cheer mattered the previous twenty-five days.

"You okay?" she asked softly.

"More than okay, but let's get going before they start to wonder."

We let go of one another and headed out of the office.

She walked a few paces in front of me and stopped until I caught up. It was a short jaunt down from the office, and I knew the place had quickly turned into a spot for my employees to hang out. They'd invited me a few times, but when a person says no enough times, the invites stop.

Skye glanced over her shoulder and smiled. "I won't say a word. I won't even look at you."

I laughed and shook my head as we reached the bar. She opened the door, and a chorus of greetings echoed through the air when Skye stepped inside. When everyone saw me, they quieted for a split second before cheering some more. Marcy glanced at me and furrowed her brows, and I shrugged as Skye wandered over to where Evie had saved a place for her.

"Okay, Skye. Tell us," Evie stood with a beer in her hand and smiled. "Do you love Fireweed Island, or can you not wait to go back home?"

Skye glanced around the bar and smiled. "This little

island is growing on me, but I'd probably miss my family."

My chest tightened at her confession, and I took a seat next to Marcy. Just another reason I shouldn't let us go down this road. I squeezed my fingers into my palm and tapped my foot as the bartender brought over a round of drinks. I requested a beer and sat back in the seat.

Marcy leaned over. "You seem tense," she whispered.

I didn't dare tell her it was because I had just kissed our new employee and was already doubting my choices in life.

"Just waiting for the word on whether we can start doing private label." I didn't look at her but glanced at Skye, who was beaming and laughing with Evie.

Skye was such a carefree spirit. The easiness of her spilled into everything she did. Whether she designed beautifully, stood in front of a room full of execs, or sat and drank a beer with everyone, she just knew how to not care.

It was an attribute I didn't have. I glanced over at Stan, who noticed me noticing Skye.

Damn.

I should have stuck to my original plan. It was going to become so obvious that I had it bad for Skye. I didn't need people to worry about me playing favorites or acting inappropriately. I clicked my jaw and took a sip of beer as

Lucas Harten came rolling over to talk to Skye.

My fist tightened, and I straightened, which didn't go unnoticed by Marcy.

Not a Harten. They were all great people. The family owned the town pharmacy, and there wasn't a reason in the world to avoid Lucas. He'd just recently moved back to Fireweed, and he was single.

I pressed my lips into a firm line as I watched him flirting with Skye. We weren't together. There was nothing to get irritated about.

But she was mine.

I let out a grunt, and Marcy laughed.

"What's so funny?" I growled at her.

"Lucas certainly zeroed in quickly." Marcy looked amused.

"I don't know what you're talking about." I took another sip of beer.

"Sure you don't, buddy." She patted my shoulder.

I laughed and shook my head, putting my beer down on the table.

Skye glanced in my direction as charming Lucas kept laying it on thick.

"She doesn't seem interested," Marcy whispered.

I shrugged. "He's a nice guy."

"So are you."

"I'm not sure about that." I kicked my legs out in front of me and held my beer.

"I know how stressed you are about everything, and it's not because you're worried about yourself. It's because you're worried about them."

I didn't answer.

"What made you come out tonight? You never do."

I turned to Marcy and smiled. "Just felt like it would be good for the team."

"Oh, right. The team." She winked.

Lucas knelt down in front of Skye and pulled out his phone while Evie elbowed her. Skye bit her lip and looked a little uncomfortable. I wasn't sure if it was because the guy she'd just kissed happened to be ten feet away from her while she was giving someone else her number or if she didn't want to give it to him.

Whatever.

It didn't matter. I took the last pull of my beer and stood, handing Marcy a few hundred bucks. "Buy the team some drinks. I'm headed home."

"Are you sure?"

I nodded, knowing nothing good would come of the night if I stuck around.

I looked at Skye, who was watching me even though Lucas was down on one knee, flirting like a champ. I gave her a quick nod and made my way out of the bar.

In the short time I'd been inside, the sun had set, and the cold air was even chillier. I pulled my coat tighter and made my way back to the office and climbed into my car. I only lived about five minutes from the office, but these had to be the longest five minutes of my life.

All I could think about was what she and Lucas could be doing this very second. It wasn't like I had any say in the matter. I was her boss. We kissed. We shouldn't have kissed. She's single.

I shook my head and pulled into my driveway and opened the garage.

Why was I getting so worked up over this? She was here temporarily.

Maybe now that she's met Lucas, he can be the distraction for her while she's here. It would certainly make things easier. I turned off my car and ran my fingers through my hair as I groaned in frustration. Why did I have to care?

Chapter Thirteen

Skye

I couldn't get the look in Levi's eyes out of my head. The moment he shot from his seat and headed out the door, I wanted nothing more than to run after him.

But I promised him I would keep our feelings hidden. If I had bolted after him, everyone would have figured something out. And then when Max rolled in . . . I shook my head at the memory.

I sat on the couch in my living room and took a sip of tea as the lights I'd hung around the mantle twinkled. I'd spent most of yesterday exploring the island and found the cutest antique and décor store, which was rumored to be owned by Anthony Hill's wife, and he only happened to be my favorite singer ever. Of course, it could just be a rumor, but it gave me time for a brief few minutes to not be obsessing over Levi.

And why was I?

Glancing at the clock, I let out a deep sigh and closed my eyes. Marcy was going to be picking me up in a few minutes for dinner at her mom's house, and I wasn't even close to ready.

I felt like a zombie, really.

The kiss I'd shared with Levi was intense and all-consuming and trying to pretend as if nothing had happened between us at dinner wouldn't be easy.

Out of complete laziness, I turned the camera on myself to see if I could get away with leaving the house. My hair was in a braid, and even though I had showered this morning, I still had yesterday's mascara on. Call it a unique talent.

I dabbed under my eyes and let out a sigh before hauling myself off the couch. When I went into the bedroom, I scanned the closet for something casual but not messy. Settling on a pair of leggings, so I could eat without discomfort, and an oversized red sweater, I felt ready to face whatever might be waiting for me tonight.

Levi didn't seem thrilled that I was talking to Larry or Landon or whatever his name was, but I couldn't be rude, and I certainly couldn't chase after Levi.

The doorbell rang, and I wandered to greet Marcy, my

savior and ride to dinner. Except, when I swung open the door, Levi was standing on the stoop.

"You're not Marcy."

He glanced behind him at his car and pointed. "I can take off."

I laughed. "No, that's okay. I just wasn't expecting to have to sit in a car with you."

Levi nodded. "Sorry about that."

"Let me grab my purse."

I dashed to get my bag and glanced at myself in the mirror again, wishing I'd at least put a fresh coat of makeup on, and darted toward Levi.

He smiled when he saw me come into view. "You look beautiful."

"Thanks." I slid by him as he shut the door, and I walked to his car.

"What happened to Marcy?"

"She was helping her mom get ready for—"

"Oh! That's right. I made a cranberry raspberry salad with pretzels. I'll be right back."

Levi stopped and turned around while I jogged back into the house to the fridge for the salad I'd made last night. I know Marcy said not to bring anything, but I couldn't show up empty-handed.

When I'd made it back outside, Levi had the car running and my door open.

I slid inside and set the salad bowl on my lap while I buckled and shut the door.

"So, are we going to talk about the elephant in the car?" he asked, glancing at me.

"The fact that I did my part to keep our kiss a secret?" I looked over at him. "Or the one about you bolting from the bar when Larry came over to talk to me."

Levi smiled and gripped the steering wheel. "I guess I don't have too much to be concerned with since you don't even remember his name."

"I meant Landon," I corrected.

Levi chuckled. "It was Lucas. His family owns the town pharmacy. He's a good guy."

I raised my brows. "Yeah? Should I return his call?"

Levi looked surprised. "He called you?"

I laughed and rested my head against the seat as we drove down the road.

"Did he?" he tried again.

"Well, if you'd stuck around longer, you would know the answer to that."

"I suppose."

"Where did you zip off to, anyway?"

"I had something to take care of at home."

"Yeah? Like what?" I asked.

"My dog needed water."

"Oh, really, by five o'clock every night, he's without?"

"Something like that."

Levi pulled the car onto the shoulder. "Listen, I've had a lot of time to think about things, and maybe you should go out with Lucas."

It was like a bomb had just detonated in the car. "What?"

"I shouldn't have kissed you."

Fury rose fast. "You regret kissing me?"

"I don't regret kissing you." He let out a sigh. "I regret not waiting until your contract is up."

"If only you and I know about the kiss, I don't see what the big deal is." I squirmed in my seat. "And for your information, Landon is not my type."

"Lucas?"

I rolled my eyes, not caring what his name was. "And I'm trying really hard not to turn into a girly girl and have my feelings hurt by the man who rocked my world on Friday night and by Sunday wants nothing to do with me."

"I've just ... I've got a lot on my mind with the

business, and the holidays never work in my favor, and I'm just setting things up for failure. I can tell."

"That's the spirit," I said, feeling nauseous.

"You know what I mean."

"I don't. I like you, and I thought you liked me. We're in the baby steps stage here, so I don't know what to make of any of this."

"Every time I'm around you, I want to pull you into my arms and kiss you. I want to feel your body against mine." He shook his head. "And when you're not around me, I wish you were."

"So why torture yourself?" I asked.

"It's what I do." He glanced in the rearview mirror.

"What are you trying to tell me?"

"Let's take it slow. No more kissing."

"Fine. No. More. Kissing." I saluted him with a smile.

He laughed and pulled his car back onto the road. "I seriously don't know what to do with you."

"You had a pretty good clue on Friday," I teased.

His hand rested on my knee, and I felt heat roll up my thigh as I secretly wished he'd move his fingers north a little.

"Will you tell me why you hate December and Christmas?" I asked, glancing at him.

His jaw tensed, and he nodded. "I will, but not today.

We've got a Sunday dinner to enjoy."

"Okay. Just promise me you'll tell me."

He nodded slowly. "I will. So, what happened at the bar on Friday?"

"You won't believe me if I tell you."

Levi grinned and tightened his grip on my knee, moving slightly upward. "Try me."

"Your brother showed up."

His mouth dropped open. "No way."

I nodded, laughing. "Yup, and he remembered me telling him that I wasn't available, so he stepped in between Lucas and me to let him know it wasn't going to work. You should have seen the look on Evie's face. It was priceless. Landon . . . I mean, Lucas . . . just looked confused."

"Man, I bet. My brother is on another level."

I snickered and nodded as Levi turned down a long driveway nestled among the woods. Snow still blanketed the ground, and the pine trees sparkled in the sunlight. It was right out of a holiday movie.

"It's such a beautiful time of year," I said happily, looking at Levi as he found a place to park behind rows of cars. "Is it that you hate snow?"

He laughed and shook his head. "No, I do like snow."

"Well, that's good."

"You're not tired of it, growing up in Maine?"

"I am a complete snow bunny. I honestly didn't expect it here."

"It comes and goes on Fireweed."

"Like me."

Levi turned off the car, and I let out a nervous breath about going inside. As far as I knew, I didn't know anyone except for Levi and Marcy. Hopefully, I wouldn't stick my foot in my mouth.

We walked up to the large cabin in the middle of the woods as I clutched the salad I'd brought. No one would ever know we were on an island, being tucked away so deep into the forest. A large Santa stood on the corner of the porch, along with three elves that looked more like gnomes than elves, and a giant fresh wreath hung on the door. Something deliciously garlic managed to sweep through the air.

"Get ready to roll out of here tonight," Levi whispered as he rang the doorbell.

Marcy opened the door and smiled, waving her hands. "Welcome to my mom's abode."

"It smells fabulous," I said, smiling. "I might move in."

Marcy chuckled. "And I'm sure she'd love to have you."

"I didn't want to come empty-handed, and this always looks festive."

Marcy took the salad from me and smiled. "So sweet of you. Come on in and meet everyone. Thanks for picking her up, Levi."

"My pleasure."

Marcy eyed him for a brief moment as we followed her inside. A small silver tree stood in the foyer decorated with a candy theme, and a sprig of mistletoe hung overhead.

I leaned over to Levi. "Does this place give you the hives?"

Levi chuckled and shrugged, taking my coat. "I plead the fifth."

I smiled as we followed Marcy into the dining room, which was right off the foyer. The table was gigantic, with enough room for at least twelve people. Poinsettias lined the buffet table, and another Christmas tree had been tucked into the far corner.

Christmas music pumped through the house, and a wave of laughter came from somewhere.

"Sounds like quite the crowd," I whispered to myself more than anyone.

Levi gently touched the base of my spine and bent down. "They'll love you."

I glanced back at him as he dropped his hand away from me right when Marcy handed my salad to a woman who looked exactly like her. They both had red hair, an off-center part, and sparkling brown eyes.

"Mom, this is Skye. She's saving us from ourselves at Shantos during the holidays. Her family's back in Maine."

"I'm so glad you could make it, dear. You can call me Joanne," her mom said, putting the salad down and coming in for a hug. "You're officially invited to every Sunday night dinner, and if you don't have family coming for the holidays, I throw a big Christmas Eve party, and we open presents all day on Christmas day. Or if you do have family in town, bring them too."

I chuckled and glanced at Marcy, who seemed pleased with the invitation. "That's really nice of you. Thank you. I'm excited because my parents and sister have never been out to the West Coast, so this is their chance."

She rubbed my arms up and down. "You're freezing. Go stand by the fireplace. Levi, take her to the family room. That's where everyone is having drinks and gossiping about who knows what."

I chuckled as my boss, who was used to giving the orders, reached for my hand and then quickly remembered not to before pretending to merely motion in his direction. I laughed and shook my head, unsure of who might reveal our secret first.

The family room was a few steps down a hall where a stone fireplace confiscated an entire wall. The room was two stories tall, with a balcony stretched from one side to the other overlooking the family room. The banister was made from twisted pieces of timber, and each rung had been painstakingly wrapped in Christmas garland.

"Hey, Levi," a guy hollered from across the room.

My eyes found the source, and my mouth dropped open as I watched rockstar Anthony Hill waving at my boss. He was hugging a woman next to him, and I stood frozen.

Levi gave a quick wave and turned to take me over to them, but I couldn't move. He spun around, and his brows furrowed as he looked at me.

"Are you okay?"

"I'm a huge fan. Please don't take me over there. I will act like a complete idiot."

Levi smiled and shook his head. "No, you won't."

"No. I'm deadly serious. I will." My cheeks flamed with embarrassment as I glanced at Anthony and his wife as they started walking toward us. "Oh, no. Oh, no."

"Skye, you're going to be fine. He's just like any other sexy rockstar God out there."

Anthony chuckled and shook his head. "Oh, Levi . . . I didn't know you felt like this."

His wife chuckled and ran her fingers over his hair.

Levi laughed. "Sophie and Anthony, I'd love for you to meet—"

"Eeep. Finally. *Finally*." Sophie's arms flailed in the air. "You've finally found your other half. Your soul mate." She rested her head on Anthony's shoulder, and I was having an incredibly difficult time not bursting into laughter. "I was beginning to wonder if you'd become one of those perpetual bachelors."

Levi smirked and glanced at me. "Well, actually . . . This is Skye. She works at Shantos Wines until the new year."

Sophie scowled. "Wait. What?"

I chuckled. "I'm just his employee. Well, technically, I'm a contract worker, but Marcy was kind enough to include me in Sunday dinner here, so . . ."

"Oh, my gosh." Sophie's hands flew to her mouth. "I am so mortified and so sorry. I should have known Levi wouldn't have enough sense to date the right woman. Not that you're the right woman. You're a woman, probably a great woman, who could be the right woman. I don't know."

I grinned, loving that I'd finally met a woman who could stick her foot in her mouth as much as I could.

I drew a breath and glanced at Anthony. "I just have to get this out of the way. I'm a huge fan of your music. And I promise I won't mention anything about it again. You're just very talented."

Sophie beamed and looked at Anthony, and my stomach knotted seeing the love for one another. It was so pure and uncomplicated. I glanced at Levi and wondered if he knew that love like that was a gift.

A goal.

Not that I was thinking about love with him. That wasn't really possible, considering I'm in Maine, and he's here, and he's a boss, and I'm not.

And ugh.

I glanced up to see Levi watching me as Anthony motioned to a grand piano in the corner. "Watch this."

The crowd of people parted as Anthony walked over to the piano and sat down. "Okay, everyone. Let's do something completely cringe-worthy and sing *Jingle Bells*."

I stood on the tips of my toes and clapped my hands. "I'm in heaven. Complete heaven. I could go now and feel like my life is complete."

Levi's brows furrowed. "Over *Jingle Bells*?"

"Over Anthony Hill singing *Jingle Bells*." I grinned, marching closer to the piano as Anthony started to play.

I spotted Maddie and a gaggle of kids around her, with a cute man standing behind her, resting his hands on her shoulders as they started to sing. I glanced over my shoulder to see Levi sitting on the couch while the rest of us started up our rendition of *Jingle Bells*.

As the tune got louder, I couldn't resist. I spun around and walked over to my grumpy boss, sulking on the couch, and pulled him up.

"Come on, Scrooge." I smiled as he rolled his eyes at me. "Do you not know the words?"

"Obviously, I know the words."

"It's actually not obvious at all because you're not singing." I swatted at his butt right when Sophie looked over. Her eyes widened, and she kept singing as I stared straight ahead of me like that didn't just happen.

Chapter Fourteen

Levi

What I hated about the month of December was simple. Everywhere I went, I was reminded of something I wished I could run from. There was no pretending or forgetting for me. It didn't matter if I was trying to buy some apples at the grocery store and Christmas music blared over the speakers or if I wanted a quiet, simple meal at Mudflats. The holiday cheer was ruthless and endless until January first.

Even something as simple as Sunday dinner at Joanne's house became a source of turmoil. Sundays were great all year long, and then come December, it was as if the world turned into the land of chew toys. Stuffed Santas here, pillow elves there . . . nowhere was safe.

"Dinner is served." Joanne stepped into the family room as Skye elbowed me off the couch.

"I got it. I got it," I grumbled as everyone went around us toward the dining room.

"Is there a reason why with each passing second here, you're getting more and more miserable? Is it me? Should I leave?" she whispered.

My Lord. She was the one bright spot in all the twinkling lights and candy canes.

I attempted a feeble smile and shrugged. "Sorry. I'll work on it."

But the truth was that all I wanted to do was pull her into my arms and kiss her again.

"Darn right, or I'll come to your house in the dead of night and decorate it."

I chuckled. "That might not be all bad."

She cocked her head. "Behave. I think Sophie is already onto us."

"Us?" I teased as we walked out of the family room.

"Buffet style. Grab a plate." Joanne pointed at the massive kitchen island covered in pots, pans, and bowls of anything imaginable. Sweet potatoes? Check. Mashed? Check. Macaroni and Cheese? Check. Creamed Spinach? Check. Rib roast? Check. Ham? Check.

Skye's eyes widened. "I guess she really didn't need the salad."

I laughed and leaned over. "But I'll be sure to have two helpings."

She smiled and reached for a plate as Joanne helped to point various dishes out, and this feast wasn't merely because it was the holidays. No. Joanne always made Sundays big. It just so happened that during the month of December, candy canes were used as garnish.

By the time Skye and I had filled our plates, we followed Marcy into the dining room, where she'd left two chairs for us across from one another. Skye froze and glanced at me as I pretended not to notice.

I took a seat next to Marcy, and Skye slid into her seat next to Maddie.

"Nice to see you here," I told Maddie and Chance. Their little ones were strung out next to them, eating away at the Brussels sprouts, which I thought was odd. But far be it from me to judge children's appetites.

"We're headed back to Hound Island tomorrow morning," Maddie explained.

"Hound Island?" Skye asked, glancing between Maddie and me.

"Oh, you should try to come visit us. My mother-in-law started an amazing lodge that has grown far beyond our wildest dreams."

Chance nodded in agreement. "Definitely come visit the property. We've just built a new wing, and I've opened another restaurant."

"Another one?" Skye asked.

Maddie nodded. "He's an executive chef for the resort."

Skye chuckled. "Wow. A rockstar and a chef at the same table. I'm pretty much in heaven."

I smiled and looked over at Skye right when one of Maddie's kids attempted to cut a Brussels sprout. The slippery green ball shot sideways and landed on Skye's plate.

Without missing a beat, Skye stabbed it with her fork and ate it, leaving the little girl in a fit of giggles.

Skye winked at her. "Thank you for this scrumptious treat."

Realizing that I was staring at Skye for probably thirty seconds too long, I sliced into my meat and took a bite.

"Wonderful as always, Joanne."

"Thanks, dear." Joanne smiled and glanced at Skye and then back at me. "How's your brother doing?"

"As far as I know, he's doing well. I think he's getting ready for another trip."

"Ah . . . research, no doubt." She laughed and shook her head. "Someday, he will find his way."

I laughed and shook my head. "I'm not holding my breath. Hey, if he's content, then that's all that matters."

Maybe if I said the words enough, I'd finally start to believe them.

"Words of the wise older brother." Marcy grinned, smiling at me.

"Right. By fourteen minutes." I shook my head. "But those fourteen minutes did a number."

Skye shuddered, and I held in a chuckle.

"Do you have any siblings, Skye?" Joanne asked.

"I do. I have a wonderful sister and brother-in-law." She smiled as her gaze softened just thinking about them. "They should be coming out here in a few weeks."

"I'd love to meet them."

She nodded in agreement. "That would be fantastic, but you can't feed them, or they'll wonder why they only get dry chicken at my place."

Joanne chuckled and took a bite of Skye's salad. "You have to give me this recipe. It's so festive and delicious."

"Absolutely." Skye looked truly in her element. In fact, she didn't need me to be here at all.

"What do you plan on doing after this assignment is over?" Marcy asked Skye.

The question perked my attention right up as I

glanced in Skye's direction.

"My goal is to go back home to Maine, find a little place to rent, and regroup for a month or so before taking on any other work." She shifted in her seat. "I've been going, going, going for a long time, and I think I'd enjoy the act of doing nothing for a few weeks. My mom just pointed out to me that I haven't taken any breaks between jobs in the last four years."

"Wow." Joanne looked impressed. "That can't be good on a relationship."

Skye grinned. "Well, I do very well at picking emotionally unavailable men, so I think it works out in my favor."

Joanne gave her a sympathetic nod.

"Except when they cheat and get someone pregnant. Then it makes me think I'm working too much."

"Ouch. That had to hurt," Anthony piped up next to me. "It sounds like a song I'd write."

Skye nodded. "Well, have at it. I'll give you any details you need to make it happen."

Anthony laughed and nodded. "We've all been there." He glanced at Sophie. "Well, not exactly there, but dating is rough."

Sophie nodded in agreement. "Sometimes, you have

to kiss a lot of wart-ridden toads before you finally find your king."

"I've been upgraded to a king?" Anthony eyed her. "And just how many are we talking?"

Sophie laughed. "After this many years, I think it's about time I upgrade you, and you know all about them."

"Ah, young love." Joanne smiled. "But it gets even better with time."

"Speaking of, where's Hal?" Her husband usually sat at one end of the table, and she at the other.

Joanne rolled her eyes. "His brother broke his ankle playing senior soccer."

Skye's eyes widened. "Senior soccer? That's a thing?"

Joanne shook her head. "Exactly my thought. And look where it got us."

I laughed and nodded.

Skye caught my gaze, and I felt a pull to be next to her again.

It was crazy the feelings that could wash over me just by being near her.

Sure, it had only been a week since we'd met, but we'd spent the first five days together, eight hours a day, which has got to be the equivalent of like twelve dates. Plus, a dinner out that went pretty deep, so in terms of the dating world, it translated into at least a month.

Okay, so I was pushing that analogy, but it had to have counted in our favor.

"Are you still planning on Christmas here, Levi?" Joanne asked. "I hope so."

I nodded. "If you'll have me."

"It wouldn't be Christmas without you." Marcy grinned as the front door opened.

In stepped Marcy's boyfriend, stomping snow off his feet and wiping flakes off his head.

"The snow is really picking up outside. Seattle's at a total standstill. The ferries are running late." He pulled off his coat. "But it looks like I made it."

Marcy hopped up from the table and looped her arm through Jay's.

"Hey, everyone," he said, noticing a new person at the table.

"That's Skye."

"Ah, you're the lifesaver for Marcy at work. "I'm Jay, by the way," Jay said, nodding before looking at me. "And nice to see you."

"You too." I glanced at my plate, not wanting to give anything away, like the fact that he'd planned on asking

Marcy to marry him in less than a week.

Skye caught my gaze and grinned right before I felt her foot on top of mine. The tip of her foot started scraping up my calf, and it took everything I had not to start laughing. She waggled her brows, and then her foot went away as quickly as it came.

I stretched my foot out to see if I could find hers but found nothing. And then I saw Anthony hop in his seat. I quickly looked over to see him straighten up and look at Sophie. And then I realized Skye was still looking at me, thinking she was playing footsie with my foot. Anthony bit his lip and scooted back in his seat and cleared his throat, looking concerned as Skye kept massaging the wrong man's leg.

"Uh . . ." Anthony glanced across the table to see Chance and Maddie and figured it wasn't either of them before looking in Skye's direction.

Anthony laughed and shook his head. "Uh, Skye?"

Her eyes pulled away from mine, and she glanced at Anthony. "Yeah?"

"Are your feet cold?"

Skye shook her head. "No. Why would you ask that?" She glanced down at her chest, which made me chuckle, and then in about a second's time, she realized what had just happened. "I am so sorry. I never meant to . . ."

The table quieted, and all heads turned to Skye.

I elbowed Anthony, who quickly put the pieces together.

"Ah, I just thought I saw you shiver," Anthony piped up.

"Oh, honey." Joanne glanced at Skye. "Are you cold? I have a sweater you can borrow, or a shawl."

Skye's cheeks were fire-engine red. "Oh, I'm okay. I think it was just a chill from when Jay came inside. Totally good now, but I'm definitely ready for seconds."

She flew out of her seat so quickly I thought she'd suddenly grown wings.

By the time I caught up with her in the kitchen, she was piling food on top of her plate and glaring at me.

"I was just playing one-sided footsie with one of the most famous rockstars in the world." She shook her head. "Kill me now."

"Believe me. I'm sure he's had much worse happen to him." I smirked. "But it was fun while it lasted."

She put another slice of meat on her plate and sighed. "See what I mean? You can't take me anywhere."

I glanced around the empty kitchen. "I'm pretty certain I can take you everywhere I'd ever want to go."

She held her plate with both hands and smiled. "We'll see about that."

"I suppose we will."

Chapter Fifteen

Skye

Fireweed was feeling more familiar by the day, and the people were friendlier with every encounter.

Except for Mr. Crabby Pants.

I honestly couldn't wrap my head around his mood swings, and honestly, as I looked around the office, I doubted that there would be one person who would care one way or another if Levi dated me, or anyone else, for that matter.

My inbox dinged with a meeting invite in less than fifteen minutes in the man of the hour's office.

I debated over hitting *Decline*, but I didn't have the energy.

After Marcy dropped me off last night, I got to thinking about Levi and his excuses, and the more I peeled back the layers, the more I felt they were just that.

167

Excuses.

By the time I fell asleep last night, I was completely fired up about it and woke up this morning just as annoyed and exhausted, nearly forgetting I was in the happiest month of the year.

But I wasn't going to let Levi wear me down. Just because he wanted to be melodramatic and moody didn't mean I wanted to spend my holiday that way.

I was only half kidding about decorating his house in the middle of the night.

It would serve him right.

The problem was that my family all had non-refundable plane tickets, so I didn't want to do anything to jeopardize my job or my rental.

And I really liked the guy, or the idea of him since he'd basically put the kibosh on us. But the cold, hard fact was that whenever I was near him, I couldn't stop looking into his gorgeous eyes or dreaming about his perfect lips.

I glanced at my phone and saw a text from my sister. She'd just found a cute snowman for her front yard and sent a picture. I smiled, thinking about how much fun Christmas was with my family. I was so grateful that they were coming out to the island.

They would be a good distraction because clearly,

whatever was or wasn't going on between Levi and me wasn't quite living up to that fiery kiss the other night.

I glanced at the clock and stood, deciding to get some coffee for whatever Levi wanted to discuss. Marcy was in the breakroom, stirring a mug of coffee as she added some milk.

"Thanks again for inviting me to your mom's last night. That meal was out of this world. I ate so much that it should probably carry me to next weekend."

Marcy grinned. "My mom loves nothing more than getting a group together at her house, and it's even better when she gets to meet someone new."

"Have you always lived on Fireweed?" I asked, sliding my reading glasses onto my nose.

"Yup." She leaned against the counter as I filled my travel mug with some coffee and reached for a sprinkle cookie. I eyed it closely before taking a bite. "I can't imagine living anywhere else. How about you? Your family is in Maine?"

I nodded, feeling my stomach clench. "I love Maine. I love my family, but I don't necessarily fit their mold. Even so, I'll probably go back and stay this time around. I'm tired of running."

"Running?" Marcy asked.

"I'm probably getting too deep for an office convo."

I chuckled. "But I'm finally getting comfortable in my own skin. I think I'm almost at the point where I can tell my parents that I don't know what life holds for me, but it might not be what they want."

Marcy squeezed my shoulder and nodded. "Absolutely, Skye. The sooner, the better. We all have different journeys, and sometimes, we're thrown some pretty big hurdles."

I chuckled. "I like to call those warning shots. I had them with my ex, and I constantly ignored them . . . for years."

Marcy nodded. "I hear ya. I'd given up completely on finding someone, and then the next thing I know, my car battery is as dead as a doornail on the ferry. I'm first in line as the panic sets in when I realize I'm holding everyone up behind me, and in swoops Jay. The man pushed my car off the ferry all by himself." She clutched her chest. "I get goosebumps just thinking about him."

"Aww. That melts my heart." I shook my head, knowing there was one person who'd done that for me, and he was grumpily sitting in an office twenty feet away.

She smiled with dopey eyes. "Me too. I asked him how I could ever pay him back, and he asked for dinner out. I didn't want him to slip away, so I made him drive us to Mudflats. Six months later, he moved in with me here on

Fireweed."

"So love does exist." I grinned.

"I believe it exists when and where you least expect it."

"I'll have to keep that in mind," I said, realizing I was running late for my meeting. "I'd better head to Levi's office for our meeting or I might get in trouble."

Marcy grinned. "Don't let his grumpy old man persona sway you. He's got a good heart under all of that."

I nodded, smiling. "I believe you're right."

As I turned around, a flutter of unexpected excitement rolled through me. Even though I was annoyed with him, I wanted to see him. With my ex, I didn't care whether I saw him or not. Probably why I'm not the one pregnant with his child.

I tapped lightly on Levi's door.

"Come in." The sound of his gravelly morning voice made me wonder what to expect on the other side of the door.

When I pushed it open, I spotted him behind his desk, staring at his computer. His hand flew up in a vague motion to come in and sit.

"Good morning to you, too," I muttered, closing the door behind me.

I took a seat and stared at him until he finally ripped

his gaze from the computer.

"Merry Christmas," I said flatly. "I know how much you love to be reminded of your favorite time of year."

His brows rose. "What did I do to deserve that?"

"You ignored me." I cocked my head. "Whether I'm your employee or your kiss buddy, I don't like to be ignored on either front."

He clasped his hands together and leaned forward. "I'll try to remember that."

"Do."

"You don't seem happy to see me, Skye. Is there a problem I don't know about?"

I straightened in my chair and took a deep breath. "Actually, there is. I didn't get much sleep last night because I was up churning a particularly concerning revelation."

"Which is?"

"I don't like being somebody's dirty little secret."

He looked shocked. "You're not my dirty little secret."

"Oh, yeah?" My brows rose. "How about last night? We pretended we were nothing more than coworkers until I played footsie with a rockstar, and thankfully, Anthony and Sophie are kind and discreet individuals. And if you'll remember, I agreed to no more kissing. So, essentially, this thing between us is DOA." I shifted in my seat. "But I'm sure that's not why you called me into your office this morning, so shoot."

Heat flared through his gaze, but I couldn't tell if it was the good kind or the bad kind.

And then he smiled. "I called you in because I heard back from the warehouse They had a few more questions and set up a meeting for tomorrow."

"That's great news." I clapped my hands together, genuinely feeling relief for him.

He kept his steady gaze on mine. "I was hoping you would come."

I looked around his office before bringing my eyes back to his. "Why?"

"Because you're amazing."

"So amazing, in fact, that the world might implode if the people in it found out we'd kissed."

"Come on." Levi shook his head. "I don't think my request is that out of line."

"Whatever. Fine. I'll come."

"Great."

I stood. "Can I go now?"

I didn't know what was wrong with me. I knew the troubles of messing around with a boss. Yet, when I was with him, I wanted to yell at him, and when I was away from him, I wanted to kiss him. This was only a recent occurrence.

"Sit."

I sat.

"I can't get you out of my freaking head. I think about you night and day. This isn't easy for me either." He stood and started making his way toward me.

"Then let's just call it what it is and see what happens."

He leaned his hip against the desk and folded his arms over his chest. "And when you realize what a jerk I am and decide you can't handle being in the same office as me, then what?"

I smirked. "We'll cross that bridge when we get to it, but I don't see you as a jerk. I see you as a man who has some serious misconceptions about life."

"Like?"

"For one, you hate Christmas, right?"

He nodded. "Pretty much."

"But you enjoy the other eleven months of the year?"

"I do."

"Well, have you ever thought that maybe you are one lucky bastard?"

His eyes nearly bugged out of his head. "Pardon?"

"Have you ever slowed down to think that maybe some of us have eleven months of endless trauma, and December is our only good month?" I stood, coming eye to eye with him now that he had sat on his desk. "Maybe the thirty days of joy and goodwill toward men are all we have to latch onto and pray it will shoot us into the right direction for the New Year."

"Is that how you feel?" he asked, watching me.

"Yeah. Pretty much, Levi. December is about the only month I can aimlessly wander around and feel the good tidings of others, while the other eleven months of the year genuinely suck for me. So I don't want to spend this December squandering this precious holiday with a man who doesn't even want people to know that he's kissed me. That is not a very joyful feeling."

Without realizing what had happened, Levi closed the space between us as his hands moved to my waist.

"What are you doing?" I looked into his eyes. "I'm not going to kiss you if I have to hide anything that develops between us. I don't need to blare a smooch on a bullhorn, but I don't—"

He pulled me closer and brushed his nose against mine with a lopsided grin. "I'm sorry. I should never have made you feel that way."

"You're a lucky man to give me an Eskimo nose kiss, you know. I don't let just any man get that close."

"I know," he said softly.

Levi's hands swept up my back as a wave of shivers followed, but he didn't kiss me.

"Thanks for opening my eyes about Christmas," he said. "I'll try not to be a curmudgeon during your one good month a year. And I won't hide whatever might develop between us, but I don't think we should kiss at the office."

"Fair enough."

He smiled.

"Now, will you tell me why you aren't a fan of the happiest time of the year?"

"Not a lot of good things have happened to me in December." His voice went hoarse on the word December, and my chest tightened.

"I'm sorry. Maybe I can help change that. Maybe getting this deal with the warehouse chain will change your mind about December," I offered.

He brushed a piece of hair from my face, and I drew a deep breath, feeling want swell throughout me. And I'd agreed to no kisses at the office, even if it might make him feel better.

"Maybe." Pain darted through his gaze, and he pulled

away slightly.

I studied him for a brief second. "There's more, isn't there?"

He nodded. "A bit."

"Tell me," I said softly as only inches of space rested between us. One sneeze or glance in the wrong direction, and his lips would be on mine, but he didn't move. "I'm a good listener."

"I know. I remember our dinner together." He smiled, but his eyes told a different story. "How about you have dinner with me tonight, and I'll tell you?"

I nodded slowly as his eyes moved to my lips.

"Are you about to break your own rule?" I whispered.

His fingers traced along my collarbone. This was it . . . our second kiss was coming. My entire body heated with excitement as I closed my eyes.

Levi's soft, warm mouth swept against mine, and every part of me lit up like a Christmas tree. His lips parted, and a little groan of need left his mouth.

The kiss dazzled me in the same way as our kiss the other night. My thoughts were going sideways, emotions rolling around like a rock tumbler, desire pummeling recklessly.

And then it happened.

The door clicked open, and a gasp emerged from behind us.

Chapter Sixteen

Levi

"I blame you entirely," Skye said, shaking her head. "I was totally on board with no kissing at work, and then you planted one right on me."

"Right. Totally on me." I chuckled, pulling into my driveway. "Never mind the fact that you're magically delicious."

She laughed. "You make me sound like a Lucky Charm."

"It kind of feels like you are."

Skye grinned in my direction, and I suddenly felt like the luckiest guy alive.

"I used to love that cereal," she gushed.

I glanced at her. "I'm just relieved it was Marcy who walked in on us."

Skye grimaced and unbuckled when I parked. "I couldn't really read her expression."

"Oddly, I couldn't either." I turned off the car and let go of Skye's hand, which I'd just realized I'd been holding since we'd left the office. "I think she's worried about December's track record, if anything."

"My word." Skye looked at me nervously. "Do you leave a trail of burning disasters every December or something like that?"

I let out a sigh and shook my head. "Not quite that bad, but it started with one event, and things never really turned around for me."

Skye smiled and nodded. "Well, I'm sorry about all of it, even though I know about none of it, and hopefully, I can change your mind on the subject. I have three weeks until Christmas Day gets here to prove to you that we can make December wonderful again."

"And then I'll have the rest of the year to prove to you that January through November has something to offer you."

"Something like that." She hopped out of the car, and I watched her zip up her coat.

When we'd made it to the front door, she shivered. "I hope you believe in heat."

I chuckled and pushed the door open. "I even have a

fireplace I'll turn on."

Skye looked over her shoulder as she headed in before turning her attention back to my house. She kicked off her boots and smiled as the sound of tapping feet headed our way.

Scarlet ran toward us with the power of a semi-truck, screeching to a halt with legs skidding on the wood floor until she ran out of steam right at Skye's ankles. She was sixty pounds of pure fuzzy canine who seemed to have never left her puppy stage.

"This is Scarlett. Boxer and question mark for the win, and we don't even know if it's a boxer."

Skye bent down and scratched her ears. "Who's a good girl?"

Scarlett's tongue unfurled and slapped Skye right in the eye.

"Sorry. She doesn't have the best manners." I snapped in Scarlett's direction, and she stopped licking Skye. "We don't have many visitors."

Skye stood and frowned. "A second ago, you said *we don't even know if it's a boxer*." She glanced around the house. "Who's we?"

My chest tightened. I didn't even think about what I'd said. "There's no one else here. Just me and Scarlett roaming our halls here."

Scarlett padded back down to wherever she came from as Skye looked around the foyer.

"Not a lick of Christmas décor." She glanced at me. "I thought you'd at least have like a wreath on the door or a bowl of pinecones by the door. Maybe a crystal jar of red and green foiled candies."

I laughed and shook my head. "For the record, I have a basket of pinecones by the back door, but I keep them there all year long."

"Okay. I certainly wouldn't want to be fooled into believing you fell for the old Christmas trap."

I smiled, feeling the urge to pull Skye into me again and kiss her, but I needed to quit acting so impulsively around her. When I invited her to dinner, I'd initially meant Mudflats, but then I realized that if I were going to open up to her about why I'd rather just skip right over the month of December, it might be nice to do it without the ears of Fireweed Island perched in every nook and cranny of the restaurant.

The fact that I was even willing to entertain the idea of confessing my history with her shocked me enough to make me question a lot of things about where I was in life.

"Well, your home is absolutely gorgeous, even if it's missing a big, fat Santa on that chair right there." She pointed at the leather wingchair next to the foyer table.

My brows quirked. "How would I put on my boots if I had a stuffed Santa there?"

She flashed a wry grin. "I never took you as a guy who needed to sit down to put on his boots."

"I never took you for a woman who'd care."

She laughed and let out a deep breath.

I glanced at her. "That sounded heavy."

Skye shook her head. "No. It felt good. That was a *good* sigh. It's just kind of nice to see where you live, kind of slowly peeling back the layers."

"I doubt I have many." I motioned for her to follow me down the hall leading to the great room. I'd designed the house to have a connected kitchen, eating area, and family room so that I could take advantage of the view. At night, I could kick my legs onto the coffee table, eat dinner, and watch the ferry chug to and from Seattle.

"What a gorgeous view. Look at all those twinkling lights. It's as if Christmas is determined to taunt you wherever you turn." She grinned, slipping her hand into mine as I flicked on the gas fireplace.

"I never thought of it that way until you so graciously pointed it out."

She squeezed my hand. "That's what I'm here for."

"I had some flank steak marinating in the fridge I'd

planned on cooking tonight. That okay with you?"

"Wow. I'm impressed."

"Don't be. I like good food."

Skye followed me into the kitchen and took a seat on a stool at the granite island. She stretched her arms up and looked at the dining room table that had a roll of Christmas wrap on top of it.

She pointed in the direction of the gold foil and raised her brows. "What's this all about?"

"I'm fully aware of the hush, hush, super-Secret Santa gift exchange at work. I've known about it for years."

"You mean the one that you told Marcy could never happen?"

I nodded. "That one, but every year, I always drop off a gift that confuses everyone."

"And they haven't caught on when there's an extra one?"

"Nope. This year, it's a unisex Tiffany bracelet."

She touched her chest. "You do have a heart, or could it possibly be a touch of the Christmas spirit?"

"I'd be more inclined to think I have a heart." I pulled out the beef and spread it onto a broiler pan.

She patted the stool next to her. "Do you mind if we talk before we eat?"

I laughed and shook my head, realizing I'd become so accustomed to coming home alone and having my routine that it didn't even occur to me to take a minute and relax.

"Would you like a glass of wine?" I asked.

"I'd love a glass of Shantos's Pinot Noir." She grinned. "And then maybe I can tell the execs tomorrow how the flavor was so intoxicating it made me sleep with my boss."

"You wouldn't."

She smirked. "I might."

"I'm not sure which part of that statement makes me more excited." I laughed, pouring us both a glass.

She popped up from the stool and eyed the couch in front of the fireplace. "Mind if we go over there?"

"Not at all." I followed her to the couch where she sat, pulling a throw over her lap.

She took a sip of wine and closed her eyes. "This is heaven."

"You like the Pinot?"

"Love it." Skye blinked her eyes open. "This is something to be proud of, Levi. Your family has to be really amazed by what you've been able to do with leveraging distribution and building bigger facilities."

I noticed something in Skye's eyes that I hadn't seen directed at me in years.

Admiration.

The last time I saw that look was with my parents.

I nodded slowly and let out a deep breath.

"Now, that sounded heavy," Skye said, smiling.

I nodded in agreement. "Kind of."

"Did I say something wrong?"

I shook my head. "Not at all. My family is pretty much Max."

She stayed silent as my chest pulled in ten different directions.

"We lost our parents several years ago."

Her hands flew to her mouth. "I'm so sorry, Levi. I'm so sorry. I had no idea."

"No reason you would." I smiled, wishing I could make Skye feel less awkward. It wasn't an easy conversation, which was why I genuinely avoided it altogether.

And the best way to do that was to stay alone.

"Scarlett was my mom's dog. So, the *we* was my parents, and I was trying to figure out what type of mutt made her so full of exuberance. She looks like a fluffy boxer, but she never misses out on a good herding session."

Skye pulled her brows together. "Herding? As in sheep?"

"Well, not specifically sheep. Mostly anything with

legs, Scarlett will try to push in whatever direction she feels is right."

Skye reached for my hand. "I'm so sorry about your parents. Were they ill or . . ." Her voice trailed off.

"No. They were extremely healthy. My dad had finally retired from our company. He loved to fly. Had his own plane, actually." Hollowness flowed through me as I looked at Skye.

"Oh, no."

I nodded. "The plane crashed. Bad weather was to blame. It was Christmas Eve. I was supposed to be on the plane with them, but I told them I would just drive because I was finishing up a few things at the office. They had a place down in Portland they'd just bought, so that's where they were flying to, and I just . . ." I didn't really know what to say.

"Christmas," Skye whispered. "I'm so sorry. I've been making light of your disgust for the holiday, and all this time, you had a real reason to want to forget it even existed."

I smiled and shook my head, realizing the woman in front of me was the most empathetic woman I'd ever met, apart from my mom.

Which was how we got Scarlett and many other strays we'd rescued over the years.

Even Max.

Granted, he wasn't a stray, but my mom understood him better than anyone, which was why she'd convinced my dad at an early age to let go of his dream to have both of his sons run the winery and to focus on the one who wanted to do it.

What they didn't realize was that I just wanted to please them. It had nothing to do with what I actually wanted. Once I'd taken over Shantos, I knew all that mattered was making my dad proud.

And then he died.

"I truly am sorry, and I'll completely undecorate your office tomorrow if you'd like." She scooted closer to me, and I shook my head.

"No. I actually like it." I wrapped my arm around her shoulder as she took a sip of wine. "Or maybe I like it because you did it."

She nestled her head on my arm and let out a sigh. "I can understand hating the holidays."

I nodded. "Well, there's more to it. I think over the years, things have just compounded, and the negative things happened to be in December."

Skye turned to look at me as her expression searched for more.

"Well, a year before my parents passed away, I had a

party planned for my girlfriend at the time. All of her friends and family and all of mine were at Mudflats, and I was going to propose."

Dread filled her expression.

"In hindsight, I know it's for the best, but it didn't help my ego. Before I even led her into the banquet room, she dumped me."

Skye's eyes got huge. "You're kidding."

"Nope."

"And you had no clue?"

"None." I shook my head. "I later found out that she was banging my best friend."

"Oh, my gosh. And that happened in December?"

"Sure did. She broke up with me in early December, and I found out about being cheated on right before Christmas."

Skye's mouth quirked slightly. "December really is *not* your month."

I touched her smiling lips. "What was that question you asked me the first night we met?" I laughed. "I think it was something like, *Do you find other people's misery funny, or is that only around the holidays?*"

She stared at me and smiled coyly. "I don't remember that."

"How convenient."

"I think so." She moved her legs onto my lap and looped her arm around my neck.

"And another fun December moment was when my brother was stuck in Malaysia."

"How so? Did he run out of money?"

I shook my head, thinking back on Max's stunt. "No, he got arrested, and he's lucky he's not still in prison there."

"Oh. My. Word."

"I got that call on Christmas Eve."

Skye laughed and held her head as her body shook. "This is horrified laughter. I promise. I just can't believe all these things happened to you in one month."

I squeezed her and laughed, realizing how tremendously horrible the month of December had been for me.

"If we really want to go backward in time, the only time I was ever bullied was when I was twelve. I had to dress up as an elf for our school play. Red tights and all."

"No." Skye hissed. "Who would do that to an almost teenager?"

"That's exactly what Bobby wondered too, and he was relentless for the rest of the year until I landed a solid punch the following December when he started up again." I laughed, remembering my mom's reaction of pure horror and my dad's reaction of pride. "And then I got detention. First and last ever, but of course, in December."

Skye let out a groan and closed her eyes. "I don't think I can handle any more of your December memories."

She rested her head on my shoulder and moved her fingers along my chest, rubbing the wool of the sweater and breathing softly.

"I'm so sorry about your parents, Levi. I can't even imagine what you've gone through and not having any other family."

I didn't say anything, but for the first time in years, I sat on my couch on a night in December and didn't feel like my world had ended.

Chapter Seventeen

Skye

My stomach still knotted when I thought about Levi. No wonder it was impossible to pretend that December was filled with good tidings of comfort and joy.

"Pesto pasta and flank steak," he said, bringing the dish to me.

The fireplace glowed in the great room, and the view of the ferry's lights and Christmas boats made it impossible to navigate to the dining room table for dinner. When he'd offered to bring over food and have us eat on the couch, I couldn't think of anything better.

As he sat next to me, refilling my wine glass and balancing his plate on his knee, I realized I'd never had this in my entire life. Sure, I'd had a long relationship, but it had never felt easy. Everything always felt forced, but with Levi,

I could share my true thoughts and not feel judged.

Or he was just better at hiding it.

I sliced into the steak and took a bite. "Mmm. Incredible, Levi."

"Thanks." He took a sip of wine and sat back on the couch. "Do you need a pillow on your lap to make it easier to eat?"

"I don't want to spill food on it."

"Ahh. Doesn't matter. They wash." He handed me a white velour pillow, which I delicately placed my plate onto.

"Thanks for sharing with me about your family." I took another bite.

"I've actually never done that before."

"Really?"

He nodded and took a bite of pasta.

I cleared my throat and wondered how to bring up his old relationship that ended in a flaming bag of reindeer poop and decided to just go for it.

"You mentioned that, in hindsight, getting dumped by your almost fiancée was a good thing?"

He let out a deep breath. "This is going to sound absolutely horrible."

I laughed nervously. "Let me have it."

"I didn't love her."

"But you were going to ask her to marry you."

Levi nodded. "I know, but my parents loved her."

"Oh, right. You're the good son."

"I made a bad habit of doing everything to please my parents."

I chuckled and shook my head. "I wouldn't call it a bad habit. You're not the one who got arrested in Malaysia."

"Fair enough." He smiled, and that was all it took for my body to light up with need.

I let out a sigh and took another bite of my steak. "I know nothing will ever take away the pain from your parents' accident, but I hope I can make the rest of this December something positive for you to cherish after I leave."

He smirked. "You had me until the last three words."

I laughed, nodding. "Yeah. I guess I could have left that part out."

My phone beeped with the familiar chime of my sister's phone number, and I wiggled to reach it out of my pocket while balancing my plate.

"It's my sister. Do you mind if I check the text?"

Levi's brows rose. "By all means. I like texts from her."

I chuckled, remembering the last thing he saw pop up on the screen from her, and shook my head.

And then I glanced at the message.

My chest tightened.

My stomach knotted.

I lost the rest of my appetite instantly.

"What happened?" Levi asked.

"My sister texted that my mom is going on and on about how to get me and my ex back together." I looked at Levi. "Christmas ought to be fun."

He laughed and took another bite of food while I expertly crafted my retort.

Does she remember that he's wandering around town with a pregnant woman who is not me?

Just as I clicked *Send*, Levi nodded. "I don't envy you. Want to read me what you're going to send first?"

I laughed. "Too late."

I showed him the phone, and he laughed. "Well, that covers one of the main issues for sure."

I grinned. "Yeah. My sister will gleefully show my mom that text, I'm certain."

"Did your ex mind you taking jobs out of town?"

I chuckled. "Apparently not."

Levi nodded. "True, but you know . . ."

"I think the reason I started taking jobs out of town was that I didn't want to face the main issue at hand."

"Which was?"

I let out a slow breath. "I didn't love him, but he offered me what my parents wanted."

"Sounds so familiar," he said, shaking his head.

"And yet, aren't we supposed to be adults?" I laughed out of nervousness. "I'm going to turn thirty in three months. I shouldn't let my parents' voices about my love life in my head."

Levi smiled. "Well, you'd been with him for a few years, so technically, you were much younger when you started up the relationship. Kind of the same age when I nearly got engaged."

I frowned. "So, how old are you? Or should I not ask the boss that?"

He laughed and shrugged. "I'm thirty-five."

"Wow. I'm dating an older man." I grinned. "Like, really older."

"I wouldn't call six years an astronomical number."

"As long as you're fine with it." I smiled.

"As you said, you're leaving to go back to Main soon, so . . ."

"Well, it's a temp job, and while I love what I've seen

of Fireweed Island so far, I don't think it's exactly a hot spot for career growth."

"Seattle's only a quick ferry ride away."

I couldn't tell whether he was teasing or not. Did he think there was a real future with me staying here?

My phone buzzed again, and I groaned. "I'm afraid to look."

I shoved my phone in his direction. "Will you read it first?"

He laughed. "Are you sure about that?"

"Yup." I closed my eyes as he took it.

"Uh-oh."

My eyes blinked open. "What? What's an uh-oh?"

"Is your boyfriend's name Jared?"

I nodded. "Ex. Yeah. Why?"

"Apparently, the kid isn't his."

I pulled the phone out of Levi's fingers and started at the text.

"Talk about sweet revenge," I muttered, focusing on the words as another text dinged. "Wait a second. He's been talking to my mom, buttering her up and telling her what a huge mistake he'd made?"

I dropped the phone on my lap and shivered at the thought as yet another text rolled over.

"Want me to look?" Levi asked.

I nodded, and he reached into my lap to pull the phone toward him.

"This is like a soap opera." He grimaced. "Apparently, she had the baby, and the real father of the baby showed up at the same time Jared did."

I felt like such an awful person because I loved every second of this, and I shouldn't. There was a poor infant now involved.

"No way." I straightened on the couch, feeling somewhat ill. "Hopefully, the baby, real daddy, and baby mama live a happy life together."

Levi's gaze met mine. "There's more."

"Of course there is."

"Your sister thinks your mom is going to call you tomorrow to convince you to hear Jared out."

I bolted from the couch. "What? How could my mom do that to me?"

"Men are tricky," Levi muttered.

"Apparently." I shook my head, taking my phone back from Levi.

"What if my Christmas luck is rubbing off on you?" Levi asked.

"Impossible. I'm setting my mom and sister straight

right now."

Levi reached for my phone.

"What are you doing?" I yanked it away.

"I'm trying to stop something you'll regret."

"I don't ever want to see or speak to Jared again."

Levi stood and looped his arm around my waist. "I understand that."

I looked into his eyes and smiled. "Then let me tell my family that."

"Tell them tomorrow," he whispered in my ear.

I frowned as he brought his gaze back to mine. "Why?"

"I might have some other plans." He slid his fingers along the edge of my top. "To distract you."

His hands ran under my top, leaving a scorching trail wherever his fingers left.

"But what about tomorrow?" I asked breathlessly. "We have a big meeting."

"Just one kiss," he said, raking his mouth along my cheek.

"I can handle one kiss." I combed my fingers through his hair as his mouth curved into a smile.

"One really long kiss."

Heat darted through Levi's gaze as his mouth met

mine. I closed my eyes, feeling the warmth of his lips and the taste of cherry and vanilla notes from the pinot. The moment whipped me back to the first night in the office when the longing between us was almost painful, but now there was no safety net of the office, only the pull to be in his arms.

His tongue danced with mine as a little moan left my lips.

"You taste so good," he whispered between kisses.

I giggled. "You can thank your wine for that. I was thinking the same about you."

Levi let out a little growl and picked me up, grasping my bum as he carried me over to the granite island, never breaking our kisses. It felt like a scene out of a romantic movie as warmth spread through me.

His hands moved along my skin under my top as I coiled my fingers through his hair, not wanting him to stop.

My phone buzzed again, and I felt him smile against my mouth.

"We could send a really informative and visual text," he said, briefly pulling away from me.

"Yeah? You think that might get the point across?" I giggled, resting my forehead on his.

"I think it could."

"But you might have to face my family at

Christmas?"

He smiled, and small lines surfaced along his eyes. "Is that a question or a statement?"

"You make me feel really good, Levi." I drew a breath. "And since we've kissed at the office twice while I'm completely sober, I know it's not just Shantos's incredible Pinot Noir, *available at fine food stores everywhere.*"

He let out a low, growly laugh. "You're pitching during our kiss?"

"Never can practice too much." I smiled, feeling his hand move around my waist and run along my spine.

"I don't know what it is about you, Skye . . ." He brushed his mouth against mine. "I feel like things are alright again in life when you're around."

When my phone buzzed again, I shook my head as a gnawing sensation worked its way into my belly.

"I should probably get going to bed," I said softly. "I don't want to screw anything up for us tomorrow. I'll call a ride share."

Levi nodded. "No. I got the app on my phone. I'll send for one. It's probably a good idea. You've got a lot to think about with your ex, and I feel like my bad luck is rubbing off on you."

He reached for his phone, but I grabbed his other

hand. "I have nothing to think about with him, Levi. The thought literally makes me ill."

"Yeah?"

I nodded and kissed Levi, wishing I could prove to him that he wasn't doomed to horrid Decembers for the rest of his life.

Chapter Eighteen

Levi

My head pounded because foolishly, after Skye left, I polished off the bottle of wine we'd opened.

And now we were walking into the woman's office that held the key to my company's future. Skye sat next to me, and we waited for the woman to enter the room.

The door clicked behind us, and we stood as the VP from last week walked in. Surprise washed over her features when she saw Skye and quickly glanced in my direction.

"I was unaware that there would be someone accompanying you today." The woman's voice fell flat.

Her name was Susan.

Important Susan.

"I wanted to bring my talented associate with me."

Susan eyed Skye. "Skye, wasn't it?"

Skye nodded. "Nice to see you again."

"Please have a seat." The VP motioned to our chairs as she took a seat behind her desk.

She didn't say anything for a few seconds. "You know, would it be possible to speak to you alone?"

Skye let out a little gasp, and I glanced in her direction. She looked as stunned as I felt.

"I—"

Before I had a chance to finish my sentence, Skye stood up and flashed a smile at Susan and then at me. "I'll be out front if you need anything from me."

The woman smiled coolly at Skye. "Excellent."

The door closed behind me, and I looked at the woman sitting in front of me.

She immediately softened and smiled at me in a way that told me this meeting wasn't what I thought it was.

"How may I help you?" I asked. "Are there specific questions that I can answer?"

She smiled and licked her lips. "As far as I'm concerned, the deal is yours."

Excitement bubbled through me. We'd done it. I couldn't wait to share the good news with my team.

"But," she continued, and my heart stalled. "I was hoping that maybe I could offer you a little something more."

"More?" I asked, shaking my head.

"Legal is already working on your PL Pinot Grigio submission, but I think our customers need two lines from Shantos. Of course, that hinges on whether you think it's a good idea." She unfastened two top buttons from her satin shirt, and I couldn't believe what was unfolding.

"I think that would be fabulous." I nodded in agreement, keeping my gaze on hers.

"Wonderful. Then maybe we can sort the details out over dinner?" Her sharp, dark brows rose.

"I . . ." I shook my head. "I don't think dinner is the best idea."

Her gaze hardened. "Oh, really?"

She stood and placed her palms on the edge of her desk, leaning over to reveal cleavage. This would probably be a lot of men's fantasy, but it wasn't mine.

It was a nightmare of epic proportions.

"If you thought the numbers played out well for one line carried by us, imagine the possibilities for two." She licked her lips again, and it only gave me the willies.

I couldn't help but think of my employees. Their families.

But Skye. A man had already cheated on her once, and I certainly didn't want her to think I'd ever do that.

She was already sitting in the lobby staring at a wall while I was stuck in here.

"What do you say?" She leaned over more, and I tried not to laugh at the ridiculousness of what had become my life.

December really was out to get me.

Insult the woman who changed the direction of my company and the lives of my employees or pretend to go along with things and ensure that Skye never found out about it.

Both were horrendous options.

"Well, Levi?" She smiled and slithered back into her seat. "What do you say? Dinner?"

"Tell me when?" I asked, feeling a large ball knot in my abdomen.

"I heard your main office is on Fireweed Island?"

"That's true."

"Do you live there?"

I clenched my jaw. "I do."

"Then I think I just might love a ferry ride." She batted her lashes, which only made me think a fly had been caught in her web. "I'm free Friday. How about you?"

I sucked in a breath and looked down at her desk, hating every part of me with what I was about to say and do.

"Friday works."

"Perfect. I'll let legal know there is no need for us to

bid on the red line. And you believe you have the capacity to provide enough Pinot Noir to all ninety-five warehouses?"

I gave a quick nod. "Absolutely."

"Great. You've just made my job easier." Her eyes fell down my chest to my lap and then up again. "I'll see you on Friday. Have your assistant tell mine where to meet you, and I'll be there with contracts in hand."

I stood and gave the nod, showing my way out the door, feeling her eyes on me every step of the way.

When I made it to the lobby, Skye's expression fell instantly. "Oh, no. It didn't go well. You look like you're about to be sick."

"Something like that." I walked past a pathetic-looking plastic Christmas tree that had a tilt, and most of its lights were burned out.

Skye walked over to me and glanced behind me. "I just figured she had the hots for you, and that's why she chased me out of there. I didn't think it was because she was going to chomp you off at the bit."

We walked outside to the parking lot, and she reached for my hand, which I pretended not to feel as I looked behind me to see the woman standing at the window.

I just needed to buy enough time until the contracts were signed.

When we both got into my Mercedes, Skye let out a huge sigh.

"What the heck happened, Levi?"

"You don't want to know."

"I kind of do, actually." She squirmed in her seat to get a better look at me, and I felt waves of nausea and guilt.

Skye didn't deserve any of this.

"I heard there is a cute Christmas shop about ten minutes from here," I told her. "Let's go check it out."

She reached her hand to my forehead and laughed nervously. "Are you okay?"

"Yup. Just thought you might enjoy it."

"Well, of course I would, but what about you?"

"I just like to see you happy."

"If you say so."

I plugged the store into my phone, and GPS came over the speakers as we pulled out of the parking lot.

"So, tell me what's going on. Judging by the look on your face, you're ready to strangle someone."

I laughed and shook my head, following the directions. "We got the deal."

"What?" Skye screamed. "Are you serious? This is awesome news."

"Yeah. It's exactly what we wanted." I nodded,

keeping my eyes on the road ahead.

"Then what's the issue?" She put her hand on my leg, and I glanced at her.

"They're offering a second private label opportunity and want us to provide it as well."

Skye's hands whipped up to her face. "And how is this a bad thing?"

"She wants dinner on Friday to go over contracts."

"By all means, eat and sign away." Skye grinned and looked like how I should be feeling, but I knew what this woman wanted.

"I don't think it's just dinner she wants."

Skye chuckled and waved her hand in the air. "Obviously, she wants in your pants."

I snorted in surprise.

"What? Like you didn't know?" She pretended to scowl.

"Doesn't that worry you?"

Skye's head lolled on the seat as her hand stayed on my leg. "If she or any woman is offering something you want, there is absolutely nothing that I can do about it. You're not mine. I'm not yours."

"Wow, Skye." I shook my head. "Just wow."

She straightened in her seat and slid her hand away.

"Did you want me to be jealous or fly off the handle of my broomstick? I could if you want me to, but I don't think that would be very productive. You've got more on your hands than just worrying about pleasing some sexy out-of-towner. You have a company that needs saving."

"You're more than a sexy out-of-towner." I hid my smile, loving the way she snuck in the sexy part. This woman didn't lack confidence, which was another amazing trait of Skye Lennox.

"We'll see. You haven't met my family yet. They just might make you wish you got down and dirty with wino lady back there."

I frowned and shook my head. "I can promise you that's not happening."

She laughed, but I wondered if she meant everything she said. Did she really think that what we had wasn't worth ignoring other females for, or did she believe all men cheated if given the opportunity?

I spotted the Christmas cottage and turned into the parking lot.

"Ah, perfection," she sang, putting her hand on my leg again. "Are you sure this isn't too much for you? Did you want to stay in the car?"

I laughed and parked, glancing at the A-Frame

cottage blinking in every color imaginable. "Isn't this kind of therapy supposed to be helpful?"

She grinned. "We'll find out."

As we climbed out of the car, Christmas music washed over me, and for the first time in years, I didn't suddenly have my chest tightened and my stomach wrenched.

Skye bounded toward me and linked her fingers through mine as she pulled me toward the stairs.

She was very resilient for someone who had just found out the guy she was seeing was about to go out to dinner with a woman who wanted to jump his bones.

When we walked into the A-frame, cinnamon filled the air, and Skye turned around with a gleam in her eyes. "Thank you for bringing me here. It's heaven. My little tree looks smaller by the day. I feel like if I got more ornaments for her, she'd look more impressive."

"Or she'll look tinier, and why are we calling your tree *she*?"

"It's got feminine spirit."

"But it's fake."

Her hands flew to her hips, and she smiled. "Your point?"

"You know what?" I shook my head, laughing. "I don't even know anymore."

She reached for a crotchety-looking Santa and held it up to me. "Does this remind you of anyone?"

"Aren't you on a roll?"

Her eyes widened. "You don't see the resemblance?"

"Maybe a little. More Max than me," I mumbled, glancing at a row of crystal ornaments.

My chest twisted into an unexpected ache as I saw the brand of ornaments that my mom always collected. It was my parents' thing. Every year, my dad would search high and low for that year's latest release, and she'd always act surprised at Thanksgiving when he'd give it to her for the tree.

My fists balled up as I shook my head in frustration. When would this get easier?

"Oh, these are my favorite ornaments in the entire world, but I just can't fathom shelling out a hundred or two for them." Skye bent down to look at the crystal ornaments, and I swallowed down the tightness in my throat as I took in her excitement.

She glanced behind her and smiled at me before her expression dropped. "We can totally leave."

"No. No way. This is good." And as I watched Skye's attention turn back to the crystal ornaments, I realized it was.

Seeing her thrill of the moment coated over bit by bit the sadness from my mom. Skye reached for a crystal igloo and let out a deep breath.

"I'm going to freaking do it." She smiled, looking up at me. "I'm going to live a little."

"It's very beautiful," I said, smiling.

"You think?" She held it up in front of her as she analyzed the facets. "I'm totally walking this onto the airplane when I go back home."

I nodded. "My mom collected this brand."

Skye's expression dropped into a mixture of horror and worry. "I had no—"

"And seeing you this happy about it makes me realize that not everything my parents touched and lived through has to be buried in a portal of wicked emotion." I smiled. "In fact, I'd like to buy it for you."

"No." She shook her head. "You don't have to do that."

"I insist." I grinned, taking the delicate igloo from Skye. "Besides, maybe I'll feel less guilty about going out with Susan on Friday."

Skye chuckled. "Well, when you put it that way, have at it."

Chapter Nineteen

Skye

I felt like I did the best job I could at playing the part of a cool, badass girlfriend who really wasn't a girlfriend. The thought of him going out to dinner with *Susan* drove me insane. Who in the heck did that woman think she was?

But I knew the pressure that Levi was under. The idea of him having to let go of employees because he didn't wink right at Susan didn't sit well with me, so if he had to go pretend to be into her for an evening, then I would just suck it up.

After all, it wasn't like I didn't have plenty of things to keep me busy on Friday night. Like I could clean or organize my little place or get ready for my family's visit in a couple of weeks. I could wander the streets of Fireweed.

Or I could spy on Levi.

I kicked that last thought out of my head the moment it snuck in.

"I think we owe a big thank you to Skye," Stan said, raising a toast in my direction.

I glanced around the bar to see Evie, Marcy, and the others nod and raise their shot glasses. Levi promised he'd swing by before heading home, but I'd believe it when I saw it.

Hark, the Herald Angels Sing played through the tavern while silver snowflakes hung from the exposed ceiling, and a tinsel tree stood on top of a karaoke machine. Most tables had a bunch of plastic holly surrounding a fake candle. It was such a juxtaposition I had to chuckle.

I raised my shot glass and smiled. "Not the case at all, but cheers to everyone."

My coworkers grinned and slung their shots back as Evie stood and walked over to the counter. I noticed the bartender light up when he saw her, which made me smile.

I glanced toward the door, hoping Levi really would show up. It was Wednesday, and he'd announced to the office that the first deal had been signed for the Pinot Grigio private label, and another deal might happen for red wine. The office had erupted into whoops and hollers, and I even saw Levi crack a smile as the group all planned a happy hour stop to celebrate.

I took a slow slip of whatever sweet holiday shot Evie had ordered and set the empty glass down. The bartender followed Evie over to us with a tray of drinks. He handed me my iced tea, and I took a sip. The thought of drinking a ton in the middle of the week didn't sound fun.

For some reason, the only thing that sounded perfect tonight was snuggling into my robe and listening to Christmas music while I debated what to tell my mom about my ex. I didn't fault her, but I wished she'd think about me. This guy cheated on her daughter, and yet, she was willing to lend an ear.

It was all a ploy. That was the thing about my ex. Jared was a master manipulator, and my best guess was that he didn't want to be alone for the holidays.

But that wasn't my problem. I was thankfully on the other side of the country.

The door swung open, and a blast of cold air hit our table as Levi walked inside. I couldn't swipe the smile off my face the moment he spotted our table. His gaze connected with mine, and I felt like I'd won the lottery. *He actually showed up.*

Evie waved, and Levi made his way to the bartender, where he grabbed a soda and came over to the table.

"I ordered some nachos and poppers for the table."

Stan clapped. "My man. Thank you."

"It's the least I could do. I'm starving."

Levi took a seat next to me and smiled.

"You don't want to party like a rockstar tonight?" I teased, glancing at his soda.

He grimaced. "After the other night, I think I'm good for a week or so."

I chuckled. "Me too."

Levi drew a breath as I reached over and brushed my fingers along his knuckles. He nodded in approval, and I grinned.

Baby steps.

"So, are you nervous about your big meeting on Friday?" I teased.

"I should probably be scared out of my wits, but I just want to get it over with." He kept focused on me. "Do you have any plans for the big night?"

"I'll probably watch Christmas movies and clean . . . or spy on you." I chuckled. "I haven't really figured out which I'd rather do."

Levi laughed. "Nice. And how's your ex doing?"

I rolled my eyes. "According to my mom, he's devastated and can't believe he'd been such a fool." I raised my hand. "Uh, I can."

Levi smiled. "You don't think she actually thinks you'll hear him out, do you?"

I shook my head and took a sip of my tea. "I can't imagine."

The bartender set the plates of food for us to share while Levi chatted with Stan.

As I piled my plate high with food, my phone buzzed.

Probably another message from my mom with reason number two hundred and thirty as to why I should talk to Jared. I set my plate down and slid my phone out of my purse.

Honey, it's me.

I chuckled as if I didn't know.

I just got off the phone with Jared, and he's so down. I really think it would be good for both of you if you called him. I think he's learned his lesson.

Fury bolted through me.

Learned his lesson?

My fingers quickly typed my response.

Mom, he's not a dog who did a potty inside the house. He was a grown man who cheated on your lovely daughter multiple times to the point of thinking he had a child with another woman. It just so happens that karma bit him in the rear when he saw the real baby daddy arrive at the hospital. I've moved on, and a goal for myself is that I don't want to be with a cheater who is only coming back to me because his alternative chose someone else.

I hit *Send* and glanced up to see Levi studying me.

"Everything okay?" he asked, leaning over.

"Define okay."

"Well, not spectacular. But maybe not horrible, either." He smiled, and I just wanted to jump into his arms like the other night and pretend none of this drama was going on back home.

"Then I'd say I'm probably not doing okay."

He cocked his head and took a bite of nachos. "You want to talk about it?"

I drew in a deep breath as Marcy gave us the side eye.

"My mom thinks I need to call Jared right this second because he's sad."

"Uh-oh." He took a sip of soda.

"I told her that wasn't happening in my typical novel-length text."

He nodded right when my phone buzzed.

I looked down and gritted my teeth.

Please, for your mother. Just to talk to him. He made a mistake.

Before I knew what I was doing, my fingers flew at the speed of light.

Mom, you're supposed to be my protector, not shove me back into an unhealthy relationship. To a cheater, no less. I'm equally parts horrified and devastated. And no, I will not be calling him. See you soon.

My phone buzzed almost as quickly as I sent mine.

He's sorry, and people make mistakes. Your father made a mistake, and I took him back. If I hadn't, I wouldn't have my precious daughters. So, forgiveness can bring good things.

My jaw dropped open as the phone fell from my fingers. Levi grabbed it before it hit the nachos as tears filled my eyes.

What was she talking about? What was she thinking, saying that?

My dad? He wouldn't.

I pretended to bend over to the floor for my napkin so I could wipe the tears away.

Why would she tell me this, and in a text?

My throat constricted to the size of a tiny straw as I wiped the tears from my eyes and attempted to look sane before popping my head back up.

Closing my eyes, I took a deep breath.

"Skye?" Levi whispered.

I blinked open my eyes to see him bending under the table with me. "You okay?"

"No. Definitely not okay."

"Is it Jared? Did he text you? I'd love to—"

I sniffled in a big snotty mess and wiped my tears away, still hunched under the table.

"No, it was a text from my mom."

"Is everything okay?" he asked, clutching my hand under the table.

"No." I sniffled. "Not at all."

"Is it your sister? Your dad?"

I sniffled again. "My dad."

"You can take the rest of the month off paid if you need to be with your family." Levi's words were filled with such tenderness, and then I realized what he probably thought.

I wiped my cheeks and let out a deep sigh. "It's not his health. It's just . . . It's—"

"Uh, does anyone know where the boss and the new hire went?" Evie laughed.

"Or why we're only seeing their butts sticking up?"

I squeezed my eyes shut. "Oh, no."

Levi looked into my eyes. "I'll handle it."

"She lost her contact lens."

"Oh, crap. I hate when that happens," Evie muttered. "But I'd call it a loss if it fell on this floor."

"I found it," I hollered, then turned and booked toward the door.

Stan chuckled. "Well, that was weird," before I made it outside.

I just needed to get home. My mom had sent several more texts and called, but I couldn't bring myself to look at anything and certainly not pick up the phone.

Night had already emerged, and the chill in the air turned to downright freezing when I heard Levi's voice behind me, calling my name

I turned around, hugging myself.

"I'll get the car and will pick you up," he said, pointing behind him.

I tried to smile, but I just nodded instead.

A shiver went through me as I thought about what my mom had said so matter-of-factly and without thinking. Did dad really cheat on her? And did she think that was okay?

I shivered again. It wasn't okay for me.

Levi pulled his car up to the sidewalk, and I darted over to the passenger's side and slid into the seat with a grunt.

"On to the house?" he asked.

I nodded, buckling and letting out a heavy sigh. "Yes, please. Mine."

"Absolutely."

He pulled back onto the road and drove toward my house, which was barely around the bend.

"Thank you for picking me up. Even though I could have walked, I'm not sure I would have made it home."

"Skye, what's going on?" he asked gently, turning into the drive. "Can I help?"

I let out another sigh and realized it was because I couldn't catch my breath.

"Well, my mom decided to drop a bomb on me while trying to convince me to give Jared another try."

"Oh, no." Levi's lips pressed into a thin line, and he

reached for my hands.

I shifted in the seat so he could cup them in his as the heater blew onto us. I needed his touch, his comfort.

Him.

A listening ear.

A caring heart.

"She said that had she not given my dad a second chance, we wouldn't have been here, and she'd never take it back." My voice quavered as I thought about my dad. Had it been once? Did he still do it? "That is the most heart-wrenching statement."

My phone buzzed again.

My eyes filled with empty tears again, but this time, Levi brushed them aside.

"I wish my mom had never told me. I wish Jared would just leave us alone. If it weren't for him, I could pretend that my life and my parents' marriage were perfect." I threw my head against his seat and groaned before turning to face Levi.

"Wow." Levi shook his head, and I chuckled.

"Yeah. Pretty much. 'Wow' does encompass my initial reaction." I tried to smile. "Followed by anger, resentment, and did I mention anger?"

"It must have happened a long time ago, Skye," Levi

offered.

"Or he got better at hiding it." I shook my head. "See? See how my head works? It's why I can't be with a cheater. I would never trust them not to cheat again."

"No, I totally understand that. I'm the same. Cheating is a game changer." He shook his head and let out a whistle. "I'm just so sorry, Skye. You didn't need to hear this."

"Or maybe I did." I let out a deep breath.

"It makes you think about giving him a second chance?"

"Oh, heck to the no. It reaffirms where I stand on the subject. Because of Jared's stupidity, my mom divulged something she probably never planned on telling me. He's just rotten to the core."

My phone rang, and I silenced it before looking at Levi. "I should probably go in and call my mom back."

Levi nodded as I climbed out of the car. He kept the car running and walked me to the front door.

"If you need anything at all, I'm under ten minutes away. I can make it in less if needed." He brushed my hair over my shoulder.

"Thank you, Levi. I don't know what I would do if I didn't have you to tell."

Chapter Twenty

Levi

Wow? All I could come up with was *wow*? I closed my eyes and stared at my computer screen. Last night, I texted Skye a few times, and she said she'd spoken with her mom. I told her she didn't need to come into the office this morning, but she said she'd be in at her normal start time.

Employees had started trickling in, and every time I heard the door click open, my hopes got dashed.

"It's me," Marcy said, poking her head into my office.

"Hey, you." I smiled, motioning for her to come in.

"I want to give you your credit card back from last night."

Before I ran after Skye, I'd given Marcy my credit card to take care of the tab.

She handed me the tiny card, and I slipped it into my

wallet.

"Is everything okay with Skye?" she asked, closing the door.

"Yeah. Well, I mean, there's some drama going on back home, but I think she's doing okay."

Marcy frowned. "Her ex?"

"Part of it. I'm sure she'll fill you in."

Marcy glanced at the seat in front of my desk and then at me before sitting. "You two seem to be getting close."

"Is that an issue?"

"You tell me."

I laughed. "I'm interested in her, and from what I can tell, she feels the same."

"But she feels close enough to tell you about her ex?"

I looked at Marcy and nodded. "The conversation just flows with her."

Her brows rose as she tried to keep a smile off her lips. "Just flows, huh?"

"It does." I nodded, folding my hands together. "And I fully recognize that she's heading back to Maine in a matter of weeks, but we're both enjoying things as they come."

Marcy nodded. "She's a great gal."

Just the mention of Skye made me want to be with her, but with what just went down with her family, I felt even less sure about Skye's reaction to Friday's meeting with the viper of private label.

I looked up at Marcy. "So, I'm not looking forward to meeting Susan on Friday."

Marcy nodded. "You think there's more to it than signing on the dotted line for round two?"

I laughed. "That's an understatement."

"Well, you're a single guy." Marcy smiled wryly.

"She does nothing for me."

Marcy nodded. "No, she's not your type."

"But Skye is."

Marcy leaned back in her chair. "Which was why I sent Max to meet her first."

"You thought he'd screw it up for me like he always did."

She nodded, grinning. "I did, but I have to confess that I'm kind of happy she isn't so easily repulsed."

I laughed. "What in the world does that mean?"

"You two seem at ease around one another."

I leaned on my elbows and shook my head. "How in the world can you surmise that from hanging out at the office?"

"You two are together eight hours a day. Not to mention, you both were at my mom's house at Sunday dinner."

"I don't know." I shook my head, knowing I felt exactly as Marcy described it.

"Well, while you sit there as confused as ever, I actually just wanted to let you know that Monday will be the office skating party at the ice rink. It wasn't easy, but I managed to secure one for a group this big. And since it's in the afternoon, I also went ahead and made a holiday dinner out of it for the team."

I groaned and coiled my fingers through my hair. "You're killing me."

"Want to know the best part?"

"I don't think I do."

"The price of admission is an ugly sweater."

I scowled and sat up. "What? To donate?"

Marcy looked extremely disappointed and embarrassed for me, which made no sense.

"What am I missing?"

"You're telling me you have no idea about ugly sweater contests?"

I leaned in and arched my brows. "Should I?"

A light tap echoed into my office

"Come on in," I said, expecting it to be Stan or Evie.

Skye walked into the office and stopped when she

saw Marcy.

"Oh, sorry. I didn't mean to interrupt."

I shook my head. "No interruption at all."

Marcy tossed me a wry grin and rolled her eyes.

"We were just talking about bringing an ugly sweater to skate."

Marcy snorted. "No, Levi. You're not bringing the ugly sweater. You're wearing it."

Skye chuckled. "Sorry. That was my idea." She bit her lip in a deliciously sexy way. "Before I knew everything."

Marcy arched a brow. "Everything?"

"With my parents," she muttered.

"Oh. Right." Marcy smiled sympathetically. "Well, I still think the ugly sweater idea is awesome, and that is the price of admission."

Skye jumped on her toes and clapped her hands together. "This will be so awesome." She glanced at me and immediately let her arms fall to her side. "You know, if you're into that sort of thing."

I laughed. "And you obviously are."

Marcy nodded and stood. "Well, I'm done with the boss. He's all yours."

Skye's cheeks flushed, and she glanced down at the floor.

Marcy closed the door behind her, and Skye took a seat.

"Everything okay?"

She nodded, and a feeble smile lined her usually perky lips. "Just felt like I betrayed my mom by not dropping everything to call Jared. She just doesn't get it."

I nodded sympathetically. "And she never will."

Skye sighed and ran her fingers through her dark hair. "I suppose you're right But it got me thinking."

I waited until she continued before I sucked in another breath.

"We only have a couple more weeks before it's Christmas, and really, we only have a week and a half before my family arrives." She tapped her finger on the armrest of the chair. "Which doesn't leave much time for us to continue to get to know one another."

"No, it doesn't."

I had absolutely no idea where she was going with this, and with Skye, it could be anywhere.

"So, I've thought long and hard about things, and I want to make this December one you won't ever forget, but for once in your life . . ." She smiled. "In a good way. If you relinquish your evenings to me, aside from Friday with the opportunist, I will do my very best to help create new holiday memories so it doesn't feel like a sucker punch every time December rolls around."

She scooted forward in her chair and waited for a response.

And the truth was that I'd happily do anything to be able to spend another minute or hour with her.

"Plus, since I'll be headed back home in January, it's partly selfish. I'd like to have a seasoned tour guide."

Hearing her utter those words about leaving Fireweed was its own sort of sucker punch.

"Whatever it is you want, I'll make it happen."

She grinned. "Well, sounds like the first thing will be going shopping to find you an ugly sweater for ice skating."

"Sounds wonderful," I said flatly.

"Do you have any thrift stores around?"

I cocked my head slightly. "Why?"

"That's probably our best bet for an ugly sweater."

"So, it literally is an ugly sweater that I'm supposed to wear."

Skye rolled her eyes and let out an exasperated sigh. "Where have you been living for the last decade?"

"In a fog."

"Well, I hope it's lifting. Let's go shopping and have dinner tonight." She stood. "Now, back to the grind."

I laughed and waved, watching her wander to the door.

We'd agreed to no kissing and complete professionalism at the office moving forward, but it was extremely hard.

"Hey, Skye?"

She stopped at the door and looked at me.

"Yup?"

"Wanna do lunch today?"

She grinned and opened the door. "But what will they think, Mr. Adams?"

I laughed. "Noon."

"Fine. Noon."

She walked out the door, and I turned my attention back to my inbox with a new message Marcy had just sent over.

Before I had a chance to read it, she popped back.

"It looks like that VP's assistant is asking for recommendations for where her boss should stay for the weekend."

I felt the color drain from my face when the words sank in.

"I'd guess the Loxxy. It's the nicest hotel on the waterfront." I shrugged.

Marcy chuckled. "I wasn't telling you so you could guide me to the right hotel." She stared at me.

"No. I know. I appreciate the heads-up. And there is a lot riding on this, but I'm certainly not going to compromise my beliefs." I chuckled. "Who knew I was that much of a catch?"

Marcy rolled her eyes. "Most of Fireweed. If you left your house more, you'd be surprised what the town folk think of you."

"Very funny."

She tapped the door frame and chuckled. "Well, just as long as you understand that she thinks you're her dessert, my job here is done."

"It's hard to be this attractive, Marcy. It really is."

"I'm sure your plight comes with many pitfalls." She turned on her heels and walked out of the office while I let out a deep breath.

I knew a lot rode on this, but the first deal was already signed, sealed, and delivered. The second line was the only thing hanging in the balance, but it would offer security and a great bargaining chip if I decided to sell the company.

My knee bobbed up and down as I looked at the *North Pole* sign. There was no way I wanted to spend my Friday night with this woman. Obviously, I'd leave it at dinner, but if that wasn't what she wanted, the deal would go up in smoke anyway.

I shook my head and chuckled. "Dad would certainly get a kick out of this."

Max walked into my office and coughed. "Get a kick out of what?"

I stared at my brother for a split second and smiled.

"Have a seat." I grinned at my brother, who shrugged and sat down.

"I just stopped by to let you know that I'm headed out on the eighteenth for my trip."

I nodded. "Okay. I'll keep an eye on your place."

"Great. Should we do like a holiday dinner before or . . .?"

I smiled, looking at Max. He was a hard guy to read. I'd always heard about how identical twins were bonded and joined at the hip, but it had never been like that with my brother. From the time we were toddlers, he didn't want to be near me. Instead, he wanted to do whatever he could to get all of my parents' attention, and he learned quickly that the best way to do that was by being bad. So, he'd climb up the bookshelves even when they'd tumble down. He'd spray water at the indoor cats with an outdoor hose, flooding the kitchen while waiting for my mom's reaction.

And once we got to high school, his behavior was even more pronounced. If there was something shady going on, Max was either the leader or the cheerleader.

"Yeah. I've got a little gift for you before you head out again. It might come in handy."

"Thanks, man." He nodded. "Has the new hire become *available* yet?" Max used air quotes to get the point across, and I couldn't help but smile.

"No. Not really."

"Ah, that's too bad. It might have been fun before I left."

My brow arched. "Skye isn't an *it*. She's a female."

"Obviously." He kicked out his feet and stretched his arms behind his head when a thought occurred to me.

Chapter Twenty-One

Skye

"You're sure we'll find an ugly sweater in here?"

I looked up at Levi, who looked miserable, but I only felt marginally bad. After all, he was headed out on a date tomorrow with a woman who wasn't me.

"I guarantee we'll find the perfect ugly sweater." I locked my fingers in between his and pulled him into the thrift shop. The door chimed, and several of the workers behind the counter shouted greetings in our direction.

Large cardboard signs with categories dangled from the drop-down ceiling. I spotted the men's section and squeezed his hand.

"This way." I pulled him with me as he glanced around, coming to a complete stop.

"Get out." He picked up an old VHS tape and turned

it over. "I haven't seen *National Lampoon's Christmas Vacation* in years."

Pure excitement filled my veins.

Pure excitement!

"This isn't just my all-time favorite Christmas movie," I whispered to him. "It's my all-time favorite movie. Period. End of story. Whenever I'm blue, I turn it on."

Levi's mouth quirked slightly. "I can't imagine you getting very blue."

I recoiled at the notion. "I get blue. Everyone gets blue. Even with the whole Jared debacle. I got annoyed, a little bit blue, and then craved an adventure, so here I am."

"Ah, a thrill-seeker." He nodded. "Nothing like Fireweed Island to bring adventure."

I rolled my eyes and chuckled. "I don't know. This has been quite an adventure so far."

"I'm getting this," he said, holding on to the movie.

"You have a VCR to play it?"

He nodded.

"Wow. I'm impressed." I chuckled. "Now, onward to our mission."

We wandered over to the men's section, and immediately, I spotted a sweater too good to be true. Not only was it supremely ugly, but the sweater was also probably about a size or two too small for Levi. Brilliant colors emblazoned the Christmas tree on the front, which looked like a shag carpet more than a tree. The sleeves were quilted red sweater patches, and the collar had a faux plaid bowtie attached.

He eyed me. "You've got to be kidding me."

I held it up to his chest, and the sleeves came right above his wrist.

"Do you secretly hate me?" he asked with a twinkle in his eyes.

"Quite the contrary. I'm dressing you to win." I grinned, checking the tag to see what a fine sweater like this was made of. "Can I count on you to pull this off at the ice skating rink?"

He smiled and nodded.

And without warning, my mom's revelation about my dad slammed into me like a freight train. I hadn't done a very good job of dealing with it, and she refused to really say anything more on the subject.

I glanced up to see Levi watching me. He tipped my chin. "Are you okay? You got suddenly quiet."

"Sorry. I just . . .what my mom said about my dad. It's like I'm getting flashbacks." I pressed my lips together in a thin line as I thought about how to say it. "Her telling me that kind of shook my world. When life would get tough, I'd always think back to my parents and think, well, they've managed. They were my beacon, in a way."

Levi draped his arms over my shoulders and pulled me in. "What your mom told you didn't take away all the wonderful years they've had and all the years they get to look forward to. Your memories are real. The feelings of love you felt between them are still real."

"But my perception isn't the same."

He nodded and kissed the top of my head. "No. You're right."

"And I just don't know why my mom assumes I want that with Jared."

"She loved your dad and still does," he said simply. "And she assumes you loved Jared."

"But I didn't. I don't think I ever did."

"Well, she must not understand that."

I nodded in silence and let out a deep breath, wondering how Levi could always make things so clear for me.

Smiling, I reached for his hands and pulled him toward me. "Now, on to my sweater."

He followed me to the women's section of the store, where I started pushing hangers and rummaging through all kinds of tops, blouses, and sweaters.

"What about this one?"

I turned around to see Levi holding up a sweater that someone had cut off to make a crop top with pieces of yarn hanging down. There were two ornaments strategically placed with red sequins highlighting the area, along with *Good Tidings* stitched near the collar.

"That is really awful, and I'm not sure it's appropriate for the workplace," I teased.

"I don't know what you're talking about. There are just two ornaments and a nice little Christmas saying."

I rolled my eyes and held it up to me. "Fine. I'll probably get frostbite on my stomach, but I'll do it."

We wandered to the cashier, where we put the sweaters onto the counter, along with Levi's VHS.

As they checked us out, Levi handed cash over before I had a chance to buy my own.

"I got it," I told him

He laughed. "No. I insist. You'll have something to remember me by."

I rolled my eyes as they handed us a bag with the sweaters and the movie. By the time we'd wandered outside, the sun had set, and the Christmas lights twinkled in all directions.

"Fireweed is so romantic," I said, turning to see Levi glancing at the nativity scene across the street at the church.

"We used to go to that church." He motioned to the tiny brick building. "Until I was about eleven."

"Why'd you stop?" I asked.

"Lots of things, not the least of which was that my brother thought it would be really funny to hide baby Jesus one December."

"What?" I gasped. "Max?"

Levi laughed and nodded. "Yup. My mom was absolutely mortified. I'll never forget her marching my brother back to church and making him hold the baby Jesus like a real baby while my dad was cracking up with me in the car."

I chuckled, imagining the scenario. "He's always been a handful, I take it."

Levi nodded, smiling. "You know what?"

He looped his arms around my waist and brought me in, dropping the bag on the sidewalk.

"What?" I asked, looking into his eyes.

"This is the first time I spoke about my parents and felt happiness." His eyes danced with light, and he shook his head. "Wow."

I smiled, feeling his arms hold me tightly.

"There is something about you, Skye." His eyes stayed on mine, and I felt like I was tipping over the edge of a cliff. My tummy tightened and dipped. My pulse raced. My palms got sweaty.

And all it took was Levi Adams holding me.

"You make me see the world differently," he said softly. "And I didn't think that was possible."

"Believe it or not, you do the same."

Levi laughed. "How's that? I showed you how to be a grumpy jerk?"

I smiled, looking into his eyes. "You've never been a jerk to me. In fact, I think you're one of the kindest and most caring bosses I've had. You have so much at stake, and you never let your employees see you sweat."

He kissed the top of my head, and my belly swirled into a chaotic jumble of nerves. It felt so unreal. The twinkling lights, the cute town, the water just across the way, and a man holding me tight and telling me that I made him feel good.

It was all a dream.

A wonderful Christmas dream.

That kept being interrupted by my mom's careless comments about my dad.

"What if one of the employees drives by, and you're hugging me?" I asked.

He smiled and shook his head. "I don't care."

"Music to my ears," I whispered, rising on my toes to give him a quick kiss. "Let's eat snacks from the freezer and watch *A National Lampoon's Christmas Vacation.*"

"I don't have many snacks in the freezer." He smiled.

"You're in luck because I do. I have spanakopita, pizza pockets, onion rings, mini quiche, wontons, and taquitos, to name a few, and I even have a digital copy I bought years ago that we can watch."

His eyes widened. "That's quite the stash."

"My family and I are big snackers. I started collecting food early."

He laughed, letting go of me. "My kind of people."

"I think you'll like them."

"But will they like me?" he asked, picking up the bag.

I nodded, thinking about the last conversation I'd had with my mom about Jared. I'd almost thought about telling her I found someone here I was interested in, but I knew that would just open a whole other can of worms.

He linked his hands with mine as we walked to his car.

"Do they know about me?"

"As in the best boss ever or . . .?"

He glanced at me as he helped me into the car. "I'd

say the *or* part."

I smiled and shook my head as he closed the door, and I buckled.

When he got inside, he fastened his seat belt, turned on the car, and let out a deep breath. "Are you going to?"

"Do you think I should?" I asked.

"Might be a good distraction for your mom. Maybe she'd forget about Jared if she knew you had a handsome suitor out here."

I laughed. "A handsome suitor? It sounds like you've already been talking to her."

"I only guessed she'd sound like mine." He pulled onto the street leading to my house, and I felt an amazing calm coat over me.

I felt the very essence of Christmas here on Fireweed. I didn't hate going to work. I loved coming home to my place and flipping on holiday music, where I just talked to myself and got to know myself again. Jared had skewed that years ago, and it was nice to remember what made me happy.

And it didn't take much.

I glanced at Levi and smiled, realizing how much I enjoyed his company.

"You're going to look absolutely smashing in that sweater next week," I told him.

"Not half as good as you."

I chuckled. "You just want to watch me freeze to death on the ice."

"And then I can come rescue you."

"If you say so."

Levi pulled into the driveway and stopped the car. "Still thinking of snacks and a movie?"

"You know it," I said, laughing. "I have to remind you of how wonderful I am since you're headed out with the bimbo of sales ... err, I mean the VP of private label tomorrow."

He smirked. "I'll tell her you said hi."

"Would you?" I faked my smile. "That would be fantastic."

I still felt I'd been doing a fabulous job of not letting tomorrow get in the way of how much I loved spending time with Levi. We were in the baby stages of this thing we had, and I knew how ridiculous it would be if I told him not to go with the lady tomorrow. I just needed to enjoy my Friday night before the rush of the holidays slammed into me.

Levi walked around and opened my door for me since I was apparently comatose in the passenger seat, thinking about tomorrow.

He'd already fished out my sweater to take inside and

left the video with his sweater in the bag.

"Okay, so I have a confession," I told him as we walked to the door.

"You have a crush on my brother?"

I chuckled. "Well, that baby Jesus story made me laugh. But no. I have a bad habit of reciting the lines to this movie."

He grinned and nodded. "I think I can get used to that."

"Good."

We walked into the house, and before I had a chance to even put my bag down, Levi brought me into his arms.

"I've wanted to kiss you all day, Skye." His mouth came to mine, and I felt like I was home.

The sensations washing through me didn't make any sense, but the emotions were welling up inside, and they were screaming to be heard.

I didn't want to believe that this was all temporary. That my job was temporary. That my life on the island was temporary. That Levi was temporary.

I started to realize that I wanted this to be my life going forward.

Yet, I knew that probably wasn't very realistic.

Maybe this was just the fling I needed to get my head

on straight.

But as our kisses deepened and his mouth pressed against mine as my heart rate soared, my stomach tensed with desire, and my world spun into a delusional bliss, I realized I didn't care. Right this second, I was willing to give up every ounce of reality because he did mean something to me, and if I wanted to pretend it could go somewhere after Christmas, then I would let myself believe.

Chapter Twenty-Two

Levi

"Okay, we have every kind of sprinkle and icing imaginable for these cookies, folks." Marcy clapped her hands as if she were the principal of an unruly high school class, but as I looked around the conference table, I was reminded that it was merely my employees. "We have two hundred plain sugar cookies that require your special touch, and then I'll deliver them to the youth center tonight."

"Two hundred?" My jaw dropped.

Marcy scowled. "What else do you have to do today?"

Stan chuckled as the other employees filed into the conference room.

As I stared at the naked snowman, reindeer, Santa, Mrs. Claus, and elf cookies, my mind drifted to last night, and I wanted a repeat. Kissing Skye was like nothing else I'd experienced, and I knew we would have gone to the next level if it weren't for today.

A workday.

But I was hoping I could show up to Skye's tonight to continue where we left off.

Just the thought of waking up with her in my arms made my chest fill up with hope. I swore my lips still tingled and were swollen from how much we kissed, in between her reciting lines from *National Lampoon's*, of course.

Until we just stopped watching.

The memory brought a smile to my lips when Marcy interrupted my thoughts.

"Really like that Mrs. Claus cookie there, Levi?"

I scowled and shook my head as Stan stood up the moment Skye walked into the conference room.

She glanced at the large mountain of cookies, and her eyes widened. "That is a lot of cookies."

Marcy scowled and huffed. "It really isn't. We have twenty employees in today, which means we each only need to decorate ten. Ten cookies isn't a lot to decorate."

Skye nodded. "No, you're right. I didn't think of it that way. I can decorate ten cookies with my eyes shut."

"Showoff," I teased, and Skye chuckled.

Marcy nodded, glancing at Stan.

"Hey, Skye. Can I talk to you for a sec?" Stan asked.

"Sure thing." She nodded and wandered over to his side of the table as I pretended to pick the cookies that I wanted to decorate.

Marcy turned up the volume to the Christmas music, which made it impossible to hear what Stan was talking to Skye about, but the way he was looking at her made my chest tighten. He'd obviously been into her, but she didn't seem into him.

I didn't think.

I glanced at Skye, and her cheeks reddened as she looked over at Marcy and then at me as Stan nodded.

"Oh, no," I muttered.

"What?" Marcy whispered, sliding some icing to me.

"I think Stan is asking Skye out."

"Uh-oh." Marcy pretended to smear red icing on Santa's belly but managed to get the table instead as she watched the two. "Thinks she's interested?"

I pretended to scowl at her, and she laughed as Skye made her way toward Marcy.

Stan didn't look too devastated, so maybe he wasn't asking her out.

Skye took a seat across from me as Marcy dished up icing for her and moved sprinkles into reach. Skye kept her gaze on the table for a few moments as Stan walked out of the conference room.

Skye's gaze connected with mine. "He asked me out. I said yes. What do I do?"

"What do you mean, what do you do?" I whispered. "Are you interested?"

"No, but I didn't want to hurt his feelings."

Marcy chuckled and shook her head. "Things just got complicated."

I smiled and smeared some green icing on an elf. "When don't they, Marcy?"

"I didn't think it would be a good idea to say no, and then he sees me with you."

"Hmm. I think this might be why workplace romances are often forbidden at most companies." I glared at Marcy. "But not this one."

Skye laughed as Evie walked in and pointed over her shoulder. "What's got Stan in such a good mood?"

I glanced at Skye. "Oh, our new hire is going out with him."

"Oh, really?" Evie cocked her head and studied me for a split second. "I thought you two . . ." She stopped herself. "You know what? Never mind. Give me some cookies to decorate."

"So, when's the big date?" I asked Skye.

She blushed again. "Tonight."

My eyes widened. "Tonight?"

She licked her lips and glanced at the cookies in front of her. "I thought since you were busy tonight, it would be a good time to choose."

Crap.

This wasn't what I'd planned for the evening at all.

"Are you headed to the tavern down the street?" I asked casually.

She shook her head. "I don't know. He was going to pick the place, and we were just going to head out from work."

Ah, good. An early bird special.

I reached for the silver sparkles and shook them on my elf while trying not to look as agitated as I felt. Had Susan acted like a professional, I wouldn't be in this predicament in the first place.

I let out a deep sigh.

"Everything okay there?" Marcy teased.

"Yeah. Totally fine."

She walked away, and Skye glanced around the table, which was now full. Her eyes met mine, and she smiled.

"It's just dinner. Promise," she said softly.

"I know. But you know, if you're into—"

Skye's expression fell. "Seriously? You think that I might be into him?"

I grinned, realizing I'd touched a sore spot.

"Well, I don't offer you the same leniency." She eyed me. "If Miss Private Label has other ideas besides a good steak and a view . . ." Her voice trailed off, which only made her more irresistible. "Why are you looking at me like that?"

"No reason." I reached for a Santa cookie as Stan came marching back into the conference room, looking completely pleased with himself.

He walked over next to Skye and took a seat. Evie glanced at me, and I pretended not to notice as I painted Santa's suit red as Marcy wandered in with some more sprinkles.

"Isn't this the best time of the year?" Marcy asked, setting down the new colors.

"The best," Skye said, nodding.

"So, your family is coming out here for the holidays?" Stan asked Skye.

She dabbed some icing onto her cookie and smiled. "They are. I'm so excited. What about your family?"

"Oh, they all live on the island. My mom would have a fit if we didn't all come over to her house on Christmas morning."

Skye laughed and nodded. She looked so at ease with Stan, and so kind. It didn't seem to matter what position she was put in. She always managed to carry herself with such class.

Now, tonight's plan hit a bit of a rough patch because I'd planned on surprising Skye at her house, and hopefully, I still could.

I reached for my fifth cookie and decorated it, glancing at the clock. I needed to meet my brother to pull this off.

"Whoa, cowboy," Skye said to me.

Stan's brows furrowed, and he glanced at her as she watched me.

"You're really getting after those cookies," she continued, not realizing she'd just called her new boss cowboy.

"I have to meet Max," I explained.

"Oh, yeah? He wants to get together before he heads out of town?"

I nodded. "Something like that."

"That will be fun," she said.

Stan glanced at Evie, who kept focused on her cookie.

"Do you want me to decorate yours?" Marcy asked. "I don't want you to keep Max waiting."

"Sure. That would be great." I glanced at Skye and smiled.

She narrowed her eyes at me and waited until Stan was staring at his cookie. "Are you mad at me?" she mouthed.

My eyes widened, and I shook my head. "Not at all," I mouthed back.

She looked a little relieved, but I couldn't exactly go around the table and give her a hug to make her feel better.

I gave a quick wave to the group and made my way to my office, where I grabbed my stuff before heading out the door to Max's house.

This was probably the world's stupidest idea, but it was about the only thing that would save my sanity. The thought of having to sit across from Susan tonight when I could be kissing Skye didn't sit well.

But I couldn't tell a soul what I'd planned with Max. This was crazy and insane, but for once, I was going to use Max's inability to tell right from wrong to my advantage.

All I had to think about was the baby Jesus kidnapping, and I knew the plan was foolproof. Max was my guy.

As I got into my car, I turned on the radio and blasted the music, hearing the lyrics sweep over me. It wasn't until I turned the corner toward Max's house that it dawned on me that I was listening to Christmas music and not getting violently ill.

Progress.

Thanks to Skye.

I shook my head and sighed as I pulled into Max's driveway. It was actually my parents' home, our home growing up. I parked and glanced at the house.

I'd always hated coming over here since my parents passed away, but my chest didn't feel like it was being weighed down by a boulder this time. My brother walked outside and gave me a wave.

I got out of the car and nodded. "Thanks again, Max."

His eyes lit up. "Should be fun."

"I was afraid you'd say that."

"What? Can a guy not live a little?"

"You have to vow to me that if things get frisky, you'll tell her that you are my brother." I squeezed his shoulders. "Promise?"

"Of course, I promise." Max scowled. "What kind of creep do you think I am?"

I didn't say a word. Instead, I just followed my brother inside.

Max had transformed our childhood home into a complete bachelor pad. There was a black leather sofa in the living room, along with a pool table. The kitchen was completely modern and updated to incorporate a beer tap and a wine fridge.

I followed him into the family room, where he had a monstrous projector screen and a dartboard set up. He pointed at the couch. "What do you think? Would this be an outfit you'd wear?"

I stared at the wool sweater and jeans. "Yeah. That works."

He stood and studied me. "Now, why is it you can't just meet with this lady?"

I let out a sigh. "I think she wants to hook up."

"And that's a bad thing, why?"

I debated what to say. I glanced at the dartboard, unsure that I really wanted to confess to my brother about Skye.

"You've met someone," Max said flatly.

I turned to face him and pushed up my sweater sleeves. "I have."

His eyes narrowed on me. "Wait a minute."

"What?"

"It's that chick from Shantos, isn't it?"

"What makes you say that?"

"The new hire."

"Technically, she's on contract."

He waved his hand. "Whatever, man. She's hot."

"Yeah. She is."

"I thought she was unavailable?"

I didn't say anything, and Max nodded. "Oh . . . so this thing between you transpired pretty quickly."

"It's complicated. She has an ex back in Maine. Her mom is pleading for her to get back with him."

"Well, that sucks."

I laughed. Leave it to my brother to manage to roll up all my feelings into three words.

"Anyway, I'll fill you in on where we're at with Shantos Pinot Grigio, the contract updates, and the terms we agreed to."

"Do you think she'll notice my signature and not yours?" Max asked.

"I doubt it."

Max nodded. "What if I tell her who I am, and she gets mad? Wouldn't that put you back to square one and you should have just told her no to this date in the first place?"

I didn't really want to suddenly confess to my brother about the trials and tribulations of owning this business, so I just nodded. "Probably."

"And you're going to be . . . where? If I need

backup."

I laughed. "You won't need backup. I'll be at Skye's house."

"Okay, man. Wish me luck."

I looked at my brother and shook my head. "You don't need luck."

Chapter Twenty-Three

Skye

Stan sat across from me at Mudflat Tavern. When he told me this was where he made reservations, I was equally jubilated and horrified. I figured the odds were such that I wouldn't actually see Levi with the vixen of Private Label or, as I liked to refer to her in my head all day, PL.

But if they happened to be seated within eyeshot, then I took that as a sign that spying was meant to be.

"Thanks for coming out with me tonight, Skye. I've been trying to work up the nerve for the last week."

I smiled and nodded in Stan's direction. "Absolutely."

"I scoured the workplace policy, and I didn't see anything about dating coworkers, so I think we're in the clear."

I chuckled. "We'd better be."

"But I have to ask something, and I'm sure it's going to come out wrong."

My stomach knotted. Stan was a nice guy. I certainly didn't want to hurt his feelings, but I also didn't want to say no to him and make him angry if he found out about Levi and me.

"Okay. I'm all ears," I answered.

The server came over, and I ordered a soda while Stan ordered a beer.

Stan leaned over the table slightly and lowered his voice, "Evie thinks there's something going on between you and Levi."

My cheeks instantly burned as I looked out the window. "Oh, really?"

Stan nodded. "I don't know if it's true or not. I haven't seen any evidence, but I don't want to step on his toes or . . ." He stopped himself when something caught his eye behind my shoulder.

I heard PL's familiar cackle, and my body stiffened when I heard his laughter match hers.

What was so funny?

Stan brought his gaze back to mine. "Well, maybe not. Maybe Evie was wrong."

My brows rose. "Wrong about what?"

"Um . . . Levi and you."

My brow arched. "What makes you think she's wrong?"

"No reason," he muttered, avoiding my gaze.

My eyes whipped to Levi's fingers at the base of PL's spine, and my own tingled. She had on a crimson-red, tiger-striped dress that fit her so snuggly I was certain one wrong move and she'd fall out of it.

"Seriously?" I gasped.

Stan looked at me and cocked his head. "What? Is your soda wrong?"

I shook my head and dropped my eyes to the menu. "No. Sorry."

"Are you sure? That sounded pretty—"

"Nope. Everything is fine." I plastered a smile on my face, but Stan looked concerned.

Stan lowered his eyes to his menu as I eyed Levi and PL. Levi was laughing up a storm and definitely enjoying himself.

The nerve.

"Hmph."

Stan looked up. "Pardon?"

I shifted in my seat and brought my eyes back to

Stan's.

I let out a deep breath. I had to confess. "I have to tell you something."

He closed the menu, and I steadied my focus on Stan.

"I've kissed Levi." I cleared my throat. "Several times."

Surprise washed over Stan's features. "Well, then you probably won't be thrilled with his date tonight. They appear to be getting along swimmingly well. And it makes what I want to ask even weirder."

I chuckled and took a sip of soda as the server came back to take our orders. After witnessing the devilish duo, I decided to order a stiff drink and a steak while Stan did the same. Once the server left, I frowned.

"I'm sorry." I shook my head. "I should have told you earlier today, but I was worried I'd hurt your feelings or you might get upset if I told you no and then Levi yes. I don't know. I suck at the dating thing and the relationship thing." I glanced in Levi's direction. "Obviously."

Stan laughed and leaned back. "Don't feel bad. I was actually going to ask you to do me a really weird favor, so it's best that this is how it's going."

Suddenly, my attention left Levi. "Well, now that sounds far more interesting than watching tiger lady and Levi schmooze in the corner. Spill the beans."

"Remember how I said I always go to my mom's Christmas morning?"

"I do."

"Well, I was going to ask you to come with me."

My brows rose. "Why's that?"

"This sounds so pathetic."

"No. What's pathetic is not being able to take your eyes off a man you have a crush on while he's with another woman at the same restaurant. I'm the pathetic one, giving all my attention to a man who clearly doesn't need it."

Stan smiled. "If it makes you feel better, you've given me more attention than Levi."

I laughed. "Actually, I have this weird eye thing I can do where it looks like I'm looking at you, but I can see to the side too."

Stan snorted and smiled.

"So, why in the world would you want me to come with you on Christmas morning?"

"To get my parents off my back about my lack of dating." He shifted uncomfortably. "And no offense, but you're not exactly my type. You're *their* type, so I thought I'd buy myself a year of bliss if they thought I had a girlfriend."

"Aww." I tucked my hands into my chest. "That is so

sweet that you wanted me to be your fake girlfriend."

He laughed. "It seemed ideal. I could blame everything on a long-distance relationship. The rise and the fall. The inevitable doom. It was perfect."

I glanced at Levi and scowled. "You still may get your chance. Things aren't looking swell on my end. I can always pop in if you need me. I know exactly what it's like to have parents pressuring you to find *The One*."

I thought about what my mom revealed about my dad's infidelity to convince me to try out Jared again, and my shoulders slumped.

"I'll remember that."

A bottle of wine arrived at their table just as our drinks arrived.

I took a big sip and shook my head.

"So, you're into Levi?" he asked.

I smiled, trying to pretend that Levi wasn't sitting across from me in the restaurant with another woman. "I am, but I know I shouldn't be. I'm leaving in January, and as you pointed out, it makes for a good excuse to end a relationship."

Stan smiled and shook his head. "I'm not exactly sure what's going on with Levi tonight, but I can tell you that I've worked at Shantos for a long time, and he's a workaholic. He's not a womanizer." He craned his neck to see Levi and tiger gal. "Or he's not usually one."

"That's nice to hear."

"Now, his brother . . ." Stan shrugged. "That's an entirely different story."

"I gathered that the few times I met him."

Stan laughed and nodded as our server brought our food.

As I caught Levi grinning from ear to ear, I ordered another drink and took a bite of steak.

"It's really tragic what happened with his parents. It shaped him into the man he is today, for better or worse," Stan said, taking a bite of steak. "He works so hard and always gives amazing bonuses at Christmas while his brother is off cliff diving and snorkeling."

"Yeah. It does seem like night and day with those two."

Stan nodded. "For sure."

I smiled, feeling immensely better that Stan and I were in the same boat. "I have to admit that I'm flattered you wanted to take me home to impress your parents."

He grinned and nodded. "And they would be impressed."

I chuckled.

Levi stood and wandered over to the lady tiger. He

bent down and whispered something in her ear, and my jaw dropped open. She reached for his hand, and he wandered away while she pulled out her phone and checked herself in the reverse camera.

"What do you see?" Stan asked.

"I see Levi's future becoming very bleak." I smirked.

"Uh-oh."

"It looks like he just whispered sweet nothings in the woman's ear and wandered off." I frowned and took a bite of the baked potato. "He hasn't even whispered sweet nothings in my ear."

"Yikes." Stan looked over to get a better look at the woman. "She seems to be enjoying herself."

"She sure does."

Levi walked back to the table and leaned next to her again, and this time my jaw clenched.

He sat down in his seat as the server set down their food.

"You know the worst part of witnessing this?" I asked Stan.

"I can't even fathom."

"Levi asked me if he should go out with her, and I was dumb enough to say yes."

Stan chuckled. "Never play the part of the chill

partner."

"Wise words, my friend."

Right when I thought it couldn't get worse, I spotted Levi reaching over to *her* with a fork loaded with halibut.

Sharing food?

I turned my attention back to Stan and chuckled. "We should make out right here."

"We could do a *When Harry Met Sally* scene to show him what he's missing," Stan suggested.

"And what he'll never get, with the way it's going."

"Oh, snap." Stan grinned.

"It's better to find these things out before you know it gets serious," I told Stan, trying to believe it myself.

I thought back to last night's kisses and then whipped my gaze in the direction of the newly formed couple, seeing the same sexual tension rise between them. Apparently, Levi was a conduit for sexual attraction, regardless of who was on the receiving end. I would never have guessed it.

I let out a defeated sigh. "I never would have guessed it."

"What, in particular?" Stan asked.

"That Levi could be so good at turning his charm on for just about anyone."

Stan scratched his head and shook his head. "I know

this might sound crazy, and I'm not just trying to stick up for him since he signs my paychecks, but I've never known him to be like that. Usually, he doesn't even notice beautiful women, let alone talk to or flirt with them."

I saw the woman take a sip of wine, and laughter rang through the air when Levi glanced in my direction. His eyes met mine, and he flashed a goofy grin while I glared at him before he turned his attention back to his date.

Yes, date. I finally had to admit to myself that Levi was having a blast with a female who wasn't me.

Bah-humbug to his strong jawline and striking eyes. That wasn't all that mattered in life.

Granted, this rendezvous between them was pretty much my doing. I could have put my foot down at any time. But oh, no. I was the understanding girlfriend who wasn't a girlfriend.

I took my last bite of steak and polished off drink number two.

The server walked over and asked if we wanted any dessert. I was about to answer no when Stan answered yes before the server trundled away.

"Just wait until you try this coconut ice cream sundae. Evie and I will sneak off here sometimes at lunch just for this."

I smiled, wondering something. "Have you and Evie ever . . .?"

Stan shook his head. "No. She's totally my type, but I'm definitely not hers."

"How do you know?"

He shrugged. "We've worked together so long that I don't think she sees me like that."

Without warning, violinists started playing in a parade, beelining for Levi's table.

"You've got to be kidding me," I said, laughing. "This blows my mind."

Surprise registered along Stan's features as he turned to watch the violinists head to their destination.

As I watched them file past Levi's table, it felt like I could finally breathe again.

And then I saw something I never expected.

Tucked far in the corner, the violinists surrounded a couple who I recognized instantly.

"Oh, my gosh, Stan. Look." I pointed in the direction of the booth.

"I'm afraid to." He grimaced.

"No. Do."

Stan turned to see Jay get on one knee, proposing to Marcy, who I never even saw in the restaurant since I was so focused on Levi and his other woman.

Or maybe I was the other woman.

Didn't matter.

Instead, I saw love unfolding in front of us as Jay popped the question to Marcy, who squealed so loudly in the restaurant that Levi dropped his fork onto his plate.

He glanced in my direction, and I gave him a dirty look.

Levi pulled out his phone and texted, but when the message didn't land on my phone, I only got more annoyed.

Jay was holding Marcy in his arms, and I let out a happy sigh for them.

"Well, I didn't see that coming tonight," Stan said, turning around.

"Yeah? What did you see happening?"

He laughed. "Honestly? The way that lady is dry-humping Levi, I assumed a glass of wine might be dumped on him or her."

"I have way more class than that," I assured him. "Besides, my family already booked their non-refundable tickets out here, and I'm depending on that house."

He laughed. "You're a lot of fun, Skye."

"Even if I'm a horrible judge of character?"

Stan smiled and shook his head. "You're not. I assure

you. He's a good guy."

My brow arched in surprise at the same time I heard Levi's voice behind me.

But I saw him sitting across the restaurant from me. And then it hit me. That wasn't Levi at all.

I groaned, feeling like an idiot.

Levi threw down a wad of cash on the table and nodded at Stan. "Do you mind if I take my girl?"

Levi's words turned my world upside down, and it felt like I could finally breathe again.

Stan smiled at me and nodded. "Have at it. I'm surprised she hasn't strangled anyone at that table yet, and I can't believe I didn't recognize Max."

I couldn't even see straight as my nightmare of an evening turned around.

He scooped me into his arms as Max glanced in our direction and shook his head.

"I should have known it was your brother," I nearly groaned into Levi's arm as he dropped his arms over my shoulders. "He and that lady are nearly undressing each other with their eyes. I feel like I've been in the *Twilight Zone*."

"And I'm so sorry about that. It never in a million years occurred to me that you'd be at Mudflats tonight."

"I'm starting to believe you about the luck rubbing off

on me." I smiled as he rubbed my back softly.

"Turns out that good ol' Susan was a fling of his, and she immediately recognized him when he showed up tonight. He texted me right away."

"What? She was using you to get to him? I'm floored." I shivered at the thought, not understanding why anyone would want Max over Levi.

I let out a huge sigh and rested my head against his upper arm. "I can't even begin to tell you how much better I feel."

"I'm glad. I'm just sorry I didn't put two and two together sooner. How's Stan? Is there going to be a lawsuit on my hands?" he teased.

I chuckled. "He thinks the world of you, actually. And apparently, I'm not his type, but he was hoping he could use me as a fake girlfriend for the holidays since I was leaving town."

"I swear the locals aren't always this weird," he muttered, skimming his lips against the top of my head.

I wasn't sure I believed him, but I felt an odd sense that I fit right in, and that didn't bother me a bit.

Chapter Twenty-Four

Levi

"Have I redeemed myself yet?" I asked Skye as we walked into my house.

Scarlet bolted toward us, circling around with yips and barks before trundling down the hall to go back to sleep. It was like she wanted to give Skye and me privacy. I smiled at the thought. Scarlett had always been extremely loyal.

Skye kicked off her shoes and shrugged off her coat before saying anything.

She smiled, and her big, beautiful eyes finally landed on mine. "You have, and I am so proud of myself."

"Yeah?" I grinned, pulling her into my arms. "For what?"

"I kept my butt firmly seated in that booth at the restaurant. No matter what I was fantasizing about, I stayed put." She put her head back and laughed. "I have matured as a person. No liquids were thrown. No punches were landed. Cameras weren't broken."

Skye tipped her head back toward me, still smiling. "But my mind ran absolutely wild with all the things I wanted to do. So, I will work on that for next time."

I nuzzled my chin into the crook of her shoulder, and her body trembled from the touch. "There shouldn't be a next time."

She leaned her head against mine as I breathed in everything wonderful about Skye. Her sweet smell was intoxicating and promised so much. The softness of her skin against mine was addicting. I wanted to feel her against me. I wanted more of this.

Tilting her head up, her eyes opened as she smiled dopily. "Mr. Adams, I fear there's no coming back from this crush I have on you."

"Crush?"

She nodded, running her fingers through my hair. "This has been the best holiday season of my adult life. But something has been killing me."

"What's that?"

"Don't you find it ironic that you live on a street called Sugarplum Lane, and yet you hate Christmas?"

I laughed. "Hate is a strong word, and no, the irony wasn't missed."

"I just had to say something." She winked at me.

"What was your favorite from when you were a kid?" I asked, leading her into the family room.

Before I realized she was at Mudflats, I'd planned on surprising her at her house and bringing her back to mine for a rain check on her favorite movie, but when she didn't answer the door, I knew she must still be out with Stan. And then I got the dreaded text from Max that she was sitting across from him at the restaurant, looking like she wanted to pounce.

"My favorite was probably when my parents gave my sister and me two loppy-eared bunnies. They were our best friends growing up. Lippy and Loppy."

"Was yours Lippy?" I teased.

Skye laughed. "How'd you guess? They were amazing. Pure white with tan ears and so sweet. It makes my heart squeeze to think about them." She glanced toward the coffee table in front of the couch, and her eyes lit up.

"Is that popcorn for us?" she asked, pointing at the big bowl of popcorn I'd made before I dashed out the door. "And is that a . . ."

Skye spun around with huge eyes. "No way . . . you bought a Christmas tree and decorated it?"

I smiled. "Okay. So, confession. Apparently, you can hire people to do things like that for you."

She chuckled and ran her hand across my chest. "Close enough. I'm in shock."

"I thought we could try watching *National Lampoon's* tonight since we never got through the whole thing the last time. I got my VCR all set up and everything."

Skye smiled and shook her head. "I don't know how you make everything feel so magical when you feel the exact opposite inside."

"It's you, Skye. I can't explain it any other way. Being with you makes me feel again." I let out a deep breath. "I'm sure it sounds crazy because we've just met."

"What do you mean?" she teased. "It's been weeks."

I laughed as she pulled me to the couch.

"I may have polished off the largest steak on the menu, but that popcorn is calling my name."

She reached for a bowl, and her gaze snapped to mine. "You're kidding me. These are Christmas bowls."

I nodded, smiling. "I actually dug them out of my basement. They were my mom's."

Skye froze with the empty bowl in her hand. "Oh, no. I don't want to break them."

I laughed. "It's melamine, so I think unless you tried

to eat them like you did the candle, we should be fine."

"I think I'd better start wearing my glasses more than I think." She rolled her eyes and scooped popcorn into her bowl as I used the remote to turn on the movie.

Skye snuggled into me on the couch, tucking her legs underneath her as I turned on the show. She happily munched on popcorn, reciting the movie as she promised, and any opportunity I found, I'd brush my fingers along her arm, kiss her cheek, and hug her.

And I no longer felt numb.

I laughed with her during the movie. I imagined what Christmas would be like with her for the rest of December, and I refused to think about January.

She was here with me now, and that was what I wanted to focus on.

As the theme song came on and the credits rolled, she turned to face me, crawling into my lap in the meantime.

Skye straddled me and caged me in with her arms.

"Is this what usually happens to you after you watch the movie?"

She giggled, and I instantly became hard.

What this woman did to me was unfathomable. I moved my arms around her waist, and she pressed her lips to mine and then stopped.

"Did I annoy you to death, reciting every line in the movie?"

I shook my head and smiled as her eyes looked longingly into mine. "You could never annoy me, Skye. I'm sure of that."

"You know what I think would just put me over the edge?" she asked.

I had no idea, but I desperately wanted to know.

I shook my head. "What?"

"If I came home one day at Christmas and my entire house was lit up like this movie. Imagine, even the roof twinkling." She sighed happily. "It would be amazing."

She crawled off my lap and pulled me up.

As our hands were looped together, she pulled me down the hall. "Is this way okay?"

I laughed and shrugged. "Any way is okay with you."

Without thinking, I followed her down the hall and realized I'd left a door open that I usually always kept locked. As she started to walk by, she stopped and turned around to look at me before staring at the large room.

"You paint?" She dropped her hand from mine.

I nodded and drew a deep breath. This was what I'd kept to myself for all these years. I'd locked away what I truly wanted to do all those years ago. When I'd gotten accepted into Rhode Island School of Design, it was my secret. I'd applied on a whim without even my parents knowing. All they knew was that I'd applied to the University of Washington to follow in my dad's footsteps.

"I do. I almost went to school for it."

She turned to face me. "What happened?"

"I didn't want to let my parents down. I'd gotten into the Rhode Island School of Design and couldn't wait to tell my parents my new plans, but when I saw the look on their faces when they saw my acceptance letter to the UW, I couldn't do it. I couldn't let them down."

"So, that's why you've been so hard on the previous graphic artists?" She smiled, touching my chin. "You knew you could do it better."

I laughed and nodded. "Something like that."

"May I go in?"

I nodded and let out a deep breath, feeling like the weight of the world had been lifted. "Absolutely."

When she stepped inside, she walked straight over to my work-in-progress.

A portrait of Skye. I held my breath as my pulse raced, wondering what she'd think.

She turned around slowly with tears in her eyes and smiled. "This is the most beautiful . . . I can't even put it into words. This is how I want to be seen, but I know I never have been."

I walked over to her, smiling, and pulled her into my arms. "You make me so happy."

She wiped away the happy tears, and her smile grew. "I'd like to make you even happier."

"Oh, yeah?" I chuckled. "How do you plan on doing that?"

Skye looked around my art room. "Is your bedroom on this floor or—"

Without thinking, I kissed her, feeling her mouth against mine. Kissing Skye in my studio was like a fantasy coming true. No one had ever been in here, and it seemed only fitting that the one and only person who made me feel again would be the one I let in.

She trembled in my arms as her lips parted, and she moaned a little, welcoming my tongue deeper as I savored her and explored her, felt her.

I deepened the kiss as her arms looped around my waist, and I knew I needed her now.

Skye broke her lips from mine, but I picked her up in my arms, cradling her as I made my way out of the studio and down to my bedroom with her giggling and throwing her head back, which only drew my lips to her neck by the time I laid her on my bed.

"Levi, you're the sexiest man I've ever met."

I growled a little smirk and shook my head as I let my fingers slide along her cheek. Her chest heaved slightly as her breathing turned more ragged from my touch.

"Skye, you're the sexiest, most gorgeous woman I've ever met." I kissed her. "And you taste so amazing."

Her body writhed as she tugged on my sweater. I quickly pulled it over my head and tossed it on the floor as she ran her delicate fingers along my chest.

"I've never been with a man who looks like this." Her eyes met mine, and I chuckled.

"Not sure what you mean, but okay."

"You have pecs," she teased. "And this stomach."

She pretended to pound on it, and I laughed, shaking my head as I traced my lips along her neck.

Skye wiggled underneath me, keeping her eyes fastened on mine as I pulled her sweater over her head.

Her lips were red and swollen from our kisses. She licked her bottom lip as she ran her fingers through my hair, driving me insane with need for her.

I took in her body and the softness of her shoulders and breasts. Everything about Skye was perfection.

Skye's eyes looked drunk with need as she bit her

bottom lip and laughed nervously. "I'm nervous."

I stopped and caressed her hair that was framing her face. "We don't have to do this."

She smiled and nodded. "No, I want it. I need to feel you inside me."

Her words literally made me ache with desire. I'd never felt a need so strong that it was almost painful.

My fingers ran along the lace of her bra, feeling her hard nipples underneath. My hands looped behind her back, where I undid the clasp and slipped the straps off her shoulders.

Her swollen breasts were full and soft as my mouth ran across her skin. Skye's breath hitched as she threaded my hair through her fingers, and my tongue played with her left nipple while my fingers teased her right.

"Levi, my God," she whispered, wriggling under me.

I sucked a little harder, feeling her fingers get a little more frantic in my hair as I moved to the other breast.

Her hands went to my pants as I licked her nipples with my tongue and attempted to help her with my pants.

I shoved my pants and boxers down as I brought my mouth to hers again while she scooted her underwear down.

Skye's eyes darkened with heated desire as she wrapped her legs around me. Her warmth immediately melted against me as I let out a groan of anticipation.

Her hands skated along my back, and I felt like I'd died and gone to heaven. I moved my hand between her thighs, and she let out a little moan followed by quickened breathing with every stroke of my thumb.

I kissed her neck as I slipped into her. She felt so good.

Skye's gaze stayed on mine as I moved in and out, biting her lip in between shifting her hips in a wicked rhythm.

"Levi," she breathed as her hand curled to my neck, bringing my lips to hers.

Skye's kiss was long and deep as her body curled into mine in an explosion of emotion as I went over the edge, feeling things I'd never felt before as I held her in my arms.

And I knew our night was only beginning.

Chapter Twenty-Five

Skye

We'd spent most of the weekend in bed instead of touring the island, and I didn't mind one bit. But he had to get to the office early this morning to work out some details with the warehouse chain, and I felt like stopping by Maddie's tea shop to jolt my Monday morning into overdrive and mentally prepare for our ice skating adventure.

As I opened the door to my new favorite spot, I saw Maddie behind the counter. She gave a quick wave.

The promise of caffeinated teas gleamed in front of me like a colorful confetti of energy to get me through my day.

I threw my hands in the air with excited anticipation. "I need fuel for ice skating and life in general."

"You've found the perfect spot." She smiled as one of her workers came from behind to wipe off one of the tables. "I suggest Fog-X."

I chuckled. "Isn't that used for cars?"

Maggie's expression dropped. "Oh, my gosh. I never put two and two together. I've just been happily peddling a tea that sounds like it's something you spray on your windshield. Maybe that's why so many men buy it. They think I'm being clever." She grinned and held up the tin.

"It sounds perfect because I'm in a complete fog this morning."

"Some Mondays are like that." She scooped out the tea and put it in a bag before dunking it into hot water to steep. "But you look beautiful and happy."

I took the cup of tea and smiled. "I am so happy, and we're going ice skating."

"We?" she asked.

"All of Shantos," I informed her.

Her brow arched. "I'm impressed that Marcy convinced him to add a holiday event to his already sparse December calendar."

I chuckled and nodded. "Actually, I made him promise to do it if we won an account, and we did."

"He got the warehouse deal?"

I nodded. "He sure did."

"Wow. I can't even begin to tell you how happy I am about that. Levi is like a sponge. He absorbs everything and holds onto it even if it makes him unable to hold any more."

I nodded, listening to his longtime friend, and was amazed at how highly everyone always spoke of Levi. "He's a really interesting person."

"And cute and available." Maddie waggled her brows.

"I'll keep that in mind." I gave her my debit card and took a sip of the delicious tea.

"Hit the spot?" she asked.

"It does. So good."

Maddie handed me the card back, and I held up my cup again. "Thanks so much for the tea recommendation. I can tell I'm ready to skate my heart out already."

"Pics, or it doesn't count."

I laughed. "It's also an ugly sweater contest, so I'm not sure I'll let anyone take photos."

She pretended to stomp her foot and chuckled.

"I even convinced Levi to wear one."

Maddie looked like she was going to fall over. "Okay, I have to see photos."

I smiled and waved as I wandered out the door and

onto the sidewalk of Fireweed Island.

The morning chill made me grateful the office was only a few blocks down the road. Even though it was a Monday, tourists filled the diners and shops along the way. Christmas music was piped outside the storefronts, and I nearly skipped to work.

By the time I got inside, my cup was empty, and I felt like Fireweed was where I needed to be.

Marcy waved her hand with her large engagement ring securely fastened on her finger, and she grinned from ear to ear, all while her ugly sweater with two kissing cats under mistletoe did its best to distract me.

I gave her a quick hug. "Congratulations, Marcy. I'm so happy for you."

"I heard you were there on Friday night with Stan." She glanced at my outfit and scowled.

I nodded and laughed. "I was. We saw the whole proposal. It was so sweet."

"You should have come over to the table. But why aren't you in your ugly sweater?"

I smiled, noticing Marcy didn't miss a beat. "First, I didn't want to intrude during your special moment. And second, I was worried my sweater might be a little too revealing for the office."

She winked at me. "Oh, that sounds intriguing."

I chuckled. "Unfortunately, it's like a crop top sweater, so I didn't really feel like exposing my midriff as I sat at my desk and plopped over my pants from all the Christmas cookies I've been eating."

Marcy chuckled and shook her head. "And Stan said you left with Levi."

I grinned and glanced toward Stan's desk. "Did he?"

She laughed. "Don't worry. Your secret isn't safe with anyone."

"Good to know."

"But Skye . . ."

My eyes met hers again. "You've been really good for him. At first, I wasn't sure what started to turn around his mood, and then I finally put two and two together."

"I can't take the credit for that. It's all him."

Marcy smiled. "I don't think so, but whatever you say."

Her words made me smile, and I nodded. "Well, thank you. I love your sweater, by the way. At least yours will keep you warm at the rink."

Marcy nodded. "I can't wait to see yours. I wish we could just leave now for the rink."

I hopped on my toes and reached for a red-foiled

Hershey's Kiss. "It won't be long. Off I go. My desk is calling me."

As I made my way to my desk, Stan waved, and I pretended to give him an evil eye for tattling. He made his way over and leaned his hip against my desk.

"I have to tell you that our dinner out did wonders for my psyche."

I laughed. "You enjoy living vicariously through others' insanity?"

"It made me realize my own insanity. I was going to beg you to be my fake girlfriend. Like, instead of just standing up to my parents and telling them I'm happy with how things are and if the right person shows up, great. But until then, get off my back. I'm thirty-five." He shrugged. "So, I got home and picked up the phone and told them exactly how I felt."

"No. Way." My eyes widened. "What did they say?"

"My mom said she thought she was being helpful with her *gentle pushes*."

"Oh, just trying to help you out," I teased. "Sounds like my parents."

"My dad was much more understanding. But only time will tell. If I can get through the rest of the holidays without hearing how it would be so much better for me if I could spend them with someone, that would be great."

I crossed my fingers and raised my hand. "Here's hoping."

"So, did you forgive Levi?" he asked.

My cheeks blushed. "I did."

"Did you ever."

My hand flew to my hip. "And how did Marcy already know?"

He looked at the ceiling. "Evie might too."

I laughed. "Of course."

"We're like family here," he assured me.

"Evie, Evie, Evie . . ." I winked at him.

"You wouldn't." He stared at me, and I chuckled.

"No, I wouldn't, because I have a heart." I grinned. "And an overwhelming desire to not meddle in people's love lives."

"I'm turning into my parents," he muttered. "Help us all."

I grinned. "They love you. That's why they do what they do. It's something I have to remind myself of after every phone call with my mom."

"Oh, success feels good." It sounded like Levi, but he'd never say something like that.

"Oh, no. The other brother has arrived." Stan stood and rolled his eyes before heading to his desk.

Max headed to Levi's office, and my stomach knotted.

I debated whether to pop in to see if Levi needed anything or let Max do whatever he was going to do or say.

As I ran through my inbox, I tapped my foot and waited for Max to hurry up and leave. But he wasn't going anywhere.

When my nosy self couldn't handle it any longer, I made my way to Levi's office. His door was open, and Max was sitting in the chair in front of Levi's desk.

"You wouldn't believe how my Friday night went," Max said as Levi's eyes caught mine and he smiled.

"Come on in," Levi said, motioning me toward him.

I glanced at the empty chair next to Max and decided to do something completely risky. I walked past Max and smiled at him as he had to me on Friday night, and I made my way to Levi, where I wrapped my arm around his shoulders.

Max's eyes widened.

"And I don't think you'd believe how mine went either." Levi cocked his head and smiled.

I chuckled as Max's brains short-circuited briefly before pulling himself together.

"Wow. Well, congratulations," Max said wryly.

"Thank you." I laughed. "And I'm so glad things

worked out well with you and the . . . I mean, for you and Susan."

He grinned and nodded, glancing at his brother. "I'm thinking of inviting her with me on my trip."

Levi's mouth dropped open. "Seriously?"

"Yeah. I forgot how well we worked together."

I hid a chuckle, realizing they might be the perfect match.

"Did you know we're going ice skating this afternoon? You should come."

"Oh, I don't do that." He shook his head.

"So, you'll jump off cliffs, but you won't skate around a slippery surface?" I scowled as Levi squeezed me tighter, probably wondering what the heck I was doing.

"You know about that?" Max asked.

"Oh, yeah. Levi's told me all about the cool stuff you've done."

Max's expression softened. "Cool?"

I nodded, and a quick smile touched Max's mouth before he straightened in the chair. "I still have my hockey skates. I'll see if Susan can come too."

Levi threw his hand in the air and smiled. "Might as well since she's a big part of the winery's future."

Max stood and started toward the door.

"Marcy can give you all the details for today," Levi told his brother who, for the first time in a long time, smiled a genuine smile.

Levi softly rubbed my back before I turned to face him. "Well, aren't you the little family mender?"

"I try." I smiled and let out a happy sigh. "Maybe Max isn't as happy as you think he is. Maybe he has the same hopes and dreams as you do."

Levi laughed and nodded. "Oh, the sensible one strikes again."

"It's only because I'm not in the thick of it. I can see things a little clearer without decades of emotions."

Levi smiled and brought me close. "No. You have a real ability to make people see that it is in their life and to somehow sprinkle a seed of possibility deep inside."

"Well, thank you for that. But I think you're giving me far too much credit."

Levi shook his head. "Nope. It's true, Skye."

I looked at the man who was making me feel really good about myself and wondered if this was it or if there'd be more to us.

As he'd said, we'd spent far more time together than most people who only count on a date here or there to get to know someone, but that didn't guarantee success. He had a business to run, and the one thing I did know from everyone was that Levi was a workaholic.

I always did my best when working, but I was anything but a workaholic.

I wasn't sure how I'd feel giving up my family in Maine, even though they drive me nuts, to stay out here while Levi heads to work early in the morning and stays late at night.

That wouldn't be the future I'd want for myself.

But when I looked at Levi, I wanted to believe that maybe with me in the picture, that might change. Maybe he'd want to come home early since I might be there, or maybe he'd decide to roll over in bed and snuggle in the morning before work rather than get into the office early.

However, I was also smart enough and old enough to know that it wasn't my job to change someone else and that maybe I should just enjoy what this was for now.

A much-needed holiday fling.

Chapter Twenty-Six

Levi

"Stop getting handsy with me," Skye muttered, smacking her assailant back down to the ice. "I mean it."

She attempted to get up again, but her legs wobbled and slid right out from underneath her, landing her right on the ice.

I pushed myself toward Skye to help as she attempted to stand again, this time fighting with the aggressor, who was now fully entangled with her. Her ice skates slipped right out from underneath her, and I managed to dive toward her to save her from crashing down onto the icy surface again.

"I leave to go to the bathroom for two seconds," I whispered, trying to help her into my arms as a defeated and deflated Rudolph the Red-Nosed Reindeer drooped with its antlers knotted around Skye's wrist.

Her eyes met mine, and she chuckled as she leaned into me.

"I had no idea you didn't know how to ice skate," I told her. "Why did you ask if I did?"

She shrugged and wobbled at the same time. "I was just curious whether I could count on you to hold me up, and you being an ex-hockey player told me yes."

I laughed as Marcy skated by and eyeballed the defeated reindeer.

I held Skye's hands and slowly skated backward, noticing her stomach was bright red from the ice.

"Do you have frostbite?" I asked.

She laughed. "Probably, but at least I'm cute."

Max sliced the ice right behind us, laughing. "I don't think I've seen anything funnier in my life. Well, there was you eating the Christmas candle. That was pretty good too."

Susan slid up behind Max, and I smiled, grateful it was never me she'd wanted.

"Are you okay, Sasha?" she asked.

"My name is Skye, and I'm fine, thank you. Just a little chilly." Skye smiled and attempted to skate toward me as I clutched her hands in mine.

Our only hope was for me to skate backward while I essentially pulled her forward.

"You've got this, babe," I said, smiling at her.

Skye's bright blue eyes stayed on mine as I skated her to the opening in the wall, where her legs finally found the rubber mat.

"Oh, thank God."

She looked like she wanted to kiss the floor but kissed me instead.

"This was the worst idea I've ever had."

I smiled, looping my arms around her bare stomach and pulling her into me. "I don't think so. I kind of like this."

Still holding her, I took a couple of steps back and sat down on a wooden bench with her falling to my lap.

"Okay. This part is nice," she muttered, holding onto my hands.

Marcy and Evie slowed at the wall, and both wore gigantic grins.

"So, Levi has finally started to crack." Evie's brows rose, and she winked at me.

Marcy nodded. "I fully approve."

I squeezed Skye a little as Stan skated to the group.

"That was quite the tumble, Skye. You okay?"

She laughed and nodded. "Totally fine. Just a little cold in the midriff."

"Yeah. That's a pretty crazy sweater," Stan said,

glancing at Evie, who did a double take at Stan.

She rested her hands on me and gave a little squeeze of hope as Stan held out his hand and Evie put hers in it.

How in the world had Skye spread her magic to those two as well?

They skated away as Marcy's eyes widened. "Love must be in the air or something."

"You should call Jay," I offered.

She winked at me. "He's already meeting us for our holiday dinner tonight."

"Good. The more, the merrier," I said, smiling.

Skye and Marcy both looked at me and started laughing.

"You really are rubbing off on him. Will you stay forever?" Marcy teased Skye before pushing off onto the ice.

My eyes met Skye's. "Yeah. Will you stay forever?"

I meant every word. The thought of her leaving in January was tough.

Skye rubbed my head and grinned. "Give me another week, and you'll probably be really tired of me. Might even pay me to leave your company."

"Don't they call that a severance package?" I laughed as Skye stood up, grateful for the rubber mat underneath her.

But then she started toward the ice again and glanced

back at me.

"Are you ready to get back out there?" she asked.

I laughed and shrugged. "I've never been a quitter."

"And neither have I."

"I know. I remember the weekend." She flashed a wicked grin in my direction, and I shook my head before following after her onto the ice.

The ice rink had been decorated for the holiday, and apart from the wily reindeer that Skye mangled, the decorations were a nice touch. I wasn't sure if it was the rink or Marcy who'd managed to convince them to put them up for us.

"Okay, hold my left hand and use your other to hold onto the wall."

She gave a nod and straightened her body, relaxing her knees slightly as I pulled her, and she steadied herself with the wall.

"It's kind of like roller skating," she muttered.

"Yeah. Sort of." I nodded as she shook her hand free from mine.

"I got this."

She started forward just as Max skated toward us with Susan.

Skye immediately reached for my hand again to

steady herself as the company showed up.

"Marcy said we can head on over to the restaurant for drinks before dinner if we want," Max explained. "So, Susan and I are gonna go."

I nodded and glanced at Skye, who looked miserable for coming up with this ice skating idea.

"We'll probably be there shortly."

Skye's eyes lit up at the thought, and she nodded.

"What's that buzzing sound?" Max asked, glancing at Skye.

"Oh, geez. It's my phone."

"Wow. You like to live on the edge." Max laughed.

Skye scowled, slipping it out of her back pocket. "What do you mean?"

"Well, that thing could have gotten crushed during your tussle with Rudolph over there."

She chuckled and glanced at the screen. I noticed her entire body turned rigid.

"Okay. See you at dinner," Max said, skating off with Susan.

"Everything okay?" I asked as Skye stuffed her phone back into her pocket.

"I don't know." She turned around, alternating between my hand and the wall for support as we made our way back to the entrance.

Skye let out a sigh of relief when her skates hit the rubber again. She handed me her phone.

"Do you think my mom actually expects me to call him, or what am I missing?"

I glanced at the text.

Can you please call Jared?

I laughed and handed the phone back, but Skye didn't find it funny.

"Sorry. Yeah, I'm pretty sure that's what she meant by the text."

"It's so infuriating," Skye said, shaking her head. "I really thought I got the point across to my mom. We finally had a really good conversation last night, and I thought we went deep. I thought she understood."

Skye looked at me for a second with her blue eyes churning with something I didn't recognize. She brought in a deep breath and sucked on her bottom lip.

"Do you mind if I tell her I'm seeing you?"

"Not at all. It might actually help."

Skye nodded and wrote a quick text and glanced up at me as Marcy made her way over.

"I think the troops are getting hungry," Marcy said, waving in our direction.

I nodded. "Max and Susan already headed over there."

"Yup. I think I might too." Marcy glanced at the little cardboard box she'd set up earlier where everyone was supposed to vote for their favorite ugly sweater. "I'll just take this, and I'll meet you there."

"See ya soon," Skye said with a quick wave in Marcy's direction.

But the truth of it was that Skye was distracted. I could see it written all over her expression. That text from her mom really threw her for a loop. She glanced at her bag on the bench and pointed.

"I'm going to put on my other top in the bathroom, or I'll freeze to death at dinner."

I leaned over and gave her a quick kiss before she untied her skates and walked toward the bathroom.

These last few days had been absolutely magical, but it suddenly felt as if it could all be wiped away once her family arrived.

Things between us were so new that I worried that it wouldn't take much to destroy our beginning. I wasn't worried about Jared. I knew Skye didn't have feelings for him, but I didn't know how much pull her parents had with her direction in life. Whether she wanted it or not, she could be back in Maine with her family and Jared hanging around in less than a month.

The thought made me sick, but it also told me I had to do everything I could to impress Skye and her family when they got here.

When Skye came out of the bathroom, she seemed much happier than before, which made the knots in my stomach lessen slightly.

Hopefully, the surprise waiting for her tonight would help remind her how much I cared about her too.

But I didn't want to get ahead of myself.

I reached for her hand, and she happily took it.

"You look like you're feeling a little better," I said.

She nodded and put her ugly sweater in the bag. "I am. I need to remember that I'm going to be thirty soon, and I'm not living life for my parents. I'm living it for me."

Stan came up behind us and laughed. "Amen."

I chuckled and saw Skye give Stan a high-five as Evie came off the ice behind him.

They started taking off their skates as we headed out the door. The air was chilly, but it actually felt warmer than the ice rink.

"This was really nice," Skye said, turning to me.

"I had no idea you didn't know how to skate." I laughed. "I mean, it was your idea."

"It didn't seem like it should be that hard. My best friend growing up was an ice skater, and I'd go to her practices sometimes, but I never did it myself. She always made it look so effortless. Now I know she was actually just good."

I chuckled. "Well, now you can chase her down on social media and tell her that."

"No need. She's my sister's BFF now. It's what happens in a small town."

I laughed as we climbed into my car. "Tell me about it."

The restaurant was only three blocks away, and we quickly found a spot close to the door.

"I think Stan has a huge thing for Evie," Skye told me, unbuckling. "And he's positive that she doesn't see him like that."

"Really?" I asked, surprised. "I always thought Evie kind of liked Stan."

Skye chuckled. "Well, maybe this thing between us will open up all kinds of doors at your company."

I laughed and shook my head. "This could get complicated."

We wandered into the restaurant hand in hand, and the hostess took us back to the private room filled with red and white poinsettias. Marcy and Jay were sitting closest to the door, and I wandered over to sit next to her when she quickly shook her head.

"Nope. You're at the head of the table."

I laughed and shook my head as I sat at the end, and Skye sat between Marcy and me.

As the employees filed into the room, finding places to sit, ordering drinks, and snacking on some of the appetizers that had been ordered, I realized that this was the first time ever that I didn't want to check my watch and make an excuse to leave.

Skye touched my hand and smiled at me as Christmas music started playing softly over the speakers overhead.

I looked around the room as Max and Susan walked into the room, holding drinks from the bar. I pointed at the other end of the table, and Max nodded, sitting at the other end. Susan sat next to him, and they immediately began chatting with some of my other employees.

For the first in a long time, I felt like I could be present and absorb my surroundings. Skye was happily chatting with Marcy, and servers were taking everyone's orders.

Once our entrée orders were placed, I gently tapped a

wine glass and stood, glancing at Skye, who winked at me.

I felt like the luckiest man in the room.

"I'd like to say just a couple of things," I started.

Marcy looked a little startled, so I smiled to make her feel better.

"I want to say thank you to everyone for joining us for the ice skating event and dinner tonight." I raised my glass toward my brother and his date. "Susan, this was their reward, of sorts, if we were able to partner with the warehouse on private label. So, thank you for solidifying our partnership."

The employees cheered and took a sip. "And I wanted to thank Skye for coming on board and providing so much insight and direction, which I apparently needed and other employees were too polite to tell me."

Skye blushed but kept her gaze on me. "But tonight is a celebration of family, and the employees here are family. Thank you for all your hard work. If it weren't for every single one of you, we wouldn't be able to expand and grow into the new wave of beverage development." I smiled. "And on that note, the hotel across the street has a block of rooms for any of you who'd like to take advantage, and tomorrow is a day off for everyone."

More cheers erupted as I sat down while Evie stood, raising her glass. "To Levi, and to Skye for making Levi smile again."

Stan stood next to Evie and glanced at Skye. "And to Skye for reminding us that we can achieve what we believe."

I smiled, nodding. That was precisely what Skye did for me.

"And on that note, our winner of the Ugly Sweater Contest goes to our fearless leader," Marcy said.

Skye glanced at me and leaned over to brush my cheek with a kiss.

"I am honored." I laughed, never wanting this night to end.

But the dinner rolled by so quickly, and before we knew it, we were saying good night, and most of the employees trundled over to the impromptu hotel stay.

"What do you think?" I asked Skye. "Would you like to stay or go?"

She grinned and hugged me as we waited to finish paying for the dinner. "Truthfully, I'd love to go home and spend the night with you."

"That sounds like a December dream come true."

Skye chuckled as the server brought the receipt to sign. I scribbled my name and left the gratuity before Skye linked her fingers with mine.

Once we made it outside, Skye let out a deep breath,

and the fog rolled into the night's air.

"Skye, I want to thank you for everything," I told her as we got to the car. "You've really reminded me what it's like to be present."

She smiled and nodded. "I'm sure the photographer I punched felt the same way."

I burst into laughter as I helped her into the car and made my way around to the driver's side. It was hard to believe we were already mid-December, and the thought of Christmas coming so quickly blew me away.

The thought of Skye leaving next month left me hollow, but maybe there was a way to make her stay.

Skye found a Christmas station and glanced at me. "Do you mind, or is this too much?"

I shook my head. "It's great, actually."

Excitement drilled through her gaze as she started belting out the tunes, and by the time we arrived at the ferry, I was singing with her.

When I drove off the ferry, I felt like my December couldn't be any more different from years prior. Once Skye's family arrived, I hoped I could convince them that I was a better fit than her ex. Logically, that shouldn't be hard, but judging by her mom's texts, I had no idea.

I glanced at Skye, who was happily looking out the

window. Her head rolled in my direction, and she grinned. "Who knew that a York Peppermint Patty drink could be so tasty?"

I chuckled as I turned down the road where her house sat, glowing in the night sky. Skye's jaw dropped as she saw the little cottage come into view, with every square inch of the home covered in twinkling lights, even the roof.

"Levi," she said softly. "You didn't."

I slowed the car and eyed Skye as she stared at the house.

"I did, and I hope I get to do it again for you, year after year."

Chapter Twenty-Seven

Skye

"Hey, I wanted to talk to you about something," Levi said, walking toward me the next morning.

"I got the dates screwed up," I whispered in horror to Levi, who was standing in my kitchen. "That explains why my mom texted last night about everything."

He leaned over and touched my chin. "Why are we whispering when we're the only ones here, and what dates?"

"For my family." I groaned. "I thought they were coming on Thursday."

"When are they coming?" he asked, taking a sip of his coffee.

"Tonight."

Levi choked on the coffee and ran to the sink, setting his cup on the counter.

"Seriously?"

She nodded. "I just . . . I don't know. I think I've been having so much fun with you that I didn't realize Christmas is only a week away."

"Do you want me to pick them up from the airport?"

She shook her head. "No. I booked them the Island Van, so they should be set."

"What time do you think they'll be here?" he asked, glancing around the tiny house.

I knew what he was thinking. With my family coming, where would he be?

"Probably around seven o'clock. I know my family. They'll be starving."

"We can make dinner for them. I make a killer lasagna," he told me, rubbing my shoulders to get the tension out. "We've got this."

I chuckled and turned to see him. "Do we, though?"

He nodded and placed a sweet kiss on the tip of my nose. "I'll go shower first."

"Thank goodness you gave everyone the day off, Boss," I hollered at him as he walked down the hallway.

"What can I say? I'm just a great boss."

My stomach clenched when he said that. I'd failed to mention that I'd told my mom that I'd started to date someone.

After she pressed about who it was, I explained that Levi was my boss. Of course, my sister was ecstatic, but my mom blew a cork.

And unbeknownst to me, it made her double down harder on the idea of Jared. Why in the world taking back a cheating ex was a better option than happily dating someone who happened to temporarily be my boss made absolutely no sense to me.

But that was the least of my worries.

Levi had a heart of gold, and I was worried about what my mom might say to him. My sister promised she'd make my mom behave, but that wasn't exactly a promise she could keep.

I wandered into my bedroom and picked out a matching Santa sweatsuit and tossed them on the bed. The same rumpled bed that Levi and I had shared last night.

Just being in his arms was enough for me, but feeling his naked body against mine as I slept next to him was a gift all its own. I chuckled to myself and pulled out some underwear and a bra from my drawer.

But I couldn't get caught up fantasizing about staying in bed all day with Levi, or I'd be in trouble. I had presents to wrap, a house to clean, and two bedrooms to get ready for my family.

When Levi's shower ended, I walked back into the kitchen to polish off my coffee and start a grocery list. I'd tried to fill the freezer with all kinds of goodies for my family, but I still needed to get milk and other fresh things from the store. Since I thought I still had a couple of days until they arrived, I was a bit behind.

Levi snuck up behind me and leaned over my shoulder and kissed right behind my ear, sending a wave of shivers through me.

I spun around and smiled. "Are you trying to make me forget about my family coming?"

He laughed and poured some more coffee.

"I'm just making a shopping list," I told him. "And then I'll hop in the shower."

"Besides the lasagna, how can I help? Do you want me to do the shopping?"

I eyed him. "Seriously?"

He shrugged and took a sip of his coffee. "Sure. Why not? I know where the stuff is. It would probably take a lot less time."

I squealed. "How are you so amazing?"

He scratched the scruff of his chin and smiled. "I ask myself that every single day."

I rolled my eyes and leaned over to kiss him. "Must

be rough."

"Okay. Well, I'm going to head out because I need to stop by and check on Scarlet. She uses the potty pad in the garage if she absolutely must, but she prefers the outdoors."

I snickered. "Who wouldn't? Did you want to bring her over here so she's not lonely?"

"She'll probably just think I'm at work."

"What about tonight, though, for dinner?"

Levi's brows rose. "Oh, you want me here for dinner? I assumed it was more of a family thing since it's their first night."

I smiled and shrugged, feeling the familiar knot arise in my tummy at the thought of not being around Levi.

"I'd like it if you could be here, but I won't hold it against you if you want to hold off."

Levi smiled and gave me a hug. "I'll bring Scarlet, and I'll stay for dinner."

"Aw, my heart." I winked at Levi, and he grabbed his wallet and headed out the door with my shopping list.

I turned on some Christmas music, got the fire started, and wandered to the closest guest bedroom where I'd stored the gifts I'd found for my family since I'd arrived on Fireweed. I'd picked up some holiday wrap and labels a week ago, and with all things Levi, I hadn't gotten around to wrapping anything yet, and since this was where my parents would be sleeping tonight, I needed to get on it.

As *Jingle Bell Rock* flowed through the house, I grabbed some scissors, tape, and wrapping paper and tossed them on the bed. I'd managed to find gifts for everyone in my family, Levi too, without having to leave the island. It was wonderful.

I hauled the gifts over for my parents first. I'd found a cute holiday sweater for my mom, some scrumptious-smelling soaps that Maddie had recommended made by her mother-in-law over on Hound Island, and some delicious teas.

As I happily wrapped the packages, I thought about my parents and how happy they'd seemed all these years. It was extremely hard for me to wrap my head around what my mom said about my dad. No pun intended.

And truthfully, the thought worried me about how I'd see my dad now.

He was my dad.

My dad didn't do things like that.

I let out a sad sigh and shook my head. My mom promised me that she'd tell my sister so I wasn't the one carrying around the burden of this knowledge.

The thought of Jared roaming around the streets of my hometown, pestering my mom about me, still irked me. The song changed to Rudolph, and my mind immediately flipped to Levi rescuing me on the ice rink.

That was what love felt like.

Oh. My. Word.

Did I just think the word *love*?

I smiled as I thought about Levi, and my heart overflowed with an enormous amount of happiness. It was like joy just oozed out of me and around me when I thought about his beautiful grinning mug.

I smiled and slapped a bow on my mom's package and reached for the next to wrap as I thought about all the trouble Levi went to in order to make my cottage look like a recreation of my favorite movie of all time.

"Who does these things?" I squealed to no one.

Clutching my heart, I closed my eyes and said a quick prayer that things would work out how they were meant to be, right when my mind had a flashback to the kitchen with Levi.

He'd wanted to tell me something right before I had my epiphany about my parents.

Crap.

I was so wrapped up in my mishap that I didn't remember to ask him what he wanted to talk to me about.

I let out a groan and reached for my phone and sent him a quick text.

A few minutes later, he replied.

*No problem. Your parents are kind of a big deal. I'll
talk to you when we have time.*

I smiled, feeling extremely guilty as I sent Levi a
heart emoji, which he returned with the same.

It wasn't quite like saying the L word, but it was good
enough for me.

As the wrapped packages piled high on the bed, I
collapsed after way too many hours of the same motion. My
back ached, I was thirsty, and I was exhausted.

I glanced at the clock and realized that I'd been
wrapping for hours, and Levi would probably be here any
minute to help me with dinner while I'd have to hobble around
like I just had back surgery. Between my ice skating antics
and lack of exercise since coming to Fireweed, I felt as stiff
as a board.

I forced myself off the bed and grabbed the first bunch
of packages to put under my miniature tree. By the third trip,
I couldn't see my tree any longer, and that was when the
doorbell rang.

I glanced at the clock. It wouldn't be my family. Too
early for them. And Levi knew the code.

"Coming," I sang, grabbing my phone.

I peered out the window and froze at what I saw.

Not what.

Who . . .

He didn't see me, so I quickly backed away from the window and stared at the wall of the foyer as my skin prickled all the way up my spine.

"What the heck is he doing here?" I waved my hands next to me and hopped up and down as I tried to imagine what to do.

Pretend I never said I was coming to the door?

Run out the back door and never return?

"Why?" I whispered to myself. "Why?"

"Um, Skye?" Jared's voice came through the front door like an annoying jackhammer.

"Yes, coming." I cleared my throat, straightened my spine, and prayed to God that I wouldn't do something that would get me locked up for Christmas.

I opened the door to see the man I was happily living without. The man who'd managed to crush my ego and sprinkle it all around my hometown as he held his pregnant girlfriend closely. The very man who only decided I was a good catch after his own ego was crushed to death in a delightful karma grip of reality.

"Jared," I said flatly, refusing to show an ounce of emotion.

His eyes twinkled, and he smiled.

He'd never been great at reading emotions or knowing I had any.

"It's been too long," he said, grinning.

"How did you get this address?" I hung on the door, glaring at him.

"Your mom."

"Ah, I see." I pressed my lips together. "Did she think you were sending me flowers or planning on showing up on my doorstep?"

"She didn't ask, just gave it to me." He shivered, but I pretended not to notice. "Your mom said she didn't have much luck getting through to you."

My jaw fell open in shock. "Which part? The one where you got another woman pregnant, only it turned out the joke was on you, or—"

He cleared his throat and shivered. "I deserve that."

"Oh, you deserve more than that, but I've grown as a person," I informed him, folding my arms over my chest.

"Yeah?" He chuckled. "I heard about the incident with the photographer."

I frowned. "How?"

"Your mom."

"I don't like you involving my parents for your gain."

"It wasn't your parents. Just your mom."

Oh, my dad just went back up a slot or two.

"Jared, I don't want to even think about why you're here, but I'm not interested. Your dumping me was the best thing that happened to me because I realized I was in denial about a lot more things than just our relationship."

He glanced over my shoulder and scowled. "Whose coat is that?"

I looked over my shoulder and hid a grin, realizing Levi had left his jacket here. "Why do you think that's any of your business?"

"You're my fiancée."

"Pardon?"

"Skye, I was stupid. I made a huge mistake. I'm sorry. If you'd just let me explain. I felt abandoned and—"

"Ah, ah, ah." I raised my index finger and wiggled it. "My mom might have lent a kind ear, but I promise you this. We are not the same person. My tolerance level is less . . ." I laughed and cocked my head slightly. "Well, tolerant."

"I flew across the country to talk to you."

"Well, it's one of many mistakes you've managed to pull off with me."

"What's happened to you, Skye?" He scowled at me and shook his head.

"I've found happiness."

Levi's Mercedes pulled into the driveway. He turned off his car as Jared looked over his shoulder to see a big dog climbing over Levi's lap to jump out of the car.

"What the—"

"Get him, Scarlet," I growled, and so did she.

"Scarlet, down. Down, girl. Scarlet. Knock it off." Levi clapped his hands twice, and Scarlet finally pulled her two front paws off Jared and licked her lips as Jared tried wiping her drool off his mouth.

"She likes giving kisses," I explained to my ex.

Jared used his sleeve to wipe the slobber off as Levi walked up to me and gave me a peck on the cheek. He had two grocery bags in his hands and went inside.

"Who the hell is that?" Jared asked. "You've only been out here a few weeks."

"Nearly three," I corrected him.

Levi wandered back out to where I stood and glanced at me and then at Jared. "Are you selling magazine subscriptions or something?" Levi's firm grip hugged each of my shoulders as he stood behind me, and I couldn't have hoped for anything better.

"No. I'm not selling anything." He glared at the man behind me.

I rested my hand on Levi's and gripped it. "Levi, this is my ex."

"No shit."

Chapter Twenty-Eight

Levi

The moment Skye laughed, I knew she recognized the phrase from Clark Griswold, and it broke the tension in the room almost immediately.

"Well, you've obviously traveled quite a ways. Why don't you come on in?" I cocked my head as Skye turned around to stare at me.

"Uh. Sure?" Jared walked into the house while Skye shut the door behind him.

"My family will be here soon."

"Good. Maybe they can help explain," Jared told Skye.

Skye whipped her arms up and folded them over her chest. "Do they know you're here?"

Jared shook his head.

"This ought to be a great surprise for everyone, then," I muttered on the way to the kitchen. "I'm making lasagna for dinner. I guess it's good I grabbed enough ingredients for two trays."

I looked over at Skye, who looked like she wanted to strangle Jared.

"Who are you?" Jared asked, walking into the kitchen.

"My name's Levi." I stuck out my hand to shake his, which seemed to throw him for a loop. Actually, just about anything did that to the guy. "Are you out here for the holidays?"

"I was hoping to convince Skye to spend them with me."

Skye's jaw dropped as I shook my head and let out a low whistle.

"Whew. That's going to be a pretty big mountain to climb. What's today? The eighteenth? You'd better get on that."

Skye chuckled.

Scarlet circled Jared a couple of times before I snapped my fingers, and she came into the kitchen and lay down on a throw rug.

I quickly put the groceries away as my mind spun a

hundred miles a minute. Never in a million years did I expect to come back to Skye's to see her ex standing on the doorstep. We only had a few hours before Skye's family was going to arrive, and I had absolutely no idea what to do other than help Skye with dinner. But on some weird level, I almost welcomed the distraction so I didn't have to think too long and hard about the offer that wound up in my inbox. I still needed to talk to Skye about it. But now wasn't the moment.

Skye looked traumatized, or worse, comatose.

Jared wandered over to her and waved his hand in front of her face.

"Not a good idea, buddy," I whispered.

"Are you alive?" he asked.

Her blue eyes flashed lightning as her gaze connected with Jared's. "Oh, I'm very much alive, and I'm trying to figure out how to keep myself out of jail and you above the ground."

Jared's brows furrowed. "Seriously?"

I grabbed two tinfoil trays and a pot to start the marinara in while I browned some sausage and fed a crumble to Scarlet.

"You've been stalking my mom. You treated me horribly," I heard Skye say as I washed my hands.

"I'm sorry. I wasn't thinking straight. I thought I was

about to be a dad, and—"

"No, no, no, no . . ." Skye shook her head. "I'm not even talking about that. You treated me horribly our entire relationship. Why do you think I chose jobs far away from you?"

"To have the experience."

Skye shook her head. "You cheated on me the entire time."

"Not true." He stared at her.

"Oh, sorry. You gave me your full attention the first six months together." She rolled her eyes. "The point is that it's over. I'd like it to end on a friendly note."

I nodded and joined in. "Friendly is always best."

"Who is this guy?" Jared asked as I flipped the Christmas album to one more suited for the occasion.

Twisted Sister's Christmas album came on, and Skye's eyes widened. "Is that Twisted Sister?"

I grinned. "Sure is."

"I can't believe they made a Christmas album. It's actually good." She wandered over to me as the sausage sizzled in the pan.

"Anything I can help with?" she asked, a smile finally touching her lips.

Jared stood at the window, noticing Puget Sound for

the first time.

"Beautiful view, isn't it?" I asked, dumping in diced tomatoes and sauce to make the marinara.

Jared nodded, looking completely befuddled.

Skye leaned over the counter and winked at me. "Look at you, all full of good tidings and cheer."

I laughed and glanced at Jared. "We've got to make the best of things."

I started layering the ricotta and mozzarella, lasagna noodles, and sauce, and Skye frowned, pointing. "Don't you need to boil the noodles first?"

"No. Way. That's old school. The key is to make the marinara just right, and the magic happens in the oven."

Jared walked over, looking a little less freaked out, and glanced at the lasagna pans.

"What is he, like your personal chef or something?"

Skye's arms whipped right back to her chest, where she folded them and glared at Jared.

Her brows rose as she spoke. "I'd say *or something.*"

I could see that just being near him made her blood boil.

A phone buzzed, and I glanced at Jared, who looked at Skye. She pulled the phone out of her back pocket and groaned.

What else could go wrong?

"They caught an earlier flight during their layover, and the shuttle is driving off the ferry now." Skye looked like her head was going to explode. She turned to look at Jared. "What am I going to do with you?"

Jared pointed at me. "Me? What about him?"

She scowled. "He's supposed to be here. You're not."

"But it wouldn't be the holidays without some unexpected visitors, right?" I opened a jug of peanuts and shook a few into my hand before tossing them in my mouth.

Jared walked over and leaned on the counter, bringing his shoulders to his ears as he leaned forward. "Dude, who are you?"

I looked at Skye, waiting for her lead. I had no idea how much she'd told her family or what had or hadn't gotten back to Jared.

"This is my boss."

Jared's frowned deepened. "Your boss?"

"With benefits," she added with a perk to her lips.

Jared slammed his fist on the counter. "Isn't that illegal? Didn't you clobber a guy for the same thing back in New York?"

"Nope. That guy's advances were unwanted. The woman made it clear that she wanted nothing to do with him."

Skye turned and looked into my eyes and smiled. "But these advances are very much wanted."

Jared eyed me before bringing his attention back to Skye. "So, this thing between you is casual."

I shook my head. "I wouldn't say anything with Skye is casual."

"The van just pulled up," Jared said, shaking his head. "What a mess."

Skye laughed and shook her head. "It wasn't one until you showed up."

"And where are your bags?" she asked, glancing toward the door.

"I left them at the hotel."

"Good call." She nodded and drew in a deep breath as I put both trays of lasagna into the oven.

I could feel Jared's eyes still on me, but I actually felt bad for the guy, and I knew I absolutely should not. He cheated on the woman I loved.

Wait. Did I say love?

I shut the oven and watched Skye pace back and forth by the door.

Yeah. Love.

Jared walked up behind her, and she spun around so quickly I thought she might clobber him.

"Would you mind giving me space?" She wiggled her body like she'd just discovered a cockroach had crawled on her.

"Either of you like a glass of Pinot Grigio?" I asked, pouring myself a glass.

"I'll take one," Skye said, glancing over her shoulder at me before readying herself to open the door.

"And Jared?" I asked.

"Fine. Yes. Good." He turned his attention to Skye as she opened the door to an eruption of family greetings.

I poured three glasses and set out four more.

"You look incredible, Skye," a young woman's voice rang through the air.

Must be the sister.

I took a sip of wine and set my glass in the corner to find it later and carried the other two glasses for Skye and Jared.

"Jared?" the same woman choked out. "What are you doing here?"

Skye laughed nervously. "I've been trying to figure that very same thing out since he arrived on my doorstep about an hour ago."

"What about—" The woman stopped herself.

"Oh, he's in the kitchen, making us all dinner," Skye

said flatly. "I can't wait to personally thank Mom for this."

"Mom for what?" an older woman asked as I rounded the bend. "Oh, Jared. What on earth are you doing here? I did not invite him."

Skye's mom and sister looked like similar versions of Skye. Her sister was a little shorter, and her mom was a little taller.

"I thought since you couldn't get through to your daughter, I could if I showed up in person."

Skye's mom scowled and shook her head. "That's not how my daughter works. If her sister or I can't get through to her, no one can. But you should know that." She narrowed her eyes on Jared as I walked into the room, handing Jared a glass of wine, followed by Skye.

Skye looped her arm around mine and smiled. "Mom, this is Levi Adams."

Her mom looked stunned. "I'm Dorothy."

Shock rattled through me. "Oh, wow. That's my mom's name. *Was* my mom's name," I corrected.

Dorothy tipped her head slightly and steadied her gaze on mine as Jared gulped his glass of wine rather than sipped it.

"Oh, dear. I'm so sorry. You're so young to have lost your parents."

Skye put her hand on her mom's shoulder and shook her head.

Dorothy moved her hand to her chest. "I'm sorry. It's—"

"My parents were taken far too young. They died in a plane crash," I explained.

"I'm so sorry, dear," she said, patting my arm.

"Many years ago. Lots of therapy. And plenty of work to keep me busy." I wanted to add that it was Skye who'd helped me most, but I thought that would be too much, too soon for her parents.

Her mom nodded. "Oh, right. Work."

She gave her daughter some side-eye as two men came into the entryway with all the luggage. I spotted her dad right away as the older fellow with the same blue eyes as his daughter.

Skye tensed slightly when she spotted him, and her mom noticed.

"We need to talk," her mom whispered, and Skye nodded in agreement as the guys set down the luggage.

"And this is my sister, Becky." Skye grinned as I introduced myself before moving to her father and brother-in-law.

"Here, let me help. What rooms should I put the

luggage in, Skye?"

"Front room for my parents and the one next to me for my sister."

"I'm Levi Adams. Nice to meet you," I told her dad, who grinned and patted my shoulder.

"Really nice to meet you, Levi. You can call me Ervin." He squeezed my shoulder just tight enough to let me know it was a warning, and I nodded, grabbing the luggage from him.

"Right this way," I explained as the brother-in-law smiled at me.

"I'm Jeffrey," he told me.

"What the hell is going on here?" Her father's voice boomed through the entire house.

I put the luggage down and turned around to see Ervin towering over Jared. "Why are you here? Didn't my wife tell you to stop calling?"

"I assumed she meant to stop calling her and figure it out with Skye."

"There's nothing to figure out. You cheated on my daughter, and you're lucky you're still walking around without a temporary limp."

Skye took a sip of wine as her mom's eyes bugged out of her head.

Her mom turned to Skye. "Well, something smells absolutely delicious."

Skye chuckled, and I glanced at her father.

"This probably isn't the best time to tell you that I invited him to dinner," I said, laughing.

Her mom clapped her hands and nodded. "Oh, this will be lovely."

Chapter Twenty-Nine

Skye

Maybe a leopard could change his spots, or maybe it was because I was my dad's daughter and the bar was held to a different standard, but I hadn't seen my dad that angry . . . ever.

I stood in the kitchen and whipped garlic butter together for the loaf of bread Levi bought at the store. Jared sulked on the couch in the living room, pretending to talk to my brother-in-law while my dad and sister were chatting in the dining room, and my mom watched Levi with eagle-eye precision in between telling me how to make garlic bread.

"This is a really lovely place to spend the holidays, Skye." She looked out the window at the gorgeous view. "I can't wait to see the town tomorrow."

I smiled. "Me too. It's just so calm and peaceful until

your ex shows up at your doorstep."

"Well, Levi certainly seems to be good-natured about it."

I smiled and nodded, thinking about Levi and this afternoon.

Having Jared show up could have turned today into a day of tears, yelling, and name-calling. Instead, it almost seemed surreal, as if it were a comedy movie that was far removed from me.

Even now, we're all functioning as grown adults without throwing jabs at one another.

And I will confess to having saved up quite a few if I ever encountered my ex again.

I just never expected it to be during the holidays, in my house, with my current boyfriend in the next room.

"Where'd Levi go?" my mom asked.

"He had to take care of a few work items."

"Right. Work." She shook her head. "I'm really not comfortable with you dating your boss, Skye."

Everything from seconds ago about being civilized flew right out of my brain. "But you are okay with me getting my heart ripped in half by a no-good, cheating, dirty scoundrel?"

"Well, I didn't say that either, dear."

I kept whipping the butter and stared at the pieces of parsley so I didn't say something I'd regret for the next week.

"It's just that . . . oh, never mind." She looked out the window.

"No, what are you saying, Mom?" I asked.

My voice rose unexpectedly.

"I just worry about you, Skye. Your sister had such an easy time finding love and—"

I put down the spoon. "I'd have a much easier time if my family didn't meddle in my love life." I pointed at Jared. "Because this right here isn't exactly easy to deal with."

"I know. I know. It's just sometimes, people make mistakes."

"Mom, nobody is perfect, but there are some things that I know I can't deal with. Cheating is one of them. Just because you can handle it doesn't mean I can."

My dad turned to face me with a completely bewildered expression. "Skye, I have never cheated on your mom. Ever. She'd make sure my body was never found."

Becky chuckled, and I frowned in bewilderment at my mom. "You said Dad . . ."

"Dorothy, you've got to be kidding me." My father stood and walked over to my mom.

My sister looked at me nervously as my pulse

quickened.

"You told Skye that I wasn't faithful?"

"She told me I should give Jared a second chance because she gave you one."

My dad drew in a deep breath, and I suddenly worried he was about to collapse from a heart attack.

Levi walked into the kitchen and saw my dad shaking his head as I prepared for a nuclear meltdown.

"Dorothy, why don't you tell Skye the exact details of the event you are talking about?" He brought his gaze to mine and arched both brows.

But I didn't see anger or betrayal in his gaze, only bemusement.

"It was the Spring Fling dance, freshman year."

"Of high school or college?" my sister asked. She basked in the details of any life event, while I'd rather not know.

"High school." My mom drew a breath. "I was home sick with a cold, but your father went to the dance with a bunch of his buddies. I knew it was a bad idea. He almost lost me forever."

"Why's that?" I asked slowly, unsure I needed the answer.

"He danced with another woman and grabbed her butt

and squeezed it."

"I did not, Dorothy," my dad said, shaking his head. "I've told you a hundred times that never happened."

My mom rolled her eyes. "The woman told me herself."

Becky cocked her head slightly. "And how old was this alleged woman?"

"Fourteen."

"And dad?"

My dad laughed. "I had just turned fifteen."

I slapped the counter and groaned. "This is the incident that you used to try to get me back with Jared? That's not cheating, Mom. You don't even know if it happened."

"Oh, it happened." My mom nodded.

Levi looked like he was about to crack up, so he walked backward out of the kitchen as quickly as he came in.

"Do you realize that I've been walking around Fireweed Island completely dismayed, thinking that Dad had an affair on you?"

"Dorothy," my dad grumbled.

"My life as I knew it did not exist these last couple of weeks." I pointed at Jared. "All for what? A guy who gets another woman pregnant but then realizes he's not the daddy, and then poof, he's mine again? I don't think so."

"Hell to the no," Becky muttered. "Don't take him back."

"Well, Skye. I don't think sleeping with your boss is exactly a great move either."

"He does make lasagna, Mom." Becky held in a giggle. "And he's really good-looking." She turned to her husband and smiled. "But not as sexy as you are."

Her husband rolled his eyes and scooted away from Jared a little more.

"Levi makes me happy. It's my time to be happy." I shook my head and let out a deep breath. "I don't know where this is going to go. Maybe it won't go anywhere, but it makes me happy in the here and now, and none of us know how much longer we have. Let me be happy."

"She's right, honey," my dad said softly to my mom. "Let her be happy."

"I stayed in a loveless relationship with Jared for years just to make you happy, to give you hope." I shook my head. "But I want to give myself hope. I want what you and Dad have, regardless of the spring fling fiasco."

My chest finally unsnarled from the days and weeks of thinking my poor dad cheated on my mom when all he may or may not have done was squeeze a little bum at the age of fourteen or fifteen. That's a bit different from thinking you'd impregnated a person.

"Loveless?" my mom asked softly.

"I never loved him, Mom. The thought of being with him made me ill because I knew he was cheating on me any chance he got." I glanced over at Jared. "Sorry, but it's true. It's why I took jobs away all the time. If I wasn't around it, I wouldn't be reminded of it all the time."

"I had no idea," my dad said, rubbing my mom's shoulders.

"Well, it's the truth, and I didn't want people to feel sorry for me." I shrugged. "So, if I'm banging my boss and enjoying myself for once, at least it's making me happy."

My mom's cheeks blushed, and my dad laughed.

Becky reached for her glass of wine and raised it into the air. "Here's to making Skye happy."

My dad and mom got their glasses and raised them, along with my brother-in-law. "To Skye's happiness."

Everyone took a sip as Levi walked back into the kitchen.

"And the view isn't bad, either," my mom muttered as we looked out the window.

"Isn't it great?"

"I wasn't talking about that one." My mom waggled her brows, and my dad chuckled, kissing the top of her head.

Levi smiled and brushed his hands along my arm. "Everything okay?"

I nodded, grinning. "Everything is more than okay."

Jared popped off the couch and set his empty glass on the coffee table. "I'm headed out."

"Ah, really?" I said flatly.

"Come on, stay." Levi smiled. "I make killer lasagna."

"That's pretty much what I'm afraid of." Jared glanced at my dad and then at Levi. "I've realized a lot sitting here, and I might not be able to make things right with you, Skye, but I'm going to change my ways."

I drew in a deep breath and let it out equally hard. "I hope so, Jared. The women you use deserve better. But honestly, you can stay for dinner. No one is going to poison you. We wouldn't waste food like that."

"No, I think I'll just get some room service back at the hotel and see about booking an early flight out tomorrow." Jared started toward the door, and I felt an unexpected pang of remorse.

My brother-in-law shook his head. "I'm sorry. I can't. I just can't. I know my sister-in-law has a heart of gold, and this little number you're pulling right here is going to eat at her all night and all through the holidays."

Jared glared at Jeffrey.

"Why don't you tell them what you're really doing tonight?" My brother-in-law raised his brows. "No? Then I will."

Jared rolled his eyes and started toward the door. As he got close, Scarlet barked at him, and he nearly jumped ten feet into the air, and my mom started laughing.

"I hadn't even seen that dog since we got here. Where'd she come from?"

Levi laughed as Jared slammed the door. "She's older and almost deaf, but for some reason, she can hear snapping and feel doors opening and closing, along with breezes."

I chuckled and looped my arm around Levi's waist. "You didn't tell me she was deaf."

"Well, we've been having to cover a lot in a short time period."

Jeffrey walked over with an empty wine glass. "This is amazing. And this is your company?"

Levi nodded, pouring more for Jeffrey. "My father started the company, and I inherited it."

"He has a twin as well, so if you're wandering around Fireweed and you spot Levi doing something incredulous, odds are that it's his identical twin, Max." I chuckled. "You know, whether it's holding up a bank or . . ."

"Using an app like Jared?" Jeffrey teased.

"Is that what he was doing?" I asked, stomping my foot.

"Yeah, he was planning his hookup here for the night. I saw the texts and everything."

"So that whole spiel . . ." I shook my head, laughing. "Wow. Just wow."

Levi kissed the top of my head, and warmth spread through me as my mom and dad eyed one another.

The oven dinged, and I moaned happily. "I am so hungry. Let me put this loaf in the toaster oven."

I shoved the bread into the countertop toaster and spun around to see Levi and my dad talking. My sister caught my gaze and smiled, walking over to me.

"So, is it safe to say that he is bang-worthy?"

I playfully smacked my sister and made sure my mom wasn't listening.

"You have no idea." I laughed. "I didn't know what I was missing all those years."

"I can still hear you," my mom hummed.

My dad glanced at us. "Hear what? Who said what?"

All the women shouted *nothing!*

I realized I was experiencing the best December ever, and judging by how much Levi was smiling, I wasn't the only one.

Chapter Thirty

Levi

I wasn't sure exactly when to bring it up to Skye. We'd all gorged ourselves on the lasagna, drunk a lot of Shantos wine, and wandered out for ice cream in freezing weather and goose down last night. I crashed on the couch with Scarlet and snuck out in the morning.

Now I was staring at my computer, wishing I could take the rest of the month off and spend it with Skye and her family.

I also knew they were here to see her, not the Levi and Skye show. My brother's plane was scheduled to take off in a couple of hours, and we'd only managed to get together at the holiday party. But we'd texted more than usual, and I felt like we were in a good place.

"Good morning, Boss," Marcy said, laughing and

waving her engagement ring around.

"It still looks good on you," I teased.

"Thank you." She wandered into my office and sat down. "You said you wanted to talk to me about something?"

I'd wanted to talk to Skye first, but Marcy was right in front of me.

"I got an offer that seems almost impossible to refuse."

Marcy frowned. "Really? Skye asked you to marry her?"

I laughed. "No, but her family is in town now."

She perked up. "Oh, have you met them?"

"They're great people. I've even met her ex." I laughed. "He's not so great."

Marcy gasped. "Her ex?"

"He showed up at her house unannounced, and it was a circus. I showed up, having no idea who he was, and then her family got there." I laughed just thinking about it. "As Jared is begging for a second shot, Skye's brother-in-law spots him on some hookup app to get some on Fireweed."

Marcy looked perplexed. "As in here?"

"Right? I've been missing out." I shook my head. "Anyway, it was really nice."

"Apart from the crazy ex-fiancé."

"Exactly. Although, it was pretty entertaining."

"I'm guessing that's not what you wanted to tell me."

I shook my head and let out a deep breath. "No. It wasn't.

She crooked a finger and waggled it. "Come on. Let me have it."

"I'm thinking about selling the company."

The color drained from Marcy's complexion. "What?"

"After securing these two private label lines, I received an offer that I can't refuse."

"But you wouldn't have gotten that offer if you weren't putting your feelers out, right?"

I nodded. "True."

"But why?" she asked, glancing around the office. "Too much Christmas stuff going on to bother you? Did I go overboard?"

I smiled and shook my head. "No. Believe it or not, maybe not enough."

"I'm not following." She shook her head.

"Some recent developments in my life have pointed me in a different direction."

"Skye?" she asked.

"Partially. Max invited me to the Maldives for the

holidays."

"And you'd go?"

"Maybe."

"What about Skye?"

"Her family is here with her. I don't want to interfere."

"So, you might sell the company and travel the world with Max?"

I laughed and shook my head. "I'm not a masochist, but I think I might take a clue from him and actually think about what I want to do with the rest of my life." I let out a deep breath. "I enjoy painting."

"As in walls?" She scrunched her nose.

"Well, I'm sure murals would be cool, but not what I meant. I mean pictures."

"Let me get this straight. You want to sell your successful business and paint?"

I smiled. "And travel."

"I see."

"I know enough about business to understand that if I want to sell, it has to be on a high. This deal gave me that crescendo. If I don't seize it, I may never be able to again. And who knows? Maybe I'll want to start something of my own. But right now, I want to paint. I want to travel."

"What about Skye?"

Skye walked into my office and smiled. "What about Skye?"

Marcy laughed and stood up. "And that is my cue to leave. But I support whatever is in your heart, Levi."

Skye watched Marcy leave the office and looked at me. "Well, that's either concerning or exciting."

I laughed. "Probably depends on who you ask."

Standing, I walked over to her and gave her a kiss.

"That's nice," she cooed. "I didn't expect you to be gone this morning."

"I had some stuff to get done and think about."

She nodded. "Wasn't that wild yesterday?"

I sat down and laughed. "That's an understatement."

"So, I gave my family an itinerary that should keep them busy until four o'clock today." She let out a happy sigh. "And there's snow in the forecast."

"You've got an amazing family, Skye."

She shook her head with a gleam in her eyes. "I really do, and I can't even put into words the relief about my dad. I've missed them while trying to run from Jared all this time."

Her words sank deep, and I shook my head. "Your mom is a trip. I'm glad you get to spend time with them for the holidays."

Skye smiled and nodded. "She is. I had no idea your mom's name was Dorothy."

"It's weird how I've programmed myself not to say it very often."

"I can understand that." She looked around the office and brought her gaze back to mine.

My body tensed at the thought of leaving her for Christmas, but I would be back, and we could keep going where we left off, and she wouldn't miss out on her family.

And maybe I'd reconnect with mine.

"I can tell you have something to tell me." She stretched her arms in front of her. "I have something too. But you go first."

"I got an offer for Shantos."

Her mouth parted, and then she shut it and smiled, letting out a deep breath. "And you're selling?"

I nodded. "I think so."

She winked at me. "You know what they say."

"I don't have a clue, actually."

"Sell when you can."

"Kind of my thoughts." I nodded, kicking back in my chair.

"So, what do you plan on doing afterward?" she asked tentatively.

"I think I'm going to take a cue from my brother and travel."

"And do your art?"

I laughed. "Yeah, and do my art."

"That will be amazing, Levi. Really amazing." She smiled, nodding. "You'll have to send me postcards."

I cocked my head slightly. "I was hoping it would include you."

She laughed and shook her head until she realized I was serious. "Levi, I have to work. In fact, I wanted to let you know that I picked up my next assignment, but it starts on December 30th. I know it's a few days earlier than expected, but I kind of have to take things when they come up."

Every single cell in my body felt betrayed as an awful ache spread through me.

I was seeing everything we'd built these last few weeks undo in a matter of seconds.

She bit her lip and sucked on it for a brief second when I didn't say anything, but I didn't know what to say. I didn't know what I thought, but this wasn't it. I guess I thought she'd stay.

My fingers rolled into a ball, and my fingernails dug into my palm. Suddenly, I didn't want to sell my business. I glanced at my inbox and let out a deep breath.

"Wow. I don't know what to say," I muttered, keeping my eyes off hers.

"Did you think I'd stay or—"

"I don't know what I thought other than I love being with you."

"Me too. I love Fireweed. I love hanging out with you." She let out a sigh. "But there's also my reality of bills to pay, my family in Maine, my career."

I forced myself to look at Skye as every single part of me broke. "No, you're right. I don't know what I was thinking. You can't just quit your career to travel with me."

She attempted to laugh. "Well, when you put it that way, it sounds rather appealing."

My gaze met hers, and I smiled. "So, we try the long-distance relationship thing?"

Skye groaned. "I didn't think we'd have to have this talk yet."

I nodded. "Neither did I."

Marcy came into my office. "Hey, I just got notified that your flight to meet your brother got canceled, but they can put you on one that leaves tonight."

Skye's gaze flashed to mine. "You're leaving Fireweed?"

"I thought I'd give you time with your family." I

looked over at Marcy. "That's fine."

She nodded and left.

"That's fine?" Skye cocked her head. "What about . . .?"

I watched her fidget and tried to let the voices in my head fight it out for me because I honestly didn't know what to do.

"I completely understand about needing to leave your assignment here early to begin the next one. And I'll always give you a glowing recommendation."

The words felt like I was dismissing an employee, not breaking up with the best thing that had ever happened to me.

"I appreciate that." She nodded and let out a breath. "Wow. So, you're going to the Maldives tonight."

"Appears so."

"And selling." She smiled as her gaze told a different story. "Good things are coming for you, Levi. I can feel it. And this December wasn't half-bad, was it?"

My chest tightened, and I wanted to beg her to stay, to pretend her responsibilities didn't exist . . . that we could just make a life together.

But what? After a few weeks?

"It was the best December of my life, Skye." I nodded. "I didn't expect it to come to such an abrupt end, though."

She shook her head. "Me neither."

"So, what are we doing?" I asked. "Why are we making this so hard?"

Skye laughed. "Because we are grownups. We went into this knowing the risks."

Part of me wondered if the boss comments from her mom did get to her.

"About the long-distance thing?" I picked the conversation up again, hoping for any kind of connection to a future.

She blew a whole bunch of air out of her puckered mouth, and all I could think about was kissing those lips, making love to her, feeling her in my arms.

How could we be on completely different pages for our future?

"We could try it. I haven't had the best luck with it."

"Don't let Jared ruin it for me." I tried to laugh, but it came out more like a croak.

"We can give it a shot." She nodded.

A shot?

Everything we'd experienced and shared sounded so pathetic and far off now.

"When is your family going back?"

"The twenty-seventh." She ran her fingers across her pants. "I was planning on flying out on the night of the twenty-ninth."

I nodded. "Okay."

"Will you be back in time?"

"Coming back on the twenty-eighth."

She looked relieved, but I didn't want to put too much weight on her reaction since I'd obviously been misreading everything so far.

"I'm glad you're going to be with your brother for Christmas."

I smiled and nodded. "I think it will be good. After all, it's just him and me."

Those words dug far deeper than I'd expected.

"Family is all we have in this world." She nodded and stood. "Well, I should get to work. I don't want to keep my family waiting after work."

I stood and walked over to Skye, the woman who'd changed my entire view on life and the same woman who had the power to crush it with one decision.

Chapter Thirty-One

Skye

"I need time to think," I said, staring at myself in the bathroom mirror as my sister sat on the toilet seat. It had been three days without Levi. I'd been spending my days at the office without him in it, and the whole thing felt wrong.

"You look like crap," Becky said, handing me a hairbrush.

"Thank you for that." I took the brush from her and ran it through my hair. "What did I do?"

"You did the responsible thing," Becky said, shrugging. "It's a bad habit."

I gave her a dirty look in the mirror and let out a sigh. "Well, let's go check out the Christmas bazaar so I can pretend I still love the holiday."

Becky laughed sympathetically and stood, rubbing

my back. "The right thing will happen."

"If you say so."

She winked at me, and I wanted to believe she had some magic wand or crystal ball.

"I know so. Now, come on. Let's not keep the parents waiting." She grabbed my hand and pulled me down the hallway to my parents and brother-in-law.

"I am so excited about this bazaar," my mom gushed. "I've read all about it in the travel guides."

I laughed and glanced at my dad. "Travel guides? They still have those?"

My dad grinned. "Some of us call it Google."

Being with my family made me feel a hundred times better, but considering I felt a thousand times worse than a week ago, I wasn't sure that was enough.

Levi was probably yucking it up with his brother and new girlfriend, tanning his already glorious body, drinking Shantos wine on a beach, and wondering why he ever fell for the temp.

"You don't look so hot," my mom whispered as she handed me my coat.

"Thanks. I feel great, though." I rolled my eyes and chuckled.

"See? I told you getting together with your boss

wasn't a good idea." My mom shook her head, and my dad frowned.

"Dorothy, I don't think Skye really needs to hear those words at this particular moment in time."

"He's right, Mom." Becky rubbed my back. "You don't kick a horse when it's already down."

"How about we just don't kick the horse, period?" I shook my head and smiled as we headed outside.

Fireweed was absolutely magical, almost as magical as the first night I showed up on the island and the first night I met Levi in a bar with a mouth full of candles and hot peppers.

The thought made me smile as we made our way down the sidewalk to the community center.

"I think this will be stocking stuffer central," my mom informed us. "In fact, I think the vendor who sells those cute little candles that look like cookies will be here."

I chuckled, realizing I'd never told my mom I'd thought they were dessert my first night here.

As we walked toward the bazaar, I felt better and better. I loved being with my family.

In small doses.

Particularly, around the holidays.

I needed this. Levi was right.

Even though it tore me up thinking about him and us. Long distance?

I kept the voices out of my head, the ones that wanted to yell at me that long distance would never work.

Because I desperately wanted it to.

I'd finally found someone who'd made me extremely happy. Because I was happy.

A group of Christmas carolers sang to the group of us wandering into the community center. Cinnamon drifted through the air, and my mom spun around to me and stopped.

"I didn't mean to say that about Levi. He's a good guy. I hope it can work out between you two somehow."

I clutched my mom's hand through our gloves and nodded. "But for the first time in my entire life, I'm not looking for approval. I'm looking to be happy."

My dad smiled and nodded, giving me a hug. "I couldn't be happier hearing it, Skye."

My parents traded a knowing look, which usually meant they'd talk about something later. I scanned the aisles of crafts, baked goods, and gifts. Maddie caught my gaze and waved me over to a booth she was sitting at with an older woman. My family came up behind me as Maddie introduced me.

"This is Hildie, my darling mother-in-law and

absolutely amazing babysitter." Maddie smiled and waved around the booth filled with soaps and candles. "And the creator of all this magic."

"She must be planning on having me watch the grandkids again." Hildie stood and smiled, shaking my hand. "Nice to meet you."

"You too. These are my parents. They're visiting from Maine."

My family introduced themselves to Hildie while Maddie looped her arm through mine and walked me away from their booth.

"What in the world is going on between Levi and you?" She glanced back at my family. "Why is he with his brother and not here with you?"

I chuckled, thinking about Max. "I try not to think about it too much, considering how he felt about Max a week ago. I would have thought he would have hung around for the holidays."

Maddie laughed. "Actually, Chance told me that Levi is so grateful to you for showing him how important Max is even though they don't see eye to eye, but I felt like there was more to the story."

I let out a deep breath and glanced around the bustling Christmas bazaar, but the truth was that I didn't feel very festive. I kept trying to psych myself up, but I missed Levi.

"He thought I should spend time with my family since they flew all the way in from Maine. Meanwhile, I accepted another temp job for the end of December out of the area." I bit my lip and shook my head. "I don't think he expected me to leave."

She nodded. "I kind of got that impression as well."

"But I can't quit working. I mean, I don't live like that. I can't just hang out here . . ."

"So, where do things stand?"

"Well, I'm absolutely miserable without him. The thought of starting my new job is less than thrilling, and I'm pretty sure I made sure we crash-landed this new relationship." I shook my head. "I just . . . I don't know. What do you think?"

"I think Levi is head over heels in love with you."

My eyes widened. "Love?"

Maddie nodded. "I don't think he was thinking about anything practical. He was thinking about forever. You were his forever. He'd already told Chance as much. So, I don't think he thought of all the other factors."

"You mean reality?" I smiled, thinking how ironic it was that Scrooge, Mr. Crabby Pants, King of Practicality, was willing to ignore all of the red flags to jump in feet first.

The thought made my stomach twist into a million knots of frustration. He looked shocked and like I'd ripped his life cord from his hands. While he dangled dreams, hopes, and fantasies in front of me, I swung a hard dose of reality in front of him.

"I have a lot of thinking to do if I haven't already screwed it up." I shrugged. "For all I know, he's found someone already and is enjoying a fruity drink in a thong."

Maddie snorted. "Does he look like the kind of guy who'd drink a fruity drink?"

I snickered. "Not the thong part?"

She smiled and gave me a quick hug. "I know it's not any of my business, but my husband says he's regretting getting on that flight."

"Thank you for that." I smiled, watching my family watching me. "I'm coming."

Becky chuckled as Maddie followed behind me. Each of them had a paper sack filled with goodies from Hildie's booth.

"Onward," I said, waving at Hildie and Maddie.

As we weaved through the crowds, I thought about Levi.

Maybe I should show up in the Maldives to surprise him. Marcy had all the hotel and flight details. It could be fun.

Or disastrous.

And if it were the latter, better to know now than later.

My pulse soared as my mind started racing with ideas. I could show up at his hotel room in a present that I pop out of. Or I could get Max in on it and meet him at a swanky restaurant. Or . . .

"What do you think?" Becky asked, holding up a seagull painting.

"I think it looks like it will make a statement in Maine."

"Perfect." She grinned and stood on her tippy toes. "What has you staring off into space?"

"I think I've come up with a plan." I chuckled. "I don't know if it's a good one, but it's a plan."

"What is it?" Becky asked.

"Fly to the Maldives for Christmas. What do you think?" I squealed in excitement.

"Buy a refundable ticket."

Chapter Thirty-Two

Levi

"Is this wild or what? Whew!" Max hollered into the air, and Susan ran her slender arms around his waist, both in swimsuits, while I sank into the sand wearing shorts and a polo. My tennis shoes were filled with sand, and I felt the old Levi coming on strong.

They were having the time of their lives, and I was stuck with them both.

"Here. Have a drink," Max said, pushing a bottle of beer into my hand.

"I'm good." I shook my head, thinking about Skye and whether or not I should sell my business.

"You're not good. You're a wreck." He shook his head. "And you're harshing our mel, man. Perk up."

I scowled at my brother and shook my head. "What

the hell does that even mean?"

Susan snickered. "Harshing our mellow. Ruining our good time."

"Pardon me for living in reality." I rolled my eyes and glared at the palm tree wrapped in twinkle lights. *Who does that? Who are they kidding? We're on a tropical island.*

Skye would do it. Skye would make it feel like Christmas in hundred-degree weather.

I was trapped on the thought of Skye Lenox. The thought of a future with her. While she was busy planning her life far away from Fireweed and me, I was busy pretending she didn't have one that didn't involve me.

"I need to get out of here," I said, taking a swig of the beer.

I nearly spat it out. It tasted like vinegar.

"That's going to be tricky considering where we are," Max said, raising a brow. He straightened, realizing I was serious. "If you and Skye are meant to be, it will be."

Susan nodded. "Just like Max and me. It just wasn't the right timing a few years back."

The thought of being without Skye for a few years made me physically nauseous . . . or it was the beer.

Chance had just texted that Maddie ran into her at the Christmas bazaar, and she seemed in good spirits. But she was confused. And she'd even told Maddie she thought I'd probably already found someone else on the island.

I shook my head at the thought. I had to get back to Skye or I'd turn back into the miserable, crotchety old man. I didn't care if she was headed to Florida or Montana for her next gig. I wanted to be there with her. She made me feel alive again. I didn't want to lose that feeling. I didn't want to lose Skye.

"It's been fun," I told my brother, "but I'm out. I gotta get back to the States. I'll see you two when you get back."

Max smiled and shook his head. "Okay, man. Whatever you need to do."

He released Susan just long enough to give me a hug before I trudged through the sand to get to our hotel. I slid my phone out of my pocket and dialed Marcy's number.

"Hello," she groaned into the phone.

"It's Levi."

"Levi!" She became awake. "Do you know what time it is here?"

"No. It's five p.m. here," I offered.

"Try five a.m. here," she grumbled. "This had better be important."

"It is. I need help getting back to Washington. I need to see Skye before Christmas."

Marcy was silent for a few seconds. "That I can help with."

"Seriously?"

"Why do you think you always give me such great raises? I'll get right on it. You might have to fly all over the world to get home, but I'll make it happen. Pack your bags."

I laughed and shook my head, feeling reinvigorated just by the thought of getting to see Skye again.

"I never unpacked. I owe you so much, Marcy."

"Does this mean I can count on you for Christmas dinner too?"

"What do you mean, too?"

"Skye had been so depressed that I made her promise that she and her family would come over to my mom's for the holiday."

"Really?" My heart tore in half.

Why did I ever leave Fireweed Island? It was like I'd patterned myself to make choices to make myself miserable, but Skye had helped me out of that bad habit.

Until my latest bright idea.

I made my way into the hotel room and crashed onto the bed.

Was this another horrible idea? Would she be happy to see me or just confused as to why I left in the first place? I was confused. I thought this would be a great way to bond with my brother, but that was just an excuse.

While I could pretend that I was shocked Skye didn't want to drop everything in her life to start on Fireweed, there must have been some small part of me that feared she would. I shook my head at the ridiculousness of the situation when someone knocked on my door.

"Coming," I growled and then realized I sounded like Scrooge. "I mean, I'll be there in a sec."

That didn't sound any better. I stood from the bed and walked over to the door, hoping in some ridiculous fashion that when I opened it, Skye would fly into my arms.

When I pulled the door open, I saw my brother Max and scowled.

He frowned. "Nice to see you too."

"Sorry. I was—"

"Expecting your fairy godmother to suddenly appear?" he joked. "I just wanted to tell you something that's been on my mind for a long time."

"How long?"

"Years."

"Okay . . ." I tilted my chin and braced myself for whatever might spill out of his mouth.

"Mom and Dad would be extremely proud of you and

your choices." He smiled and shrugged. "But I think they'd be even prouder knowing you made a choice to make yourself happy."

"Are you talking about Skye or Shantos?" I asked.

"Both." He took a step into my hotel room and wrapped his arms around me. "I know I haven't been the best support system, but I'm trying to get better." He patted my back and took a step back. "I know this trip out here was meant to make me see your commitment to family, and I do. But it's time we start making our own, don't you think?"

I smiled and nodded. "I think you're right."

"I know I'm right, but one piece of advice."

"Yeah?" I cocked my head slightly to listen, liking this new version of my brother.

"Don't overthink it."

I pressed my lips together and nodded. "Good advice."

"I thought so." He buffed his nails on his bare chest. "Now, duty calls, and Merry Christmas."

I laughed, waving down the hall as my brother trundled back to the beach.

Right when I got to my bed, my phone rang with Marcy on the other end yelling to grab my stuff and get to the airport STAT.

I did as she said, grabbed my bags and dashed out of the hotel.

I had one shot and several flights ahead of me to make this work.

And by the time I'd finally dragged myself off the final flight into SeaTac Airport, I'd traveled for two days straight.

It was Christmas Eve, and I was absolutely exhausted.

I rolled my suitcase to the rideshare waiting for me and fell asleep until the driver dumped me out at my house.

Marcy opened my front door and let go of Scarlet, who ran toward me.

"Thanks for watching her while I was gone."

"I think you spent more time in the air than you did on the island." Marcy chuckled, shaking her head.

"I'm pretty sure you're right."

She gave me a quick hug as Scarlet circled us both.

"Are Skye and her family still going to be at your mom's tomorrow?"

Marcy grinned. "Last I heard, they are. I hope you don't mind, but I lent your Mercedes to Skye to use so she could drive her family to my mom's. I figured you could just drive your truck over."

I chuckled. "It's good you told me so I didn't think

someone stole it."

"Stole it? Where would they take it? We're on an island."

I smiled and nodded. "Thanks again for everything. You're an amazing friend."

"Well, I can't say thank you enough for that bonus that plopped into my account this morning. That was truly unexpected."

I laughed as the first snowflake fell. "You did all the work for the direct deposits. I just told you the numbers."

She winked at me. "Which is the most important part. It was really generous of you."

"Consider it my parting gift," I said, walking into the house with Scarlet right behind me.

"So, it's true? You're going to go ahead with the sale?"

I smiled and nodded, feeling like the biggest weight had been lifted. "Yeah. I am."

"Good for you, Levi. It's about time you did something for yourself."

"Thanks, Marcy. Even though I'm almost an old man, I think it's time I start living for myself."

"If you're an old man and we are the same age, what are you trying to tell me?" Marcy giggled and shook her head.

"You know what? I don't want to know. Merry Christmas Eve, Levi," she said with a quick wave as she trundled to her car. "And get some sleep. Tomorrow is a big day."

I shut the door and walked to the family room, where the view was breathtaking on this Christmas Eve, and for the first time in years, I was present enough to notice.

And I knew I had one person to thank for it.

I'd spent so much of my life focused on what I could do to honor my parents' legacy and lift their story that I forgot to write my own.

Until Skye came into my life, I'd stopped letting myself imagine. Dream. And now, it was nearly impossible to stop.

But the one thing I knew was that Skye was in all of them. Every single thought, wish, and dream I had for the future included Skye Lenox, and I only prayed I hadn't blown it.

Scarlet hopped on the couch next to me and rested her head on my knee.

If there was one thing that I understood now more than anything, it was that I'd given the brush to too many people in my life. I'd let them paint the picture of who they wanted to see instead of who I was.

But Skye saw through all of that. She quickly

understood what I so desperately misunderstood about myself.

I didn't hate the world. I didn't hate people. I hated the choices I kept making in life.

And I think that similarity between us helped to unravel us a little bit too. We both came to an end that we weren't ready for, but this time, I knew what to fight for.

Chapter Thirty-Three

Skye

"I love your red velvet dress," Marcy said, giving me a giant hug. "You look absolutely beautiful. Too bad Levi isn't here to see you."

"His loss," I joked, feeling the sting of my own words.

I'd tried everything in my power to fly to the Maldives, but even with Marcy's magical powers of travel and persuasion, she couldn't find any flights that would get me there in time.

So, I decided to make the best of it, dress up, and enjoy my family for the last while that they were here. I knew I'd be busy for the next month with my new assignment and wouldn't be able to see them until at least February or March.

"Hi, Becky," Marcy sang, giving my sister a hug while I looked around Joanne's house in the woods. It felt absolutely magical, even more so than the last time I was here.

The house was beautifully decorated with red and white poinsettias lining the staircase and an enormous Christmas tree centered in the living room. She'd obviously continued decorating since the last Sunday dinner, and it felt like a winter wonderland.

I glanced at the table and laughed to myself when I remembered playing footsie with the wrong guy at the table. The thought left me with one more reason I missed Levi.

Joanne came down the hall dressed in a Mrs. Claus apron with her arms extended for a hug, which I happily gave before introducing my parents.

My mom handed two trays of food to Joanne, and they both wandered toward the kitchen as Jay took my dad and brother-in-law into the living room.

"It's so good to see you outside of the office," Marcy said.

"I know. I feel the same." I shook my head, holding my sister's hand. "It's hard to believe that I'm not going to be working at Shantos this time next week."

Marcy frowned and nodded. "It is, but I hope you'll still come back to Fireweed. I know Levi would be devastated if you didn't."

The thought of not seeing Levi again was more than

devastating. It was unthinkable. There wasn't an hour that went by when I didn't think about him. The way he smiled at me. The way he teased me or touched me to remind me that he was thinking of me.

Just the little things.

I missed him so much it hurt.

And it didn't help that the last two days, he basically went incognito, barely a text returned or a call answered.

All I could think about was the look on his face when I told him I'd taken another assignment. The moment the words slipped out, I regretted them. Why couldn't I take a little time off? Why did I think I had to take the next job?

I knew why, and the answer scared me.

"Okay, let's find a place to sit until my mom calls us for dinner." Marcy squeezed my arm. "If you think my mom's Sunday dinner is incredible, wait until you experience this feast."

"She's not kidding," I told Becky. "This dining experience is next-level."

Marcy gave me a hug as we weaved through the kitchen, where my mom was happily chatting with Joanne. There were several people I didn't recognize huddled around the kitchen nook as we made our way to the family room.

I reached for a strawberry and thought about my

current mood. I was one of those people who waited all year for Christmas and was sad when it was over. All December, I was in bliss, making my own way, not worrying much about what my family thought or expected, and reveling in the fact that I'd finally let my heart open up to a man who liked me for me.

And then I turned him down. So many people would have jumped at the chance to put a pause on work and gallivant around the world with a new partner.

But as I sat in his office, I realized I was starting to fall into my old ways again. We hadn't talked about what I wanted or even what he wanted until a set of circumstances forced it out of us.

I needed to be heard, but I didn't think it through. And I didn't listen. But I knew now more than ever that when Levi Adams came back to town, I'd make him promise to come to visit me, and I'd vow to see him. We would make this work.

As long as he hadn't found some beach bunny on vacation who'd happily take him up on his idea of traveling the world.

Which was honestly a good one.

Oh, what was I thinking?

As I made my way to the family room, I glanced behind me and noticed everyone had disappeared.

"Becky? Marcy?"

When I turned back around, Scarlet plowed toward me at a full gallop. I knelt down to hug her, and I let out such a happy squeak that she jumped backward. Somehow, she must have heard me. She bounded back, and I held onto her, somehow feeling closer to Levi.

Scarlet had a red velvet bow around her neck, and I nuzzled her hard while wishing Levi were here. It was so nice of Marcy to watch his pup, but I should have been the one to offer. I closed my eyes, enjoying the warm, fluffy fur, and took in a deep breath.

"Hey, are you going to just make out with my dog the whole time, or do I get any of that?"

I couldn't believe my ears.

Opening my eyes, I looked up slowly to see Levi Adams towering over me.

"You'd better not be Max." I playfully narrowed my eyes at Levi when he opened his arms for a hug.

And then it hit me.

Levi was really here. It wasn't a dream.

"What? How?" Tears filled my eyes, and I jumped up from Scarlet, wrapping my arms around his neck. "You came back?"

"It wasn't easy, but the moment I got there, I knew

I'd made the worst decision, Skye. I missed you so much." He breathed into my hair, and my body to shivered from the warmth along my skin. He took a step back and shook his head. "And if I missed out on seeing you in this . . ." He didn't have to say another word. The look in his eyes said it all.

I wrapped my arms around him as if he'd vanish on me and closed my eyes, breathing in everything about Levi. "I missed you so much, Levi. I don't know how or why things ended the way they did, but our relationship deserves better."

"I know, baby," he said softly.

I opened my eyes to see Levi taking me in, and I knew this was the best Christmas present ever.

"You really turned my holiday around," I teased, still feeling like this was a dream.

"Skye, you've made my life infinite times better, and I don't expect you to stop your life to be with me. I'm sorry for how I sprang things on you. All I want is to make your life better the way you've made mine. I'm excited about wherever your next job is taking you, and I hope you'll let me come with you. It will be an adventure for both of us."

I ran my hands through his hair and hugged him again. "Seriously? You'd come with me?"

"I'm selling the company, Skye. I'm leaving it behind. I'm starting fresh, and I want that to begin with you."

"It's not exactly the Maldives," I said, grimacing. "But it will be beautiful."

"Okay, let me have it." Levi smiled. "Where are we going?"

"North Dakota . . . for thirty days, to work with an oil company out there."

To say he was shocked put it mildly. "North Dakota in the winter?"

"I hope you like snow."

"I hope you like bitter cold," he whispered, nuzzling his nose against mine.

"Better snuggling conditions," I told him.

"I could snuggle with you for the rest of my life and do nothing else and be completely satisfied." He laughed. "But only if you wanted to."

I laughed, feeling his arms around my waist as Scarlet sat against my heels. "I've been thinking about your offer to travel. I think I can figure out how to fit it in between working."

He tipped my chin up as his gaze fastened onto mine. "It sounds like we're finally getting the hang of planning our own future."

I chuckled, knowing how truly unusual that was for both of us.

"What made you come back?" I asked softly as our foreheads touched.

"You know how you told me that sometimes, the people who loved Christmas as much as you did had a bum rest of the year, so Christmas was your one joyful time?" he asked, brushing my hair away.

I nodded slowly. "It rings a bell."

"Well, I didn't want to ruin your one good time of the year with my absence," he teased, and I laughed, resting my head against his chest.

"Don't let it go to your head, Mr. Adams."

"In all seriousness, I realized that I wanted to be the one who made every month of the year special for you, the way you made December amazing for me," he whispered as I lifted my head off his chest.

I looked into his eyes and knew I wasn't leaving Fireweed Island without him and Scarlet, but I hoped we'd be back soon.

"You've given me the best Christmas present ever, Levi," I said, feeling my heart expand bigger than I knew possible.

"Skye, you showed me how to embrace love and experience joy again this holiday season. It's something I'll never be able to thank you enough for."

"You're the only person I can truly be myself around, Levi. That's enough for me. When you left, I realized how much of my life I'd spent catering to how others wanted me to live my life. You never did that. You just let me be me. Even when it came to my new assignment."

"I love you, Skye."

He brought his mouth down to mine and kissed me gently as Scarlet started whining behind me.

Levi's mouth fell from mine as we turned around to see my entire family, Marcy's family, and several other people I didn't know start clapping and cheering right before yelling Merry Christmas.

Levi pointed above us and smiled. "Look up."

I slowly raised my head to see a sprig of mistletoe dangling above, and I knew I'd do everything in my power to make Levi love Christmas forever and ever.

"I did that." He grinned. "You may think I'm crazy, Skye, but you're my forever, and I hope I can be yours."

The group behind us started singing Christmas carols as Levi kept me in his arms, and I knew I'd found my forever too.

Chapter Thirty-Four

One Year Later

Levi

"Max still reminds me of Cousin Eddie from *National Lampoon's*," Skye whispered, and I couldn't keep in my laugh.

Max and Susan turned their eyes to us across the dinner table, and I just grinned as Dorothy and Ervin helped themselves to more rib roast.

It felt good to be back on Fireweed, but this Christmas, we decided to spend it on Sugarplum Lane. I never in a million years imagined that I'd host Christmas dinner, especially for my girlfriend's family, while my brother and his girlfriend happily agreed to spend time with us.

It was amazing what happened when I started living my life for myself and opened up my heart.

"Can you hand me the garlic mashed potatoes?" I asked Skye's sister.

"Of course." She handed me the bowl, and I set it down next to my plate.

The truth was that I was just trying to buy time. Skye's dad kept giving me the side-eye, waiting for me, and I kept hoping for the perfect moment.

"Where are you going after the New Year?" Dorothy asked us.

"Skye wanted to go to Hawaii," I said, smiling. I hadn't been since I was a kid, and Skye had never been.

"That sounds incredible." Her mom smiled and nodded. "Erv is taking me to the Bahamas in March."

"That's awesome," Skye said, smiling. "In March and April, we should be back in Maine."

"Yeah?" Her dad looked pleased.

"Yup. We might even sniff around for a small place to buy." She waggled her brows.

Her mom let out a happy yap, which somehow resonated with my deaf dog. Scarlet shot up and howled, making Susan look like she had lost her hearing.

I felt for the tiny box in my pocket and the envelopes for everyone under my legs on the chair.

Grabbing my butter knife, I tapped it against the wine

glass and looked at Skye. Her beautiful blue eyes sparkled with joy as I took a deep breath and stood from the table.

I scooted Skye's chair out and got down on one knee in front of her.

Skye's hands flew to her mouth as I pulled the ring box from my pocket.

"Skye, I feel like you were put in my life by some very important angels of mine. The moment I first saw you, I knew there was something different about you."

She smiled wider and sniffled.

"You knew there was more to me than most cared to understand, and I thank you for pausing your own life to help me unwrap mine. What I'm trying to say, Skye, is that I want to spend the rest of my life with you. I want your family to be my family. I want us to create an even bigger family like we always talk about. Skye Lenox, will you marry me?"

Skye jumped from her seat and nearly toppled me over as she hugged me with all her might.

"Yes, a million times over," she said, wrapping her arms around me. "You've made me the happiest woman alive."

I smiled, kissing her in between, pushing Scarlet off us while attempting to stand up with Skye still in my arms.

Our family erupted into congratulations, and I smiled,

reaching for the stack of envelopes.

"As I mentioned, Skye and I will be in Hawaii for two weeks, and I'd love it if you all could join us for the second week. Hotel, food, and airfare are covered."

Dorothy looked like she was about to fall off her chair while Susan elbowed Max like he'd better up his game, and Becky cried while getting up to hug us.

"You are the best." Becky squeezed Skye and me, and I looked around my home filled with Christmas decorations, food, and family, and I realized how lucky we were to find our forever.

Becky sat back down, but Skye led me from the table toward the window. She looked into my eyes and smiled, and I knew I was the luckiest man alive.

"Thank you, Mr. Adams," Skye whispered. "And Merry Christmas forever."

Dear Readers,

Thank you so much for reading *Forever Christmas*! I can't believe it's the sixteenth book in the Island County Series. It was as magical (if not more) for me to write this book than even the first one in the series. I never expected this series to be so cherished by readers, so thank YOU for making this possible. I hope you loved Levi and Skye's story. It just made me full of joy while writing.

If you're new to the series, *Finding Love on Forgotten Cove* is what started it all. For those who've read all of *Island County* or *Silver Ridge* books, my latest series *The Sunshine Breakfast Club* has been an absolute blast for me to write. I've included an excerpt of *Dash of Love* (book 1) below. If you love small town romance, plenty of humor, a matchmaking club going undercover as a book club, family secrets, and lots of romance, this is the perfect series to start. It's available now! I've also completed the *Cloudberry Inn Series* and all books are available to read. *Imagining You* is the first in the series, and you can check it out below as well. I have over sixty books for you to binge read, so feel free to snoop around my Amazon Author page and hit follow!

But thank you so much for reading my Christmas book. It put me right in the holiday spirit in the dead of summer when I wrote it, and I loved every second. I hope you did too! And on that note, I so appreciate all the reviews and ratings. They really do help new readers find me. I hope this book made you as happy to read as I felt writing it.

Feel free to pop on over to my Facebook group (Karice Bolton Book Buzz) to see what's on the horizon! I'm just so grateful to you all.

Many thanks,

Karice

BOOKS BY KARICE BOLTON

SUNSHINE BREAKFAST CLUB

DASH OF LOVE

PINCH OF LOVE

SPRINKLE OF LOVE

CHRISTMAS OF LOVE

MR. MISTAKE SERIES

MR. MISTAKE

MR. ACCIDENT

MR. WRONG

MR. RIGHT

ISLAND COUNTY SERIES

FINDING LOVE IN FORGOTTEN COVE

LOVE REDONE IN HIDDEN HARBOR

TANGLED LOVE ON PELICAN POINT

FOREVER LOVE ON FIREWEED ISLAND

TEMPTING LOVE ON HOLLY LANE

CHANCE AT LOVE ON MYSTIC BAY

IRRESISTIBLE LOVE AT SILVER FALLS

LUCKY IN LOVE ON HOUND ISLAND

MISTLETOE MISCHIEF

ACCIDENTAL LOVE ON MEADOW COVE LANE

DISCOVERING LOVE ON CRANBERRY LANE

CHRISTMAS ON FIREWEED

IMAGINING LOVE ON WILLOW ROAD

CHRISTMAS CRUSH ON FIREWEED

WAITING ON LOVE AT HAWTHORNE AVE
FOREVER CHRISTMAS ON SUGARPLUM LANE

BEYOND LOVE SERIES
BEYOND CONTROL
BEYOND DOUBT
BEYOND REASON
BEYOND INTENT
BEYOND CHANCE
BEYOND PROMISE
BEYOND the MISTLETOE

CLOUDBERRY INN SERIES
IMAGINING YOU
REMEMBERING YOU
LEAVING YOU
LOVING YOU

SILVER RIDGE SERIES
A HAPPY TRUTH ABOUT LOVE
A LITTLE SECRET ABOUT LOVE
A FUNNY THING ABOUT LOVE
A SURPRISING FACT ABOUT LOVE
A SIMPLE WISH ABOUT LOVE

LUKE FLETCHER SERIES
HIDDEN SINS
BURIED SINS
REDEMPTION
MIA

BLOOD TORN DUET
BLOOD TORN
BLOOD CURSED

V MAFIA SERIES
BLAKE
DEVIN
JAXSON

THE WITCH AVENUE SERIES
LONELY SOULS
ALTERED SOULS
RELEASED SOULS
SHATTERED SOULS

THE WATCHERS TRILOGY
AWAKENING
LEGIONS
CATACLYSM
TAKEN NOVELLA (A Watchers Prequel)

AFTERWORLD SERIES
RecruitZ
AlibiZ
UprisingZ

Contact Karice

Don't forget to join Karice's newsletter by visiting

her website at karicebolton.com and don't miss out

on all the updates and sneak peeks by joining her

Facebook Group (Karice Bolton Book Buzz).

To contact the author, please visit her online at

www.karicebolton.com or via

Twitter/Facebook/Pinterest @KariceBolton.